MISTRUST

KATHLEEN HELMS

Laurel -
this is #3
I think I gave
you A.I. Smith (#1)
#2 is called
loyalty I don't
have any
author copies
but it is on
Amazon is
your want
it

Kathleen
Hel

ZZYYZX PUBLISHING

Mistrust / Kathleen Helms - 1st ed.

Library of Congress Control Number: 2020924640

Ebook ISBN 978-1-7361836-0-1

Paperback ISBN 978-0-9600923-9-0

For my daughters

Hannah, Hayley, and Paige

Despite my best efforts, I find it impossible
To condense a lifetime of love
Into a few short words

PROLOGUE

A trickle of sweat dripped down Jodi's forehead and into her left eye. She blinked rapidly and tilted her head to the left, trying to force the salty drop out of her already stinging eyes. She felt tears mingle with the droplet of sweat, then trickle down her burning cheeks. She couldn't wipe the tears away. Her hands were tied tightly behind her back. A bandanna prevented her from calling out. The room she was in, her bedroom, was dark. Her eyes flitted around searching for something to focus on. Her thoughts mimicked her eye movements, disjointed and unsettled. Jodi forced herself to close her eyes. She took one long breath in through her nose and let it out slowly. She followed this breath with a second, and then a third. A semblance of calm came over her.

The masked men had her boyfriend, Travis, in the living room. She had known the moment she had told Travis her secret that it had been a mistake. They had been together just over seven months. Jodi still wasn't sure what had motivated her to share the truth with him. It had been just over a week ago. That perfect July morning had found them in bed, drinking Irish coffees, and planning their day. She had felt so safe in that moment, so secure in Travis' arms, that she had just blurted it out. The next day she had told him she was going for a run. Instead she had sent a small package containing everything to her sister, Brandi. Then, tonight, the men had come.

She could hear them interrogating Travis in the living room. He was moaning and pleading with them. Jodi knew they would get nothing from Travis. He had nothing to give them. There was silence for a moment, then a muffled *whump*. Jodi flinched as she heard Travis' body fall from the chair. The door to the bedroom opened and a shaft of light streamed across the floor. Jodi tensed. They had returned for her.

1

LOYAL TRUESDALE

Loyal downshifted and pulled the light blue buggy into the parking lot of the Wolf Creek Resort. He parked the buggy next to Maggie's bright yellow one, cut the ignition, and maneuvered himself out of his vehicle.

"That was great," Loyal said to Maggie as she walked up beside him.

"Yeah, I've never been on a buggy run I didn't like," said Maggie. "And nobody broke on this one, which makes it even better."

"Dinner and awards at 5:00, right?" said Loyal.

"Yep."

"I'm going to shower and change," said Loyal. "I'll find you at dinner."

"Sounds good," said Maggie. "I think I'll do the same."

Loyal climbed the stairs and entered his hotel room. He set his keys on the counter, removed his belly band containing his Kahr PM9 and placed both next to the keys, then grabbed a beer out of the fridge and sat in the chair by the window. He took a long appreciative sip, then leaned back and slowly reviewed the day's events in his mind. He was in Big Bear, California attending his first official Meyers Manx Club event. After his abrupt retirement from the Carlsbad Sheriff's Department the previous April, Loyal had been searching for things to occupy his time. Saturday morning breakfast with Bruce and Winnie Meyers, Maggie, and assorted Manx Club enthusiasts, was one of the things he had added to his routine. On an overcast Saturday in early June, Winnie had mentioned that she knew of a buggy for sale. It was older, and needed a little work, but she thought it would be perfect for Loyal. Loyal had purchased it and hired Bruce's grandson, who was visiting from Colorado, to help him get it fixed up. Loyal was good at lots of things, but he was not an experienced mechanic. Bruce's grandson was, and he had spent two weeks instructing Loyal.

These events led Loyal to find himself in the mountains of Big Bear, participating in the *Meyers Manx Big Bear Bash*. The event was held every July in the mountains above Los Angeles. Bruce, Winnie, and Maggie had all encouraged Loyal to attend. Winnie had even worked her magic and found him lodging at Wolf Creek, which was typically sold out a year in advance. This morning had started with coffee and doughnuts, then a driver's meeting, and eventually the run. This had been a scenic off-road drive through the mountains. As Loyal sat and sipped his beer he had to admit... he was hooked.

Loyal finished the beer and stood. He tossed the empty bottle and headed to the bathroom for a much needed shower. Buggy rides on off-road trails equaled dirt on the driver. Twenty minutes later Loyal was clean, his hair combed, and he was dressed in a gray Big Bear Bash T-shirt and blue jeans. He had purchased an extra large T-shirt so it hung loosely over the PM9 that was once again on his waist. He locked his room, pocketed the keys and his phone, and descended the stairs. The dinner was being held in a large outdoor area at the rear of the lodge. Loyal rounded the corner and stopped. It was a few minutes before 5:00 and the tables were packed. As he was searching for an available seat he heard his name. He turned to his left and saw Maggie waving and calling out to him. It took Loyal a moment to work his way through the closely set tables. He sat in the chair Maggie had indicated, set his phone and room key to the left of his place setting, and took a look around the table. Bruce and Winnie Meyers sat at the head of the table to his left. Maggie was to the left of Winnie, directly across from Loyal. Continuing to the left were Jim and Nancy Chamberlain and Lori Ann Dario. Mike Dario, Lori Ann's husband, and Andy, a young man from Australia, were at the other end of the table to Loyal's right. Andy's girlfriend Cassidy, and Verne, who was a regular at Saturday morning breakfast, sat to Andy's left.

The one unfamiliar face sat beside him to his right. The woman appeared to be in her early forties. Brown wavy hair loosely framed her pale face, and flowed mid way down her back. Her dark brown eyes locked on Loyal's when he turned her way. When she smiled at him the corners of her mouth curved in an inviting manner. Loyal smiled back and held out his right hand. "I'm Loyal," he said. She shook his hand and said, "Brandi."

"You a buggy owner?" Loyal asked.

"Nope," said Brandi. "I'm here with Verne."

"Lucky guy," said Loyal.

Brandi's smile widened slightly. "We are long time friends," she said. "Verne's a married man."

Before he had a chance to respond, Loyal felt a tap on his left shoulder and turned to look into Bruce's twinkling blue eyes.

"How was the run?" Bruce asked.

"So much fun," said Loyal. "I smiled the whole time."

"That's what dune buggies are all about," said Bruce, "fun and freedom."

Their conversation was interrupted by the ringing of a bell and the announcement that dinner was ready. Three taco bars were stationed on the periphery of the dining area. One of the perks of sitting at Bruce and Winnie's table was being fed first. Loyal offered to fill a plate for Bruce. Maggie did the same for Winnie. Within ten minutes the entire table was re-seated and dining on street tacos, rice, and beans. Drinks were served by the wait staff.

After a few bites of food and a long sip of beer, Loyal turned to Brandi.

"You remind me of someone," he said.

"Really?" said Brandi. "Who?"

'I can't remember her name," said Loyal. "She's an actress. You look so much like her you must hear it all the time." He paused. "She starred in that HBO series Weeds."

Brandi smiled. "I do get that a lot," she said, "Mary-Louise Parker."

"Yep," said Loyal, "that's the one."

Conversation continued at the table through the meal. Bruce told entertaining stories of his adventures throughout the years. The time passed quickly and before Loyal knew it the time had come for buggy awards. Prior to the day's runs, the club had held the *Show and Shine*. All the buggies that were being entered were parked on the grounds of the Wolf Creek Lodge. Club members spent several hours walking amongst the buggies and voting on many categories. Loyal had not entered his buggy. It still needed lots of work. He had, however, spent the morning wandering among the buggies and voting for his favorites. He was pleased to see that a few of his choices were winners. When the awards were completed and the crowd was dispersing, Verne leaned over Brandi and asked Loyal if he wanted to join them at a local bar called The Cave. Loyal thanked Verne for the offer, but declined. He walked Maggie to her room and thanked her again for convincing him to come to the buggy event. Just as she was turning away his phone pinged. He pulled it out of his pocket and smiled when he saw the sender of the message.

"Judging by the look on your face that must be good news," said Maggie.

"It's my stalker," said Loyal.

Maggie laughed. "How is that working out?"

"Pretty well," said Loyal with a smile, "pretty darn well."

2

TRINITY GLASS

Trinity Glass read the text message response from Loyal and leaned back in her chair with a smile. It was after 1:00 in the morning, yet she was finding sleep elusive. Her room at the Courtyard by Marriott Stafford Quantico was stuffy and warm. She had been working out of the Russell Knox Building at Quantico for the last eight days. Her immediate supervisor, Douglass Caldwell, was here as well. They had been working long hours with less than satisfying results. Tomorrow, or more correctly today she thought as she glanced at the time, would be more of the same.

Trinity kicked her bare feet up on the coffee table and allowed her body to slump even further into the soft armchair. She closed her eyes and thought about Loyal. Their separate cases had converged the previous April and they had spent seven days working toward a common goal. Both had felt the spark of interest, but broken ribs and Trinity's abrupt recall to Washington had left things up in the air. In mid June Trinity had found a few free days and spent them with Loyal. It was early days yet, but she could not deny the attraction. Nor did she want to. With thoughts of Loyal in her mind she drifted into sleep.

Less than four hours later Trinity's alarm delivered on it's promise and woke her. She fumbled for her phone, silenced the noise and, with eyes closed, sank back into the chair for a brief moment. She then re-opened her eyes and maneuvered her stiff body out of the chair. Trinity dressed in sweats and a T-shirt. She spent about 20 minutes stretching, then laced up her Brooks Ghost 11 running shoes and headed out the door. Just over ninety minutes later, Trinity was back in the hotel room, showered, and in the process of drying her long vibrant hair. Once that process was complete she applied a minimum amount of makeup, slipped into her navy blue business suit, and exited the hotel. Despite July's warmth and humidity she walked the two miles to the Russell Knox building.

Trinity grimaced as her steps echoed out over the gleaming floors of the Russell Knox Building. She realized the importance of image, hence the business suit, low slung heels, carefully applied makeup, and neat bun at the base of her skull. She much preferred more casual clothing, and smiled at her imagined image of the looks on peoples' faces if she were to enter the building in a T-shirt, yoga pants, and hiking sandals. The smile remained on her face as she entered the dining area, ordered scrambled eggs and decaf, then found a seat by herself at a small table in the corner. She was five bites and two sips into her breakfast when her phone announced an incoming message. A glance at the screen revealed a text from Caldwell. As usual it was terse and to the point.

My office, 10 minutes

Trinity pocketed the phone and scooped a few more bites of egg into her mouth. She drained the coffee, dropped the tray and dishes where indicated, and began the walk to Caldwell's office. At just over 718,000 square feet it was an understatement to say that the Russell Knox Building was large. The entire campus encompassed more than 100 acres. Trinity's journey from the food and beverage area to Caldwell's office took her past offices for the Defense Intelligence Agency, the Defense Security Service, the U.S. Army Criminal Investigation Command, and the Naval Criminal Investigative Service. Trinity watched the time and knew that just over eleven minutes had passed when Caldwell's assistant showed her into his office. Without looking up he said, "You're late."

"It's a big building Doug," said Trinity. "I was having breakfast."

Caldwell looked up and met Trinity's blue eyes with his own dark green ones. "I know where you were," he said.

Trinity sat in the chair facing his desk and said, "Have you got something?"

Caldwell nodded. "Security breach at the border in San Diego. Intel from Homeland Security, sent through the NSA database for facial recognition, is just over ten days old." Trinity's eyes widened. "I know," Caldwell said. "It is an unacceptable delay and I'm dealing with it." He paused a moment. "Still, it's what we have been looking for. Be ready to fly in two hours."

3

LOYAL TRUESDALE

L oyal woke early Sunday morning. He showered, shaved, and got dressed in cargo shorts and a Tommy Bahama. He left his room and descended the stairs to the parking lot where a sea of buggies awaited him. Loyal wandered among them, taking mental note of designs and accessories that caught his eye. As he rounded the corner and entered the area where the previous evening's dinner had been served, he caught sight of Bruce and Winnie. The popular couple was sitting alone at a table. Each had a cup of coffee and a doughnut in front of them. Loyal approached and asked if he could join them.

"Sit down," said Bruce, patting the chair next to him.

"Unusual to find the two of you alone," said Loyal as he sat down.

"It is still early," said Winnie. "There will be a crowd before too long."

"I'd love to hear some stories from Baja if you are in the mood," said Loyal. "My trip to Mike's Sky Ranch was one of the best I've ever taken."

Bruce smiled and began to speak. Instantly Loyal was transported back in time to the dusty roads of Baja. Bruce was in the middle of describing a devastating crash when Loyal's phone rang. With an apology he looked at the screen. When he saw the caller was Maggie, he tapped accept.

"Maggie," he said.

"Loyal." Maggie sounded upset. "We need your help. Can you come to the Honey Bear Lodge? Room 119."

"What's wrong?" Loyal asked.

"I'll explain when you get here," said Maggie. "Hurry." She disconnected the call. Loyal turned to Bruce and Winnie. "I've got to go," he said. "Can we finish the story later?"

It took Loyal less than ten minutes to drive to the Honey Bear Lodge. He parked his buggy behind Maggie's and slid out. She met him at the door of room 119.

"What's going on?" said Loyal.

"Brandi is missing," said Maggie.

Loyal followed her into the room. Once he entered he saw that it was more of a suite. His eyes took in the small living room. Just past the living room was a tiny kitchen. Verne stood by the dining room table, a distraught look on his face.

"Maybe she went for breakfast, or a walk?" Loyal said.

Verne shook his head. "Her bag and phone are gone. The room is spotless."

"Could she have gone home?" Loyal asked.

"I've known her for years, she would never do that," said Verne.

"When was the last time anyone saw her?" asked Loyal.

"Last night, just after midnight," said Verne. "I dropped her here after we left the bar." Loyal walked past Maggie and glanced in the bathroom and the bedroom just beyond it. Verne was right, the place looked like the maid service had already been through. Loyal returned to the living room. "Start with when you left the awards ceremony last night," he said, "tell me everything."

It took Verne about five minutes to describe his evening with Brandi. They had gone to The Cave for drinks. A decent country band had been playing, so they had hung around to listen. Verne had nursed one beer, Brandi had polished off four Jack and cokes. "She was pretty drunk by the time we left," Verne said. "When we got back here I helped her inside and got her situated in the bedroom. I locked the door and went back to my hotel. It is about two blocks away. When I got to my room and emptied my pockets I realized I still had her room key." He paused and slowly shook his head. "I should have taken it right back. I figured she was passed out and wouldn't move until this morning. When I got here about an hour ago this is what I found."

"What is her story?" Loyal asked.

"Her sister and the sister's boyfriend died just under a week ago," said Verne. "Home invasion gone wrong. I thought she could use a diversion, so I asked her to come here with me."

"Have you contacted the Sheriff?" Loyal asked.

Verne shook his head. "They won't do anything. Nothing is out of place." Verne paused and rubbed his eyes with the back of his left hand. "She wouldn't have just left Loyal. I know her."

Loyal sighed. "I'm sure you have tried calling her."

"Straight to voicemail," said Verne.

"Ok," said Loyal, "let's search the room and go from there."

BRANDI KENDRICK

Brandi was stretched across the length of the backseat of the vehicle. She was blindfolded, and her wrists and ankles were bound. The men had not gagged her. She kept quiet so they wouldn't have a reason to. Her head was swimming, mostly with alcohol residue, but also with questions. She had no idea what was happening. She had been passed out when they blindfolded and bound her, and had only awakened with the movement of the vehicle. She hadn't a clue about how long they had been traveling, or which direction they were going. She could hear the mumbling of male voices from the front seat. They were speaking quietly. Brandi lay still, breathing evenly and quietly. All she could do at this point was wait.

TRINITY GLASS

Trinity was the only passenger in the Citation X Elite. She sat in the leather swivel seat and pored over the file Caldwell had assured her she would find when she boarded the plane. As promised, it had been sitting squarely in the center of the spring loaded fold down table. One of the flight crew, a man named Rodger Stuart whom she had met many times, had indicated its presence when he had escorted her personally onto the plane.

"Captain Fraser is already seated," he had said as he led her up the folding stairs. "You requested no other staff, so you'll be on your own back here. I've been instructed that this information," he had indicated the file on the table, "is not to leave the plane. You'll have just over 4 hours to review it." Stuart had pushed a button and the folding stairs had slid neatly back into place. He had checked to make sure the bulkhead door was secured and sealed, then turned and said, "As always, Western Flight's cameras will be disabled when we land. Stay on the plane until your car is brought to the ramp. I'll deplane and transfer your luggage." With that, he had turned and stepped into the flight deck to join Captain Frasier.

Trinity stretched her arms toward the ceiling of the business jet. She pushed the file away, stood, and walked to the rear of the plane. A small fridge was located just outside the lavatory. She opened it, perused the contents, and selected a water bottle and a green apple. She returned to her seat, took a long sip and a bite, and returned to the file. The breach that Caldwell had been referring to was six Chinese Nationals crossing from Mexico to San Diego over the span of three days. All had been using false passports, which had been red flagged. Rather than detain, Homeland Security had kept them under surveillance. That is, until they had lost them seven days ago. Trinity took another large bite out of the apple and chewed hard. She was frustrated that Homeland Security had held onto this intel for so long. She understood that various agencies preferred to keep their information close to the vest, but at the same time realized the importance of interagency cooperation.

Trinity pushed the file away again and leaned back in the plush chair. She swiveled to the right and glanced around the interior of the Citation. Working for the government definitely had its perks. Although her assignments were often filled with danger, she always traveled in comfort and style. Trinity closed her eyes and forced her mind back to the Chinese Nationals with falsified passports. The file was dense and detailed China's long history with the United States regarding military and industrial secrets, high level industrial espionage, stolen intellectual property from government contractors, exploitation of commercial entities, and an extensive network of scientific, academic, and business contacts. China's intelligence agency, The Ministry of State Security or MSS, was established in 1983. Its mission was the preservation of China's National Security through gaining commercial, technological, and military secrets. It was believed that China was involved in espionage around the globe.

Some crimes against the United States were listed in the report. During the Presidential election in 1996 Chinese agents had directed money from foreign contributors through the embassy in Washington to the Democratic National Committee. Ghostnet, a large scale cyber spying network targeting 103 countries was revealed in 2009. Shadow Network, a series of cyber-crimes against India, was revealed in 2010. Both cyber-crimes were traced back to China. In 2015 the United States Office of Personnel Management was the target of a data breach targeting the records of 18 million people. The Equifax data breach of 2017 compromised the private records of 147.9 million Americans, 15.2 million British citizens, and 19,000 Canadians. These two extensive cyber-crimes were traced back to China as well. As recently as 2018 the Deputy Director of the MSS, Yanjun Xu, had been charged with economic espionage by the United States.

Trinity ran her hands over her face and rubbed her eyes. She thought about the brief bios of the five men and one woman who had crossed the border into the United States. One, Keping Xie, was a former top ranking general in the People's Liberation Army. The female, Mei Hua Feng, was a medical researcher who had affiliations with several research hospitals in the United States. The other four men, Chen Zhao, Guang Lin, Tung Shen, and Peng Wei were unknowns. All she had were their names, likely false, and the pictures from the passports. Trinity took a long breath in and blew it out slowly. She checked the time and saw that she had less than two hours until she landed in Carlsbad. She picked up the file again and went back to the beginning.

LOYAL TRUESDALE

Loyal, Verne, and Maggie conducted a very thorough search of Brandi's rooms. They looked under chairs, the couch and the bed, between the mattress and the cushions, and in every cabinet and cupboard. No inch was missed. After an hour Loyal sat heavily on the couch with a sigh. "There's nothing here," he said. "It is *too* clean."

"What do you mean?" said Maggie as she sat down beside him.

"Someone has already been through here," said Loyal. He glanced towards Verne. "I"m starting to give more credit to your theory," he said. "We are going to treat this as foul play until we discover anything that refutes that theory. What more can you tell me about the sister's home invasion?"

"It happened at Jodi's house in Carlsbad," said Verne. "Someone broke in, tortured and then executed them, then set the house on fire. The neighbor's called in the fire, and the fire fighters got it out pretty quickly." Verne paused. "I guess Jodi and Travis were pretty roughed up. Brandi never gave me details."

"I've got someone at the Sheriff's Department I can reach out to for details on the home invasion," said Loyal. "You two go to the office and make sure she didn't check out. Then double check at Wolf Creek to make sure Brandi isn't there. Keep trying her phone. If you don't find her report it to the Sheriff. I'm going to head down to her house." He recited his number for Verne. "Text me her address."

Loyal drove back to Wolf Creek and checked out. He saw Maggie and Verne moving in and out of the crowd of buggy enthusiasts asking about Brandi. He tossed his phone in the passenger seat before he drove away. His buggy was a stick shift and loud. He wouldn't be bothering with his phone while he was driving. Loyal filled the tank and began the drive back to Carlsbad. The road down the mountain was windy and smooth, perfect for the buggy. Loyal let the sun and wind, the sounds and smells, wash all thoughts from his mind. He simply enjoyed the drive.

At the base of the mountain, when he merged onto the freeway, Loyal brought his mind back into focus. He settled in, one lane to the left of the slow lane. He focused his thoughts on Brandi and mentally reviewed his limited interactions with her the previous evening. They had only spoken a few words to each other. He wished now that he had accompanied Verne and Brandi to The Cave. He would have a better sense of the woman if he had spent more time with her. A honk to his left brought Loyal out of his thoughts and back to the present. A truck with three teenagers packed onto the bench seat was next to him. They were all waving at him. The girl in the passenger seat leaned slightly out of the window. Smiling broadly she said, "Cool car!" Then the driver accelerated, and they were gone.

BRANDI KENDRICK

Brandi felt the forward movement of the vehicle cease. She lay quietly while the occupants of the driver and passenger seats exited the vehicle. She heard both doors close. A moment later the rear passenger door, the one closest to her head, opened.

"We know you are awake," whispered a male voice. His head was close to her ear, his smoky breath warm on her cheek. "You will do exactly what we say. Understand?" Brandi nodded.

"We are taking off the blindfold and the restraints," said the voice. "You will stand and walk with us to our destination. If you struggle or cry out, you will be killed." He paused a moment. His breath was still wafting against her cheek. "Do you understand?" he asked again. Once again, Brandi nodded.

TRINITY GLASS

T rinity put the file back on the table and focused her
gaze out the window of the business jet. Captain
Frasier had announced their impending landing at
McClellan Palomar Airport in Carlsbad. She watched as the
towns of Escondido and San Marcos slid smoothly under her
view and the edge of Carlsbad appeared. Her mind wandered
briefly back to the previous April and the thick fog that had
enveloped the fuselage of the Lear she had been traveling in.
This time the air was clear and the sun was shining brightly.

The landing was smooth, as always. Trinity waited as Rodger
stowed her luggage in the Toyota 4Runner she had requested.
He re-boarded the plane, unlocked the safe where her gun and
phone had been stored during the flight, and handed them
back to her. She holstered the Sig Sauer Compact 45 and sent a
quick text to Loyal letting him know she had landed. She then
stuffed her phone in her briefcase, thanked Rodger, and

deplaned. In mere moments she was in the 4Runner and exiting the airport. The drive to the condo she had requested was short. She parked, carried her belongings into the condo, grabbed a Perrier from the fridge, and immediately sat at the dining room table with her laptop open in front of her.

Since she had not been allowed to keep the file, or take notes or photos, Trinity had committed much of it to memory. She started with descriptions of the Chinese Nationals. She had memorized their names and details of their appearance in much the same way one would memorize a song or poem; repetition. She let the mental melody flow now, from her brain, through her fingers, and onto the keyboard. She described the angles of their jaws, the size and set of their ears, the bridges of their noses, and the angle, size, and set of their eyes. All had fairly long hair, which Trinity assumed would have been cut as soon as they drifted off the radar of Homeland Security.

When she had finished with the descriptions, Trinity pushed away from the computer and stood. A glance at the kitchen clock told her over an hour had passed. She took a long inhale, reached her arms over her head, hinged at the hips, and let her arms dangle by her toes. She stayed in this position through several more long inhales and exhales. With the final exhale, she hinged back up and stood straight, then gave her body a small shake and sat back down. She took a long drink of the Perrier, gave a small burp from the carbonation, then turned to her computer again. Caldwell had provided the file as background so that she would be prepared for her meeting with

Homeland Security agents the following morning. It was Trinity's habit to always be over prepared. The habit consistently returned positive results. She positioned her long slender fingers over the keyboard and began to type.

LOYAL TRUESDALE

L oyal was driving South on Interstate 15, approaching Lake Elsinore, when his stomach gurgled and reminded him that he had not yet eaten. He saw an In and Out sign and exited the freeway. As usual the drive-through line was long, but the wait was fairly short. Loyal ordered a double-double with grilled onions and a lemonade. Eating while driving the buggy was a somewhat difficult proposition, so Loyal pulled into a shady parking spot to eat. He took this opportunity to Google map the address Verne had sent to him. The street was Caminito del Reposo, a cul-de-sac just East of Interstate 5. Just as he was setting his phone down it dinged twice, announcing the arrival of two text messages. The first was Verne, saying they had looked everywhere they could think of and had not located Brandi. Loyal sent back a quick text

ok, halfway to her house. Make sure you make a report to local law enforcement. Even if they don't believe you it gets the ball rolling.

.　.　.

The second was from Trinity letting him know that she had just landed in San Diego for work, and was hoping to see him. To this text Loyal responded

Sounds great. Let me know when you are free.

Loyal set the phone in the passenger seat with a smile. He ate the last bite of his burger then slid out to dispose of the trash. He was still smiling when he slid back in the buggy and drove away.

Just over an hour later Loyal pulled up in front of Brandi's home. The houses on Caminito del Reposo were duplexes, Brandi's being the right half of the conjoined homes. Loyal slid out and went straight to the front door. He rang the bell, then knocked. Neither action produced a result. Loyal stepped back to the sidewalk and studied the small home. There was a grassy area to the right of the house; a cement walkway leading to the rear. Loyal walked down the walkway to the back of the house. There was a small patio that held two chairs and a small table. Several potted plants were strategically placed around the small area. Loyal was surprised to see that none of the homes had any type of fencing. All the backyards were open to the greenbelt area.

The blinds in Brandi's sliding glass door and back windows were closed. The house felt empty to Loyal. He turned and surveyed the greenbelt. A small clump of trees stood just to the left of Brandi's home, less than 50 yards from her patio. Loyal walked over to the trees and turned to look back at Brandi's house. It was a clear view. He walked behind the trees and hunkered down. Again, he had a perfect view. Loyal looked at the ground around him. Under a few leaves he saw a lime green disposable lighter. Loyal used his right hand to lightly sweep the leaves away. Not far from the lighter he discovered an open and empty matchbook. Loyal swept his hand along the leaf cluttered ground once more, and found a few cigarette butts.

Loyal paused for a moment, then straightened and returned to the buggy. He rummaged around in the duffel he had taken to Big Bear and found a ziplock bag containing a few q-tips. He returned to the clump of trees and kneeled down again. Using two q-tips, he gently lifted the lighter, chopstick style, and placed it in the ziplock. He repeated this action with the matchbook and the cigarettes. He slipped each item into its own corner of the bag to keep them separated, then sealed and folded the bag and slipped it into his pocket. Not an ideal evidence collection bag, but it would have to do for now. Loyal straightened and walked back toward the front of Brandi's house.

LOYAL TRUESDALE

A s Loyal rounded the corner of Brandi's home, a voice called out, "I have 911 dialed and I'm ready to press call." Loyal stopped abruptly and looked at the source of this comment. A middle aged woman stood about 30 feet from him. She was dressed in a black business suit with a gray blouse beneath the jacket. Her hair was cut short, her makeup thick and perfectly applied. Her face was set in a hard expression. She did not look the least bit afraid, in fact she looked to Loyal like a particular lawyer he had dreaded being cross examined by when he was on the force.

"I saw you snooping around back there. Who are you and what are you doing?" she asked.

Loyal held up his hands in a placating gesture. "I'm just looking for Brandi," he said. The stern woman said nothing. Loyal filled the void with, "I met her at a buggy event in Big Bear this weekend. She gave me her address. She said to stop by."

The woman appraised Loyal for a moment. "You don't look like her type. Brandi prefers her men younger than you."

Loyal sighed. "I'm a retired detective with the very department you are abut to call. I apologize if I spooked you. I really just wanted to see her again."

The woman's features remained hard and untrusting. "I saw you digging around in the trees back there. You won't find Brandi there. What's really going on?"

"I'm really just looking for Brandi," said Loyal. "And I'm leaving now." He paused, then added, "If you see her will you tell her Loyal stopped by?"

The woman stared hard at Loyal for a long minute, then uttered a reluctant, "If I see her."

"Thanks," said Loyal. He turned and walked to the buggy. He slid in and started it up. As he exited the cul-de-sac he saw the woman in the rearview mirror. She was standing, ramrod straight, holding her phone up in a way that made Loyal suspect she was recording his departure.

TRINITY GLASS

Over two hours passed before Trinity lifted her hands from the keyboard. She rolled her shoulders and wiggled her fingers, then stood and retrieved a plastic USB drive from her briefcase. She had mentally regurgitated all the details that she could remember from the file she had ingested on the plane. She saved all the contents to her computer and the zip drive, then slid the zip drive into a secure pocket in her briefcase. Her stomach gurgled. She went back to the refrigerator and examined the contents more closely. She was relieved to see that all her requested items had been neatly stored inside. She grabbed a pre-made Trader Joe's Greek salad, opened all the packets, and dumped everything into a bowl. She used two forks to give the salad a few tosses, then put one fork in the sink and used the other to eat.

With her hunger sated for the moment, Trinity turned to the task of unpacking her suitcase and storing her personal items in the appropriate places. When that task was complete she took an extra long shower and dressed in sweat pants and a loose T-shirt. She ran her fingers through her long damp hair, then let the uncombed tresses hang loosely down her back. She returned to the kitchen, heated some tomato basil soup and grilled a pepper jack sourdough, and returned again to the computer. She re-read the file as she slowly ate her meal. Her relaxed brain released a few more tidbits of information, which she added to the file. She then re-saved the information on both her computer and the zip drive, which she returned to its secure place in her briefcase. Trinity was exhausted. She lay down on the couch and drifted off.

LOYAL TRUESDALE

L oyal popped onto Interstate 5 and in ten minutes was parked in front of his apartment on Roosevelt Street. He remained in his buggy as he contemplated typing out a text to Patrick O'Keefe. Pat was a Detective with the Carlsbad Sheriff's Department, and a friend of Loyal's. Things had been a bit tense between them since the previous April when Loyal had overstepped the bounds of friendship by asking favors of Pat that could have jeopardized his position with the department. Loyal needed information that Pat could help him access. He decided to give it a try and tapped out a short message.

You free for lunch? Usual spot?

Loyal sat in his buggy and waited for a response. It took over five minutes, but finally came through.

. . .

Ok. 1:30

Loyal looked at the time. It was 1:15. He'd barely make it on time if he left right now. He looked longingly at his front door. A few minutes at home would have been nice. With a sigh he restarted the buggy and began the drive to Plant Power.

Plant Power was a small restaurant that Loyal and Pat had originally chosen because it was vegan and they did not think they would see any of their fellow officers there. They still appreciated the lack of police presence, but had also come to really enjoy the food. Loyal pulled into the small parking lot at 1:32. He found no spaces, so drove to the Vons grocery store that was adjacent and parked there. He walked quickly back to Plant Power and found Pat waiting for him.

"Hi Pat," said Loyal, "thanks for meeting me."

Pat's gaze settled on Loyal for a long moment. He looked directly in Loyal's eyes. "I was walking past the radio room at the station on my way to come meet you," Pat said. "Heard a call from a woman reporting a man poking around her neighbor's house. He fit your exact description, said he was a retired detective, and told her his name was Loyal." Pat's blue eyes narrowed. "She gave his license plate number, and guess what? It *was* you. What's going on this time, Loyal?"

Loyal sighed. "It was me, but I can explain. Let's get our food and I'll tell you everything."

"I don't think I want to eat with you today," Pat said. "It's clear you invited me because you need something. I can't keep risking my job for you Loyal."

Loyal nodded. "It was wrong of me to ask Pat. You've been a good friend."

Pat nodded back. "I've gotta go." He turned and was gone before Loyal had a chance to reply.

13

TRINITY GLASS

T rinity woke with a gasp. Her face was smashed into the couch cushions, air was scarce. She rolled and took a deep shuddering breath. When she was calmed she tried to remember the dream from which she had just escaped. The first part came easily. She had been in the desert. Which one, she did not know. It resembled the Sahara, miles of dunes with nothing else in sight. She had been struggling to climb to the top of a large dune, hoping to see some type of refuge in the distance. The climb had been arduous, her feet slipping and sliding on the unstable sand. In the end she had crawled to the top and, finally, stood to take in her surroundings. There had been nothing but desert as far as her eyes could see.

Trinity sat up and rubbed her eyes. She stood, went to the kitchen, and poured herself a glass of water. Leaning against the counter, she drained the glass and carefully placed it in the sink. Her thoughts went back to the dream. She remembered now, she had been standing on top of the dune when it began to implode, the sand swirling and sucking at her feet, pulling her down. She had clawed at the silty mass, but could find no purchase. It had been sucking her down into its depths, slowly suffocating her, when she had awoken.

BRANDI KENDRICK

R estraints and blindfold removed, Brandi was able to see that they were parked near a marina. The two men with her were Asian. They said nothing more to her, simply led her to a gate labeled J. One of the men slid a fob in front of the gate and it unlocked. They led Brandi down the dock, stopping in front of a very large boat. A metal stairway led them off the dock. They walked quickly to the cabin and entered the living room area. An L -shaped couch and a coffee table dominated the room. Before Brandi had time to notice more, she was quickly blindfolded and restrained again. Her captors pushed her onto the couch. She lay quietly, listening. She heard more male voices, and then a female voice. All were speaking a dialect she did not understand.

LOYAL TRUESDALE

Loyal watched Pat drive off, then returned to his buggy without ordering any food. He slid in, then picked up his phone and called Verne. He answered on the second ring.

"You find her?" Verne asked.

"Not yet," said Loyal. "Sounds like you didn't have any luck either."

"No," said Verne. "Just finished with the Sheriff. He took the report, but said they can't really do anything for two days."

"Still, it is important that you made the report. It gets her into the system," said Loyal. "Do you happen to have Brandi's sister's address?" he added.

"I don't know the house number," said Verne. "It's on Morgan Road, just West of the junction of El Camino Real and College. It's partially burned, you should be able to find it."

"Thanks," said Loyal. "That is my next stop. What are your plans?"

"Just leaving Big Bear," said Verne.

. . .

Loyal disconnected and google mapped Morgan Road. It was about 15 minutes from his current location and looked to be a short residential street. He ran his hand through his hair and thought about Pat O'Keefe. Their friendship had been strained since the previous April when Loyal had asked a few too many favors of the young man. Loyal had been hoping to get the official report on the home invasion and murders, but realized now that wouldn't be happening. Instead, he called Phil, a Carlsbad firefighter he knew through Maggie, and left a message asking for details about the fire on Morgan Road.

Loyal drove West on Interstate 5 and exited on Cannon Road. Traffic was heavy on Cannon and Loyal's progress was slow until he made the right turn on Faraday. A left on Camino Hills Drive, a right on Browning Road, and a right on Morgan Road and he had arrived. The house was easy to find as it was the only partially burned house in the neighborhood. It was located about half way down the short street on the right hand side. Any crime scene tape that had been there had been removed. Loyal could see that the scene had been released by both The San Diego Bomb and Arson Unit and the Carlsbad Sheriff's Department. Loyal continued past the house and drove the length of Morgan Road. At the base the road curved to the left and became Lindsay Drive. Loyal pulled the buggy to the curb, parked, and slid out. He had no badge or search warrant, just his instincts and the gun on waist.

Before he had taken a step his phone rang. He saw it was Phil and answered.

"Thanks for calling Phil," said Loyal. "I'm just approaching the house now."

"Don't go any further Loyal," Phil said. "I'm off today. Let me meet you there. Don't go on the property without me. The tape is removed, but this is still an active investigation."

"I'll wait on the sidewalk in front," said Loyal.

16

LOYAL TRUESDALE

He was almost to the house when his phone rang. Loyal recognized the number as the Carlsbad Sheriff's Department. He silenced the phone and placed it back in his pocket then continued towards the house. Loyal paused on the sidewalk in front of the partially burned building and took a long look. The house was a single story. The driveway was positioned down the length of the house, the garage attached toward the back. The front portion of the house had been preserved by the firefighters. The center of the house was clearly where the fire had started. Loyal removed his phone from his pocket, saw that he had a voicemail but ignored it, and snapped a few photos. He looked around, the neighborhood was quiet. Movement down the street drew his eye and he saw a marked unit turning onto Morgan Road. He replaced his phone and watched the unit approach. He casually walked over and approached the passenger window of the vehicle as it slowed in front of the residence. He looked in and saw Officer Demkowski.

"Hey Truesdale," Demkowski said. "What are you doing here? I thought you were retired."

"I'm doing some consulting work. An arson investigator is meeting me here."

"Ok," said Demkowski. "I'm still going to need to turn this in as a field interview."

"Understood," said Loyal. "Nice seeing you man."

Demkowski gave a wave and drove away.

As Demkowski rounded the corner Phil arrived in his truck. He parked and slid out.

"Hey Loyal," he said.

"Hi Phil. Thanks for meeting me."

"Sure."

"Haven't seen you since the wedding. How's Elsie?"

"She's pretty good," said Phil. "Still dealing with her Mom's death, but overall things are good."

Loyal turned towards the house. "You have any idea what went on here?"

"I was one of the first responders," said Phil. "We got the fire knocked down quickly. At first we thought it was a regular structure fire until I found the first body." He paused. "It was bad, Loyal. The guy's hands were still bound. He'd been shot in the head. We backed off and called in homicide."

"Who took the call?" Loyal asked.

"Hammond."

17

LOYAL TRUESDALE

P hil and Loyal did not go inside the burned building. Instead they walked down the driveway and to the back of the house. There was a small fenced yard and a tree filled greenbelt beyond the yard. Phil remained by the fence while Loyal slipped into the greenbelt, walked up the slight hill, then turned and surveyed the home from behind. The small hill provided a good view of the back of the house. Loyal moved a few feet to the left and found a spot that was obscured by plants and trees but still offered a decent view of the house. He knelt down and looked at the ground. It didn't take long to discover an empty matchbook and three cigarette butts. He had no more ziplocks in his buggy, so he found a large leaf and scooped the matchbook and butts onto it with a stick. He then made his way back down to the fence line and rejoined Phil.

"You have anything in your car I could put these in?" he asked Phil.

"Yeah," said Phil. "I have a first aid kit. I'm sure there is something in there." As they walked back down the driveway to

Phil's truck Loyal asked, "Who's the lead in the arson investigation?"

"Larry Weber," said Phil. "You know him?"

"Yeah," said Loyal. "He's actually a good friend of mine."

Phil dug around in the first aid kit and came up with a few small ziplock bags. Loyal slid the matchbook and the cigarettes into the bags, thanked Phil again for meeting him, and walked down the street and back to the buggy. He placed the ziplocks under the seat, then slid in the buggy and drove towards home.

18

PATRICK O'KEEFE

After walking away from Loyal, Pat had driven straight back to the station. He had parked, entered, and climbed the stairs to his small office without a glance at anyone. He was currently sitting behind his desk, computer open, but his mind on Loyal. He was feeling guilty about the way he had spoken. When Pat had first been hired Loyal had made a point of being welcoming. Pat admired Loyal's work ethic, tenacity, and strong moral core. Nearly a year ago Loyal had gotten mixed up in a case that had ended up getting him suspended. Then a heart attack had sidelined him. Just as he was coming back from that he had involved himself in a case where he did not belong. It was during that time that he had asked Pat for help and information. Pat had helped him, but had risked his own career to do so. True to his word, Loyal had not revealed the source of the help. There were times however, that Pat felt Captain William's gaze and knew that the man suspected him of helping Loyal.

. . .

Pat leaned back in his chair and ran his hands over his closely cropped red hair. He let out a sigh, closed his eyes, and tipped his face towards the ceiling. He was in this position when he heard a knock on the open door. He opened his eyes to see Captain Williams in the doorway.

"Got a minute?" the Captain asked.

Pat nodded and waved him in. Captain Williams closed the door behind him and sat in the chair opposite Pat.

He leaned forward, his forearms coming to rest on the metal desk, and said, "You have any idea what Truesdale is up to? We had a call about someone snooping around a house. Description fits Truesdale and license plate is registered to him."

Pat shook his head. "No." He paused, then added, "He called today and wanted to meet for lunch. I heard that call about the suspicious person too, on my way out. I asked him about it, but decided I really didn't want to know. I left kind of abruptly. Feel bad about that."

The Captain leaned back in the chair with a sigh. "We ran the name of the resident of that address. She was reported missing this morning in Big Bear. I called Truesdale. He didn't answer. What the hell is he up to now?"

19

LOYAL TRUESDALE

L oyal parked in front of his apartment. Before he exited the buggy he listened to the voicemail. It was short and to the point. Captain Williams would appreciate a return call. Loyal shelved the idea of calling back and instead carried the evidence he had collected up the stairs. He walked through the small apartment and opened windows to let in the fresh coastal air. He stood at the small kitchen window and called Larry Weber. The call went to voicemail and Loyal left a brief message telling Larry he was interested in the arson on Morgan Road and asking if he could call at his earliest convenience. He went in the bathroom and grabbed a pair of disposable gloves, then walked back to the kitchen for a box of ziplocks. With those items in hand he returned to the dining room table where he had placed the matchbooks, lighter and butts. He carefully repackaged the items in individual ziplocks and used a sharpie to note the date, time, and locations where they had been found. Through the clear plastic he could see that the matchbooks were identical. Both were from The Jolly Roger restaurant in Oceanside Harbor. Loyal looked at the

clock in the kitchen. It was nearly 4:00. A beer and and some
mahi fish tacos sounded pretty good. Loyal changed into slacks
and a fresh shirt. He considered taking the Altima, but decided
the buggy would be more fun on such a beautiful Summer day.
By 4:30 he was on his way.

Loyal followed the long lazy loop that connected the offramp
from Interstate 5 to Harbor Drive. The two lanes merged into
one and led down a small hill into Oceanside Harbor. Loyal
never tired of the view. Both the North and South sides of the
Harbor were visible for a brief moment. Sparkling blue water
held boats of all sizes which were bobbing gently on the sea.
Masts, most without sails attached, reached skyward. The rock
walls of the harbor framed the exit out to open sea. At the base
of the hill Loyal veered to the left and drove past some restaurants and shops on his right, the wide expanse of sandy beach
to his left. He parked the buggy at the far end of the South side
of the harbor and slid out. Not wanting to risk a citation, he
purchased an all day permit from the payment machine and
stuck the paper under the windshield wiper. On the drive over
he had decided to park on the South side and make the long
walk around to The Jolly Roger which was located toward the
far Northern end of marina, the Oceanside Yacht Club and
some condos the only buildings beyond it.

Loyal walked at a steady pace, but kept his eyes open for
anything unusual. He did not believe in coincidences, and
finding matchbooks from the same restaurant at Jodi and Brandi's homes suggested surveillance. The South side of the harbor
was crowded and had a party atmosphere. Trailers filled the

parking lot, the sand was dotted with sun umbrellas, and the ocean full of swimmers. Shoppers and diners filled the shops and restaurants. The crowds thinned as Loyal reached the Northern part of the Harbor. This area contained the slips, which were full of boats of all types and sizes. He reached The Jolly Roger in just under an hour.

The Jolly Roger had a very popular happy hour from 3:00-7:00, and it was in full swing on a Sunday evening in July. He made his way through the tables to the large wooden bar and found an empty stool at the far end. Loyal and his second wife, Angela, had been happy hour regulars at The Jolly Roger during their three years together. They had both loved the ambiance and the serene views of the harbor. They had even briefly considered buying a boat, but had decided against it when they had calculated the cost. Loyal swiveled on his stool and raised his hand to signal Ted, the long time bartender, that he was ready to order.

Ted approached Loyal with a wide smile and stretched his hand across the bar for a shake.

"Loyal, man," he said. "Great to see you. It has been a while."

Loyal returned the shake and smile. "Yeah, sure has," he said. "Great to see you Ted." Loyal glanced around the crowded restaurant. "Looks like not much has changed."

Ted laughed. "Nope. Same old thing. What are you drinking?"

Loyal thought about Trinity and her fondness for IPA's.

"What IPA's do you have?" he asked.

"Belching Beaver 78, Ballast Point Sculpin, Stone IPA, Stone Ripper, and Lagunitas," said Ted.

"I'll have the Stone Ripper," said Loyal. "In a schooner please."

Loyal's seat afforded him a nice view of the harbor. He gazed out the window, silently reading the clever names on the boats docked at the slips. Ted returned quickly with the schooner. Loyal sipped and let his mind drift back to Trinity's brief visit the previous month. She had arrived on a Friday night, quite late. They had slept in on Saturday morning, then decided to visit Stone Brewery in Escondido. Upon arriving they had learned that public behind-the-scenes tours were available for a small fee. The tour had been fascinating, and had culminated with the tasting of six different Stone products. Trinity's favorite had been Ripper. After the tour she and Loyal had hung out in the lush garden area of the restaurant sipping beer and nibbling on pretzels and deep fried Brussels sprouts. The taste of the beer he was drinking now brought back those memories of Trinity.

20

LOYAL TRUESDALE

L oyal drank the beer slowly and felt himself begin to relax. Ted returned to ask if he wanted anything to eat. Loyal ordered two fish tacos, which were delivered in a timely manner and delicious. As 7:00 neared, and with happy hour ending, the bar area began to empty out a bit. Loyal stayed where he was. He ordered another beer. Ted delivered it, and having few customers at the large bar, stayed a moment to chat with Loyal. Ted did not know Loyal had retired and Loyal did not mention it. He told Ted he was working on a case and had found a few Jolly Roger matchbooks at the scene.

"You see anyone unusual around here lately that smokes?" he asked Ted.

Ted leaned across the bar and spoke in a low tone.

"I think I might know who you are looking for," he said. "A group of Chinese people docked about a week ago. They have the biggest boat in the harbor, expensive as hell."

"I need to see them," said Loyal. "What slip are they in?"

"They are in J," said Ted. "Very end of the slip." He paused, then added, "But you will see them in here pretty soon. They always eat at the same time and table." He pointed across the room towards a secluded table at the rear of the restaurant. "They eat there at 8:00."

Loyal glanced at his phone. It was 7:15. He ordered another taco and a glass of water, setting the second schooner of beer to the side. When Ted returned with his taco and water Loyal said, "I need to get to their boat."

Ted smiled. "My dinghy is tied up in the transient dock just outside that exit door." He pointed to a door located at the side of the restaurant. "You can borrow it." Ted leaned across the bar again. "They eat fast Loyal. You'll have forty minutes at best."

"Thanks Ted," said Loyal. He moved the beer back in front of him and ate slowly, attempting to assume the role of local barfly.

Loyal nibbled on the taco and mentally reviewed everything that had occurred since he had received the frantic call from Maggie. He regretted giving Brandi's neighbor any information about himself. He hadn't thought she would actually call law enforcement about him. The fact that she had presented a problem. He knew from his years on the force that the San Bernadino Sheriff's Department would have entered Brandi's information in a national database even if they suspected no foul play. When her neighbor called in about Loyal, the Carlsbad Sheriff's would have run Brandi's name and discovered that she had been reported missing earlier in the day. Loyal was sure that was why Captain Williams wanted to talk to him. He hadn't done anything illegal up to this point. His plan to sneak onto the boat while its occupants were at dinner definitely crossed the line. Loyal reconsidered what he was planning. He didn't even know Brandi, had no allegiance to her. He wondered, for a moment, if perhaps it would be best to simply finish the taco and second beer, walk back to the buggy, and go home. When he saw the group that walked in and sat at the table in the back he dismissed that thought, stood, turned off and pocketed his phone, and walked to the dinghy.

21

BRANDI KENDRICK

Brandi lay on the couch and tried to remain calm. Her wrists and ankles were still bound with zip ties. The bandana was still wrapped around her head, but had slipped a bit so that she could just see out of the corner of her right eye. It was an extremely limited view, and slightly blurry because her eyelashes were in the way. She had counted five men and one woman, all Asian. They had dumped her luggage and found the small black backpack that Jodi had sent her just over a week ago. It's contents were spread on the coffee table. Brandi had not been able to understand the content of the conversation going on between her captors, but she could tell by tone and body language that they were arguing. There was one man who appeared to be the leader of the group. At one point during their discussions he had looked at his watch, said something, then walked towards the door. The other men had followed him off the boat. The woman had remained. She had stood still, staring at Brandi for an uncomfortably long period of time. Eventually she had exited through a different door.

Brandi had heard her footsteps as she went up the stairs to the bridge.

22

LOYAL TRUESDALE

L oyal sat on the right rear edge of the dinghy near the engine. He started the engine with one hard pull. For a moment he thought the momentum from the pull was going to send him over the edge and into the water. He teetered, then regained his balance. Remaining on the edge of the craft, he shifted into reverse and eased away from the dock. When he was clear, he turned towards the bay, paused to shift to forward, and eased out into the darkening water. He made one pass around the entire perimeter of the harbor for two reasons. The first, to become accustomed to handling the dinghy, the second to get a good view of the boat Ted had told him about. It wasn't hard to locate, it was definitely the largest in the entire harbor. Daylight was rapidly fading, but he was able to make out a silhouette standing at the bridge, smoking. The end of the cigarette glowed with each inhale. He wasn't sure, but thought it was a female.

After he completed one pass around the harbor, Loyal steered the dinghy in the general direction of the large vessel. As he neared he saw that the figure was indeed a female. She glanced his way, stubbed the cigarette out, turned, and descended the stairs back to the cabin. Loyal watched with his peripheral vision as she unlocked the door and entered. Once she closed the door, Loyal pointed the dinghy at the back of the yacht. He revved the engine to get speed, then shut it off for silence. The dinghy drifted straight to the back of the yacht. There was a small shelf-like area and a hand rail, which Loyal grabbed and tied the dinghy to. He then stepped out of the dinghy and onto the yacht. He walked as quietly as possible to a circular porthole and risked a peek inside. He let out a slow breath. Brandi lay on the couch. Her wrists and ankles were bound with zip ties, her eyes covered by a loose fitting bandana. She appeared to be asleep. Loyal hoped she wasn't drugged, as that would make getting her out of there even more difficult. Her captor sat in a freestanding chair opposite the couch, her back to the door.

Loyal stepped back from the porthole and rapidly considered his options. Calling 911 was the safest, but if the five men returned they could easily leave the slip and be far out to sea before help arrived. Loyal hadn't liked the look of the men when they had first entered the restaurant. The oldest one, especially, had a military air about him. They all walked with tension, like coiled springs. Now, seeing Brandi bound and blindfolded, Loyal knew that something very bad was going on. He eased the PM9 off his waist, checked that there was a bullet in the chamber, and moved silently to the door. He paused a moment and a thought passed through his mind. Entering this boat, as a private citizen, with his gun drawn could get him in a lot of trouble. He replaced this thought with the image of Brandi on the couch. She needed help. Hopefully he wouldn't lose his concealed carry permit over this. With a slow exhale, he placed his hand on the thin silver handle and eased it downward. It was unlocked. Loyal eased it gently open and entered the cabin.

23

BRANDI KENDRICK

Through her limited right eye vision, Brandi saw the cabin door easing open. Although her adrenaline spiked when she saw who was slipping through the doorway, she remained absolutely still. She could not even begin to imagine how the man she sat beside at dinner the previous evening had found her. She didn't care. He moved silently, gun in front of him, to the chair the woman was sitting in. With a swift movement he placed the gun against her temple and at the same time covered her mouth with his hand. The woman's eyes widened, but she did not flinch. The man, Brandi recalled that his name was Loyal, whispered something in the woman's ear. She nodded and he eased his hand off her mouth. Keeping the gun trained on the woman, he eased around in front of her. He reached out and pulled the bandanna off of Brandi's head. His eyes briefly met hers, then focused again on the woman. He moved to the galley, grabbed a knife out of a drawer and eased back toward Brandi. She held her hands out towards him and he cut the zip tie. He did the same with her ankles. Brandi rubbed her hands and feet grateful for the full blood flow returning to them.

"Zip tie her hands and feet," he said. Brandi picked up two long zip ties from the pile on the coffee table and followed his instructions. The woman looked at Brandi with hate filled eyes.

"Let's go," he said as he started towards the door.

"Wait," said Brandi, "I need my things." She returned the items to the black back pack and slipped it over her shoulders. She then picked up a pile of clothes from the floor, stuffed everything into her small suitcase, and followed Loyal out of the cabin.

24

LOYAL TRUESDALE

L oyal watched as Brandi zip tied the Chinese woman's wrists and ankles. Her movements were swift, her hands calm. He had expected hysteria and was surprised and pleased that Brandi seemed to have her wits about her. He wasn't thrilled when she stopped to gather her things. She swept a dozen or so small black and silver rectangular boxes into a small black backpack and put it on. She then grabbed a small suitcase and followed him out the door. Loyal slipped the PM9 back into his belly band. He led Brandi to the dinghy and helped her in. He then joined her in the small craft, pulled the cord to start the engine, and reversed away from the yacht.

Less than a minute after they had motored away, Loyal heard shouting coming from the yacht. He revved the engine to full power and aimed the dinghy at the South shore. Over the noise of the dinghy's engine, Loyal heard another, even louder engine start up. The moon and the harbor lights provided enough ambient light for Loyal to see that several of the men were in a dinghy of their own and coming after them.

"Duck down," he said to Brandi. "Brace yourself. We are going to hit the shore hard." Loyal braced himself as best he could and the dinghy hit the shore at speed. The motor screamed, then shuddered as it was embedded in the sand. The collision threw Loyal forward in the dinghy. He landed on top of Brandi, then pushed quickly off and sprang out of the small craft. He reached his hand out for hers and pulled her out. She still wore the small backpack and had her suitcase in her free hand.

Loyal and Brandi sprinted to the buggy and slid in. He could hear the thump of their pursuers dinghy as it slammed into the sand. A quick turn of the key and the buggy was running. Gunshots rang out as Loyal slammed it into gear. The tires made a squeal as he let off the clutch and sped away. Loyal drove out of the harbor and merged onto Interstate 5 heading South. He kept the buggy steady at 65mph. Just past Cassidy Street he took the exit that merged onto Highway 78 heading East. He glanced at Brandi. She sat in the passenger seat eyes facing forward. As if she felt his eyes on her she turned her head to look at him. She smiled that slow, sexy smile and said, "Thank you."

25

TRINITY GLASS

Trinity stayed awake until the last wisps of the dream had eased out of her mind. To help this process along she had re-read everything she had typed earlier in the day. She was fairly sure that the Chinese Nationals who had crossed the border with falsified passports were connected to the work she and Doug were doing. China was using very clever means of spying and stealing intellectual property in and from the United States. It was suspected, and Trinity and Doug were trying to prove, that the five Chinese Consulates scattered across the US were actually spy networks. They were located in New York, Los Angeles, San Fransisco, Houston, and Chicago. Trinity suspected that the six people who had crossed the border ten days previously were heading to the consulate in Los Angeles. As she was easing her tired body into bed Trinity thought about calling Loyal simply to hear his voice. Instead she closed her blue eyes and fell back into sleep.

26

BRANDI KENDRICK

Brandi felt Loyal's eyes on her and turned to look at him. She smiled and said, "Thank you," although she doubted he could hear her. He nodded and smiled back.

"Where are we going?" Brandi asked loudly, over the engine noise and wind.

"Valley Center," said Loyal. "Maggie's house."

"Can you exit on El Camino Real?" asked Brandi. "I need to grab something."

"Those guys were shooting at us," said Loyal. "We don't have the time to stop anywhere. They might be close behind us."

"I have to stop," said Brandi. "Please. It will only take a minute. It's the 24 hour fitness right off the freeway. By the movie theater."

The look on Loyal's face told Brandi that he wasn't happy, but he took the offramp and parked in front of the gym. Brandi jumped out and ran to the entrance. She entered the gym and went straight to the woman's locker area. She keyed open a locker and grabbed the contents, and stuffed it into her jeans pocket. She paused a moment, eyeing the backdoor of the gym. "Do I really want to stick with Loyal?" she asked herself out loud. She spent a full minute considering her options. Ultimately she decided that Loyal was competent. Sticking with him, at least for the time being, made sense. When she returned to the buggy Loyal gave her a questioning look, but said nothing. He simply put the buggy, which he had left idling, into gear and drove out of the lot.

With the engine noise and wind whipping around their heads, conversation was not easily managed. Brandi scrunched down in the seat and let her mind drift. She still had no idea how Loyal had managed to find her, but was certainly grateful. She glanced behind her at her suitcase in the back seat. The movement caused pain in her back and she remembered that she was still wearing Jodi's backpack. She wriggled out of it and stowed it in the footwell where she could keep en eye on it. She glanced at Loyal again. His eyes were focused on the road. She didn't know what he had planned after they arrived at Maggie's house. For a moment she wondered if she would be better on her own. With her eyes still on his profile she realized that she wasn't worried about what was in store for her. Loyal had rescued her, she trusted him.

27

LOYAL TRUESDALE

L oyal steered the buggy down Maggie's long driveway. He had turned on his phone and called her from the parking lot of the 24 Hour Fitness while Brandi was inside. She had picked up on the sixth ring.

"Did you find her?" she had asked.

"Yes," Loyal had said. "Can we come to you?"

"Of course," Maggie had said.

The outside lights of her house shone brightly now, welcoming them. Loyal parked in front of the house. The front door opened and Maggie and her German Shepard, Storm, stepped out. She paused to instruct Storm to stay on the porch, then hurried to the buggy.

"Are you all right?" she asked Brandi.

The woman nodded.

"Come on," said Maggie. "Let's get you inside." She reached to help Brandi out of the buggy. Brandi grabbed the backpack from the footwell, allowed Maggie to help her out, then slipped the backpack back over her shoulders. Loyal followed the two women and the impossibly large dog into the house.

. . .

As they stepped into the light of the entryway, Maggie glanced at Brandi's chaffed wrists. Her eyes widened. She removed the suitcase from Brandi's hand, set it in the entryway, and led Brandi to the living room.

"Sit here," she said. "You must be starving. I'll make you something to eat."

"May I use your restroom?" asked Brandi.

"Of course," said Maggie. "It's just down the hall."

Brandi rose from the couch and walked down the hall. Loyal noticed that she took the black backpack with her. He followed Maggie and Storm into the kitchen. She turned to him and said in a low voice, "What happened?"

"She was kidnapped," Loyal said. "I found her on a boat in Oceanside Harbor. She was tied up and blindfolded."

"I noticed her wrists," said Maggie. "Have you called Verne?"

"No," said Loyal. "And I don't want to yet. I have no idea what is happening or why she was taken." He paused. "The people who had her are really bad news. I haven't had a chance to talk to Brandi yet. We need a safe place to hunker down for a few days."

Movement caught Loyal's eye and he turned to see Brandi coming back down the hall. He turned back to Maggie. "Can we go to Peter's?"

"No," said Maggie. "I don't want to involve him in this."

"We need someplace remote," said Loyal. "Mike's Sky Ranch?"

"Too many people," said Maggie. She thought for a

moment. "I have friends who have a house South of San Felipe. They rarely use it anymore and I know where the key is hidden. You two should go there."

28

BRANDI KENDRICK

B randi returned from the bathroom and sat on the faded brown couch in the living room. She picked up a framed picture that was placed on the coffee table. Maggie and a man were in the foreground, the yellow buggy in the background, the man's arm protectively around Maggie's waist. Both were smiling. Their hair was windblown. Verne had mentioned that Maggie's husband had passed away several years ago. She supposed this was him. Brandi set the frame back on the table gently and turned so that her right ear was facing the kitchen. She could hear Loyal and Maggie whispering to each other, but could not tell the content of the conversation. The refrigerator door was opened, then closed. Brandi closed her eyes. She was exhausted. Her stomach rumbled and she realized she was starving as well. The last food she had eaten was the street taco meal in Big Bear. She rose from the couch and entered the kitchen.

Maggie was in front of the stove using a spatula to stir something in a skillet. Loyal leaned against the kitchen counter. Both had their backs to Brandi. Maggie was speaking in low tones.

"I'll give you some of my old Baja maps and I can hand draw some for you too. You can cross at Pinto Pass, the border wall isn't complete there yet."

Brandi cleared her throat. "You guys making plans without me?"

Loyal and Maggie both turned toward her.

"We need to hide you away for a few days until we figure out what is going on," said Loyal. "Maggie knows a place in San Felipe. I think we should go there."

Maggie reached into a cabinet and brought out a plate. She removed the skillet from the heat. She placed a flour tortilla on the pate and scraped a steaming mound of scrambled eggs on top of it. She placed a fork on the plate and handed it to Brandi, then looked back at Loyal. "You hungry?" she asked. He shook his head. "I had fish tacos earlier." Maggie grabbed some salsa out of the refrigerator. She turned to Brandi and Loyal, "Let's sit on the back deck and talk this out," she said.

29

PATRICK O'KEEFE

Pat squirmed closer to his wife, Olive, and wrapped his arm around her as far as it would go. She was 8 months pregnant, her belly large. He loved the little snuffling noise she made as she slept. He closed his eyes and breathed in deeply through his nose, enjoying the smell of her hair and skin. His mind went back to the conversation they had had earlier in the evening after they had put their two young children to bed. Pat trusted Olive more than anyone else in his life. He had always been honest with her. When he had helped Loyal the previous April he had told her everything. This evening he had told her the entirety of events that had happened earlier in the day.

"You have always trusted Loyal, Pat," she had said. "Has he given you any reason not to continue to do so?"

"That's what I can't figure out," he had said. "His actions don't look good, Olive. The Captain coming to ask me about him is big. It is his way of putting me on notice that if I have communication with Loyal I better report it to him."

"I can't tell you what to do Pat," she had said, her large green eyes steadily holding his gaze. "I trust you to do what you think is best."

The problem, Pat thought to himself now, was that he didn't know what was best. Loyal was a good friend and Pat wanted to honor that friendship. At the same time, he was a husband and father of two, with another on the way. He could not jeopardize his career. Pat let out a slow soft breath. He re-closed his eyes and concentrated on the sound of Olive's breaths. He supposed he would know the right thing to do when the situation presented itself. At least he hoped he would.

30

TRINITY GLASS

Trinity woke uneasily. She wandered around the condo for a bit, eventually settling on the couch in the living room. She was used to being able to manipulate her dreams. Prone to nightmares as a child, she had learned to change the outcome of her scary dreams. The fact that she had slid so easily into the dreamland sand was unnerving. She sat on the couch and let the silence in the condo soothe her. She let her thoughts drift and, predictably they settled on Loyal. She was looking forward to seeing him and trying to figure out how she was going to fit it into her schedule. Eventually she stood and made her way back to the bedroom. She double checked that her phone alarm was set for 6:00 am. The meeting was set for 10:00 the following morning in San Diego, so she figured she needed to be on the road by 9:00. On impulse, Trinity opened Loyal's contact information and tapped the call symbol. The call went straight to voicemail. Trinity disconnected without leaving a message. She set her phone on the nightstand and lay back on the bed. In the past three months of regular texts and phone calls Loyal's phone had never gone straight to voicemail. A feeling of unease settled slowly over Trinity. She closed her eyes and let herself drift into an unsettled sleep.

31

LOYAL TRUESDALE

Maggie's back deck faced West. The view was stunning, illuminated by the full moon hanging in the sky. The deck was built out of rough hewn wooden beams held together with oversized hardware. A custom made table and accompanying chairs sat squarely in the center of the deck. Potted succulents dotted the area and a slate covered fire pit sat to one side. Maggie set the plate and the salsa in front of one of the chairs and indicated that Brandi should sit. Loyal took the chair next to Brandi. Maggie settled in opposite Loyal. Storm circled a few times then settled at Maggie's feet with a small thump and a large sigh.

Loyal watched as Brandi dumped a liberal amount of salsa on her scrambled eggs, folded the tortilla around everything and took a large bite. When she had chewed and swallowed, she looked across the table at Maggie.

"Thank you," she said. "This is delicious."

"You are welcome," said Maggie.

The group was quiet while Brandi ate. She finished quickly and leaned back in her chair with a sigh, her eyes closed. Loyal turned slightly so that he was facing Brandi.

"Tell us what happened," he said. "Everything you can remember."

Brandi opened her eyes and looked at Loyal.

"How did you find me?" she asked.

"We'll get to that," said Loyal. "You first. Start from when you left the dinner with Verne."

Brandi sat up a little straighter. She leaned her forearms on the table, her hands were clasped.

"We went to a bar called The Cave. We listened to a band and had some drinks." She paused, then continued. "I must have had one too many. I don't remember leaving the bar. When I woke up I was in the back seat of a car with my wrists and ankles tied and a blindfold over my eyes. They freed me for the walk to the boat, and told me they would kill me if I struggled. As soon as we were in the boat they tied me up again." She rubbed her wrists at the memory.

"What are those things in the backpack?" Loyal asked.

Brandi shrugged. "I don't know. Jodi sent them to me right before she was killed. She told me to keep an eye on them."

"Those people on the boat were professionals," said Loyal. "My phone is turned off and location services are disabled, but we can't stay here long."

Maggie stood. "Let me dig around for some maps for you." She leaned across the table and picked up Brandi's plate.

"You need anything else?" she asked. Brandi shook her head then stood.

"I'm going to lay down on the couch while you guys make plans if that's okay."

Loyal followed Maggie into the kitchen. She placed the plate in the sink then motioned for him to follow her. They passed through the living room where Brandi was already curled up on the couch, Storm settled on the floor below her. They passed through another door and entered what Maggie referred to as her radio room. Loyal had been shocked the first time he had been in the room. Radio equipment was everywhere. Maggie went straight to some steel shelving at the back of the room and started rooting around. Loyal noticed a small box on the ground.

"Is that a safe?" he asked.

Maggie glanced back and nodded. Loyal removed his PM9 and belly band.

"Can you hold on to this for me?" he asked. "If I take it to Mexico I won't be able to bring it back." Maggie knelt and opened the small safe. She secured Loyal's weapon, closed the safe, then rose and turned back toward the shelving. When she turned back toward Loyal she was holding some papers in her hands.

"Maps," she said. "Let's go back on the deck and I can show you where you are going."

Loyal and Maggie sat opposite each other again, the pile of maps on the table between them.

"Have you ever been to San Felipe?" she asked.

Loyal nodded. "Yes, but it was over 35 years ago. I don't remember much."

"It's a long drive," said Maggie. "You've been awake a long time already, I think you should stop and rest at Canyon Guadalupe." She opened the first map and turned it so that it was oriented towards Loyal.

"We are here," she said. "I'll lead you to here." She tapped the map with her finger. "I'll explain the route very clearly, but after that you guys are on your own."

32

BRANDI KENDRICK

B randi was awakened by a gentle tap on her shoulder. She rolled onto her back and found herself looking into Maggies dark green eyes.

"Time to get going," said Maggie quietly.

Brandi sat up and shifted so that her legs hung off the couch. She took a moment, then stood.

"Everything is already loaded and ready to go," said Maggie. "Loyal's with the buggy." She paused, then added, "You should use the restroom again. It is a long drive."

Brandi walked down the hall and went into the bathroom. She faced the mirror and took a long look at herself. She thought again about her situation. She had always taken care of herself, and wondered if putting herself in someone else's hands was wise. She was sure she was still being hunted, and would be as long as she had the backpack. Staying with Loyal, at least for the time being, seemed like the best choice. She ran some cool water into the sink, cupped her hands, and splashed it on her face. She leaned at the waist, hung her head, ran her hands through her hair, then straightened with a small flip of her head. She used the restroom, washed her hands, and with one last look at her image walked out the bathroom door. Just as Maggie had stated, Loyal was waiting by his buggy. It was a four seater, and the back seats held two gas cans, two sleeping bags, a small cooler, her suitcase, and a small duffel bag.

"Where are we going?" asked Brandi.

"Mexico," said Loyal. "We need to disappear for a few days." He gestured at the passenger seat. "Hop in."

Brandi settled into the passenger seat without saying anything further. The full moon illuminated Maggie as she slid into her yellow two seater and slipped a faded ball cap onto her head. Both engines rumbled to life and the journey began.

The two buggies drove East out of Valley Center, through the Rincon valley which housed the massive Harrah's Casino, and up the 76 grade to the base of Palomar. Brandi felt on her chest and shoulders for the black backpack that she had turned backwards and now wore on the front of her body. Thoughts of Jodi entered her mind. She saw her sister's face in her mind's eye for a brief moment, then pushed it out. She wasn't ready for that yet. Brandi closed her eyes and leaned her head back against the seat. She breathed in deeply through her nose, savoring the unfamiliar mountain scents. The wind caught her loose hair and whipped it wildly about her face. The strands stung where they hit her skin. Brandi gathered her hair to the base of her neck, wound it into a tight bun, and kept hold of it with her left hand. The loose layers from the front still batted at her face, but it was bearable. She turned to her left and studied Loyal's profile for a long moment. He looked to be in his mid fifties. He wasn't what she would consider handsome, but not unattractive either. At forty-two years of age , Brandi considered herself on the outer edge of young-ish. She preferred to date men her age or slightly younger. Still, she thought, there was something about Loyal. She turned her gaze back to the front and considered this for a moment. She finally landed on his steady manner. He had a reassuring way about him. Despite all that was happening, she felt safe.

33

LOYAL TRUESDALE

Loyal kept his buggy about half a football field behind Maggie's. Her taillights and the full moon provided plenty of illumination. He glanced to his right. Brandi was sitting in the passenger seat. She wore the black backpack backwards, with the pouch across her chest and the straps around her shoulders. She had balled her hair up at the base of her neck and was holding it in place with her left hand. Loyal reached beneath his seat and pulled out a baseball cap. He reached out and set it in her free hand. She flinched at the unexpected touch, then, upon seeing what he was offering her, smiled that unbelievable smile. With a swift movement she tucked her hair through the open space at the back of the hat and settled the cap firmly on her head.

Loyal mentally reviewed everything he and Maggie had discussed while Brandi had been sleeping. Maggie was in the process of leading them through the desert to a small border town called Ocotillo. She had provided them with maps, a GPS full of waypoints in Mexico, two five gallon gas cans which they had filled at a gas station on La Jolla Indian Reservation, sleeping bags, water, a cooler full of snacks, and $500 in cash. He recalled her words when she had handed over the GPS, "Ed and I input every one of these waypoints together, Loyal. Please bring it back safely."

Maggie turned right at Scissors Crossing, then left toward Ocotillo. Loyal and Brandi followed. Even in the depth of the night, the desert was visible. The glow of the full moon produced enough ambient light for Loyal to see the dilapidated trailers and shacks just off the two lane road. The land beyond was barren and rocky; the silhouette of jagged hilltops visible in the distance. They passed a tiny airport on the left, not much more than an airstrip really, the orange windsock extended and glowing in the moonlight. On the right he saw a sign that said *Agua Caliente*. Even with his extremely limited knowledge of the Spanish language, Loyal knew the words meant *hot water*. The thought that "hot water" could very well be exactly what he was getting mixed up in burbled to the surface of his mind.

The road began rising slightly in elevation. They wound through a series of switchbacks. When the road leveled out again, Loyal could see a farm of massive electricity producing windmills in the distance. They grew larger and larger as the buggies approached them. The road led them right through the center of the farm, giant windmills towered above them on either side of the buggy. For a brief moment Loyal considered how small and insignificant they all were in the scheme of things. He pushed this thought aside as they slid under the last windmill and left the farm of giants behind.

34

BRANDI KENDRICK

B randi saw the moonlight sparkling off the windmills when they were still some distance away. She did not immediately recognize the towering machines for what they were. She had never seen anything like this before. The windmills stood, some slowly spinning, some still, like gigantic sentries guarding the desert from intruders. Brandi imagined one slowly tipping over, its long blade impaling her and stopping the buggy in its tracks. With a quick shake of her head she removed the intrusive thought from her mind and breathed a sigh of relief when they had left the windmill farm behind them.

The buggies had kept a consistent pace of 55 to 60 miles per hour for the entire trip. Up ahead Maggie's brake lights flashed red and she slowed. Brandi felt the buggy decelerate as Loyal did the same.

"Scoot down and pull your hat down low over your head," said Loyal. Brandi silently followed his directions. Moments later they passed a checkpoint of some kind. It was closed, but Brandi assumed there were cameras. She glanced at Loyal and saw that he had his head down and his left hand on his forehead shading his eyes. Minutes later they entered the town of Ocotillo. Brandi looked around in amazement. "This is a town?" she said out loud, though Loyal couldn't hear her over the engine noise. Scattered broken buildings and fences lined the road. They passed a few small houses that actually looked inhabited and maintained, and a building with a sign that said *Lazy Lizard Saloon*. Although the dingy bar was clearly closed, Brandi's mouth watered at the thought of a cocktail. After another mile or so they passed under a freeway and Maggie pulled into a dirt lot on the Western side of a Chevron and a shuttered cafe. She pulled her yellow buggy to the far side of the lot and parked. Loyal pulled up beside her.

With the buggies ignitions turned off, silence surrounded them. Maggie slid out of her buggy and motioned for them to do the same. Brandi watched as Loyal unfolded himself and raised his arms in the air for a long stretch. She paused a moment, then did the same. All three gathered in the space between the buggies.

"This is as far as I go," said Maggie. "You will continue on this road, cross over the train tracks, then turn East on the 98 toward Calexico. You will drive about eleven miles then turn off the main road onto Pinto Pass. The GPS has a proximity alarm set and will vibrate and beep when you are within 50 yards." She paused and took a moment to look both Loyal and Brandi in the eyes. "There are surveillance towers everywhere out here. They are mostly watching for people trying to enter the US, but someone leaving in this way is going to attract their attention too. Don't stop for anyone. You won't get arrested crossing the border into Mexico. Keep going no matter what. No one from this side will follow you into Mexico."

Brandi turned to look at Loyal. He said nothing, simply nodded at Maggie and held out his hand. Maggie took it and the two shook. Maggie turned to Brandi and gave her a small smile, then walked around her buggy, slid in, started it up, and drove away. Brandi and Loyal watched until her taillights disappeared around a corner. With Maggie's departure the silence was complete. Loyal and Brandi looked at each other for a long moment.

"You sure about this?" Brandi asked.

Loyal nodded. "Keep that hat low over your eyes," he said. Then he slid in the buggy. Brandi walked around to the passenger side and did the same. They shared another long look, then Loyal started the buggy and drove slowly out of the dirt lot.

35

LOYAL TRUESDALE

L oyal drove out of the dirt lot. He crossed the train tracks and turned left onto 98 East toward Calexico. The desert stretched out on either side of the road, barren with the exception of random dots of creosote, a low growing bushy green plant that thrived in the desolate environment. He also noticed randomly placed blue cans, about three feet in height, with orange and blue flags attached to them. Loyal knew these to be water containers for Mexican travelers. The surveillance towers Maggie had mentioned were easily visible as well. Wispy clouds, illuminated by the moon, floated above the towers. To Loyal they looked like ghosts hovering silently above the desert.

As promised, the GPS beeped, which neither passenger could hear above the engine and the wind, and vibrated, which Brandi felt. She held the GPS up near Loyal. He nodded understanding, and slowed to look for the entrance to Pinto Pass. He saw it just as he passed it. With no other vehicles on the road,

Loyal simply stopped in the lane, reversed to the entrance, and turned onto the small rutted track. It was a narrow two track path that led toward the border with Mexico. Loyal could see that a section of the border wall had been built in the distance. Just as he was mulling over what they would do if they could not cross at Pinto Pass, he heard a huge engine sound and spotlights lit up the buggy. He glanced up and behind and saw that a huge helicopter was above them. A magnified voice rang out from above them.

"Stop, Turn back. You are approaching an International Border. It is illegal to continue. Stop. Turn back."

The message repeated. Loyal sped up. The downwash from the helicopter swirled around the buggy and the desert floor. Dust rose and obscured Loyal's vision. The buggy bounced as he struggled to keep in on the narrow winding two track path. His adrenaline spiked, and for a moment, he worried about his heart. His hands gripped the steering wheel so tightly he felt his fingertips growing numb. Then, just as abruptly as it had appeared, the helicopter banked and turned away from them. The border had been crossed.

Loyal had memorized Maggie's instructions. He crossed Mexico's Highway 3, and maneuvered through the mile or so rough patch beyond that. Suddenly, like a mirage, the dry lake bed of Laguna Salada was in front of them. Loyal pulled to a stop and let the buggy idle as he took in the breathtaking view. It was that bewitching time right before dawn when the sun's rays were just teasing the night away. The expanse of the lake bed lay stretched out before them. The sand was silvery-white and reflected both the emerging light and the illumination from the moon, which hung low in the sky. What struck Loyal was that there was nothing but sand. No trees or low growing scrub brush dotted the lake bed, it was pure, unadulterated sand. Loyal turned to look at Brandi. She was staring unblinkingly at the view. She appeared to be mesmerized. As if she felt his eyes upon her, she turned to look at him. Their eyes met and held. "Ready?" asked Loyal. Her answer was that slow, sexy smile.

36

TRINITY GLASS

T rinity woke several hours before her alarm was set to go off. She knew from the moment she opened her eyes that she would not be returning to sleep. In an instant she went from deep sleep to complete awareness. The pre dawn light glowed through her partially opened blinds. The light had an otherworldly quality about it. It was straw colored and not muffled by fog, promising another bright and clear July day in Southern California. Trinity eased out from beneath the covers and sat up on the edge of the bed. With a gentle exhale she stood and walked into the kitchen. She filled the tea kettle with water and placed it on the stove. She poured some coffee beans into the grinder and depressed the lid. Although she was expecting it, the jarring noise of the beans being pulverized caused her to flinch. She poured the ground beans into a French press and when the kettle sang, she poured the hot water over the beans.

. . .

Ten minutes later Trinity could be found on her small patio cradling a warm cup of coffee. She sat in a wrought iron chair, a small matching table to her right. The patio faced West, so the sun rose slowly behind her. It's gentle early morning rays gradually illuminated everything around her. As she sipped, Trinity thought about her upcoming meeting in San Diego with agents from Homeland Security. She hoped they would be forthcoming with information about the six individuals who had crossed into the United States from Mexico. Sharing was not a high priority between agencies. For the past two months Trinity and Doug had been working on trying to expose Chinese spies working in the Chinese Consulate buildings in the United States. While the Chinese were not great innovators, they were excellent at copying and then reproducing at a greatly reduced price point. Intellectual property belonging to the United States was being stolen on a large scale by spies working for the Chinese government. Worse than that, however, was the theft of America's military and government secrets. It was the spies selling that information that Trinity and Doug were tasked with ferreting out. Trinity thought the odds of the six Chinese Nationals who had crossed the border with forged passports being involved with spies in the consulates to be quite high.

When the last drops of coffee had been drained from the cup, Trinity rose and went back inside the condo. She rinsed the mug and placed it in the dishwasher. She laid her yoga mat on the floor of the living room and spent the better part of an hour on her yoga practice. She was just relaxing into Savasana when her alarm went off. Trinity pushed back the frustration that threatened to enter her nearly calmed mind. She rose, stretched, found her phone, and silenced the noise. She returned to the mat and lay down on her back, legs outstretched and arms to her side. She deepened her breathing and tried to clear all thoughts from her mind. She was nearly successful. The only thought that lingered was an image of Loyal Truesdale.

37

BRANDI KENDRICK

Brandi wasn't going to lie to herself. The helicopters had frightened her. The relief she had felt when they had abandoned the chase had been palpable. Now, with the awesome expanse of the dry lake bed spread out like a glowing blanket in front of her, she felt only excitement. She felt Loyal's eyes on her and turned to make eye contact.

"Ready?" he asked. All she could think to do was smile. Loyal smiled back, gave her a slight nod, and eased the buggy forward onto the smooth sand.

Driving on the lake bed was like nothing Brandi had ever experienced. She knew they couldn't be going more than 65 miles an hour. Loyal had told her that was the buggy's most economical speed. Speeding across the sand now, however, it felt like they were going at least 100. The sand was so smooth it felt like the buggy was a few feet off the ground and simply floating in the air. Brandi took off the hat and let the wind blow through her hair. The sense of freedom was exhilarating. She raised her arms in the air above her and a laugh gurgled up from somewhere deep within her. She turned to look at Loyal. His focus was on the track in front of them, but she could tell that he was smiling too. Brandi gathered her hair back into a ponytail and replaced the hat. She turned to look behind the buggy. A giant dust plume, glowing pink in the early morning light, sprayed out behind them. She remained in that position for a long moment, mesmerized by the shifting, glowing sand. It wasn't until she developed a crick in her back and neck that she turned back to face forward.

Brandi looked to her right and saw the rounded mountains of the Coastal Range. They rose nearly 2,000 feet above the dry lake bed. The sun, rising in the East, illuminated them with its gentle early morning rays. Brandi looked at the rugged beauty surrounding her and thought, sadly, that it had been a very long time since she had seen the sun rise. Her next thought landed on Jodi who had loved the earliest part of the morning. The two sisters had been as different as two people could be, and yet had loved and protected one another fiercely. Brandi felt tears threaten. She blinked rapidly, pushing them back, refusing to allow even one drop to spill down her dusty cheeks. She patted the backpack that spanned her chest. Jodi had trusted her. Although her sister was no longer alive to know it, Brandi made a silent vow that she would not let Jodi down.

38
────────

LOYAL TRUESDALE

lthough he had been awake for nearly twenty-four
hours, the drive on the dry lake bed rejuvenated
Loyal. The clean air, the smooth ride, the floating
sensation, and the relief to be across the border all combined to
create an elixir of energy within him. He found himself smiling
as he drove. The lake bed was flanked by mountain ranges, but
it was the rounded mountains of the Coastal Range on the West
that Loyal was focused on. Maggie had instructed him to begin
looking for the spot where the track across the lake bed split
about the same time as the mountains on his right began to
look more jagged than rounded. At that point he was to take the
the path heading towards the jagged heights.

The rising sun made the fact that it was Monday morning
obvious to Loyal. Beyond that bit of knowledge he had no idea
what time it was. He took a moment to look over at Brandi. She
was looking straight ahead and blinking rapidly. He supposed
that with all the sand swirling around them that she had gotten

some in her eyes. He rooted around under his seat again and came up with a pair of sunglasses. He tapped her thigh gently with the glasses. Brandi flinched, then looked down at her leg and saw the glasses. She took them from his hand and gave him a brief smile as she slid them on. Loyal turned his attention back to the track ahead of him. Before long he saw the transformation in the mountains begin. The peaks stretched tall against the clear blue sky. The rounded edges became jagged. Loyal kept his eyes open and soon saw the V in the track. He stayed to the right, heading toward the jagged peaks.

As they neared the mountains the topography began to change. The smooth road became rougher and Loyal was forced to slow down in order to evade rocks and maneuver over bumpy areas. They began climbing in elevation. The higher they went, the rougher the road became. Scrub brush reappeared on all sides of the track. After about 6 miles of winding and increasingly rough roads they came around a bend and the narrow canyon widened out. Palm trees were everywhere. To Loyal it looked like an abandoned movie set. Then Loyal saw the sign.

Welcome. Guadalupe's Canyon Hot springs. Information 400 meters.

Loyal felt tension he had not been aware he was carrying drain out of his body. He was both exhausted and excited, the two emotions competing for control of his depleted body and mind. He stopped the buggy and turned to Brandi.

"This place is a natural hot springs. Maggie suggested we rest here and continue to San Felipe this evening."

Brandi simply looked at him from behind the sunglasses and nodded. For a moment Loyal considered asking her if something was wrong. But as he thought about her situation he realized everything was likely wrong, so he remained silent and drove the rest of the way into the campground.

P atrick O'Keefe entered the Carlsbad Sheriff's Department at 6:48 on Monday morning completely unprepared for the shit storm that was about to engulf him. He waved hello to Fatima, who was just settling in behind the reception desk, and then made his way up the stairs and to his office. He had been in charge of the newly formed Computer Forensics Division for just over six months. The job was perfect for Pat who, while an open and engaging person, preferred working with data rather than people. He settled himself behind his desk and booted up his computer. His main focus at the moment was using Stingray, a warrantless cell phone surveillance device, to track a cadre of suspected drug dealers. The Carlsbad area had seen an increase in overdose deaths during the past few months. The deaths were blamed on fentanyl, an extremely powerful opioid used by drug dealers to cut their illegal wares. O'Keefe had captured some powerful and incriminating texts and conversations. The information would be inadmissible in court, but Narcotic Detectives were hoping that it would lead to evidence that could be introduced at trial.

Pat was just opening some files to review when Captain Williams entered his office, closed the door, and sat in the chair opposite him.

"I'm going to lay it all out for you O'Keefe," he said. "After you hear it all you might want to reconsider whether or not you have any idea what Truesdale is up to."

Pat opened his mouth to respond, but closed it when the Captain held up a hand.

"One, Brandi Kendrick was reported missing in Big Bear yesterday morning." The Captain held up his pointer finger as he said this.

"Two," his middle finger joined the pointer, "Truesdale was seen snooping around at the same woman's house yesterday afternoon. Three," his ring finger joined the group of extended fingers, "a field report filed by Demkowski has Truesdale at the scene of a double homicide and arson that occurred a week ago." The Captain paused, his eyes boring into O'Keefe's. "One of the homicide victims was Brandi Kendrick's sister. Four," his pinkie finger joined the rest, "shots were fired at the Oceanside Harbor last night. An eyewitness camping there described a man and woman very similar to Truesdale and this Kendrick woman running away from the person firing the gun. They got away in a dune buggy similar to the one Truesdale owns. Five," the Captain added his thumb to the rest of the fingers, his open palm facing O'Keefe, "a dinghy found beached on the shore was traced back to Ted Fogerty, a bartender at The Jolly Roger. He says Truesdale told him he was working an active case. The bartender let him borrow the dinghy to do reconnaissance on a private yacht in the harbor. There's damage to the dinghy and Ted wants to know if the Department is going to reimburse him for damages."

The Captain paused, his eyes never leaving O'Keefe's. "Imagine Ted's surprise when he was told that Truesdale retired in April." The Captain leaned his forearms on O'Keefe's small steel desk. He reached out and slid O'Keefe's computer slightly to the left so that nothing was between the two men. "You have anything you want to tell me?" he asked.

40

BRANDI KENDRICK

Brandi remained in the buggy while Loyal secured them a campsite. She wondered if she should translate as she watched him talk to an older Mexican man who sat on a stool in front of a small shack. A refrigerator lay on its side beside the man. Loyal and the man spoke for a few minutes and seemed to be communicating just fine. Loyal reached into his pocket and handed the man some money. The man pocketed the cash and then spent a moment gesturing, clearly giving Loyal directions. Loyal returned to the buggy and slid in. He turned to Brandi and said, "Maggie recommended a campsite called La Cueva. It's just over that way." He pointed toward a cluster of palm trees, then started the buggy and shifted into first gear. Brandi said nothing. She simply closed her eyes and leaned her head against the seat.

La Cueva turned out to be a pretty neat little campsite. The small area, which contained a table, benches, and a barbecue, was completely enclosed by small palm trees. A palapa provided shade for the table and barbecue. There was a flat spot that would have been perfect for a tent if they had had one. A cement walkway led down to their private hot tub which was filled with water that was piped down from the top of the mountain. The water came out of the mountain at 152 degrees. It cooled to about 101 degrees as it traveled through the pipe system down to the campground. Each campsite had its own hot tub. La Cueva was unique in that the hot tub was surrounded by boulders, some which hung slightly over the tub creating a cave-like feeling.

When Brandi saw the hot tub she removed the small backpack, stripped down to her bra and undies and stepped right into the steaming water. She pulled her hair up underneath the ball cap and slid down so that only her head was above the water. When she closed her eyes all she could hear was the sound of the wind rustling the palm fronds above her. Brandi felt as if she was suspended in space and time. The warm water, the rising steam, and the whispering palm fronds all combined to give her a mystical feeling. If she had been a woman of faith she might have described it as spiritual. Whatever descriptive word she chose, ethereal, heavenly, magical, unworldly, it didn't matter. The feeling was pure lightness and calm, something she had not felt for a very long time. With a silent thought of gratitude Brandi welcomed the peace.

Loyal's voice brought her out of her trance like state. She opened her eyes and turned to focus on him. He was kneeling next to the hot tub and quietly saying her name. She turned towards him and smiled.

"This place is like the garden of Eden, Loyal," she said, "except it has palm trees."

His smile was brief. " We are only staying here for the day. I want to get on the road to San Felipe by midday. I laid out the sleeping bags." He pointed up towards the campsite. "It would be smart to have a snack and try to get some sleep."

Brandi let out a long sigh and stood. She stepped out of the tub and stretched a long, leisurely stretch, well aware of Loyal's eyes on her. Slowly she slipped back into her clothes. They clung to her still wet skin. "Ok Loyal," she said, "whatever you think is best."

With that, she picked up the backpack, turned, and made her way back up the walkway to the campsite.

41

TRINITY GLASS

T rinity arrived at the front doors to the offices of Homeland Security on Front Street in downtown San Diego at 9:45. She had parked in a downtown parking garage on Broadway then walked to the building on Front Street. She had high hopes for the outcome of today's meeting and was feeling the familiar adrenaline spike that came with the hunt. On the drive to San Diego she had tried calling Loyal again. Once more the call had gone straight to voicemail. Trinity was concerned about him, but was forced to table that concern to concentrate on the meeting at hand.

Trinity showed her ID to the guard at the entrance and gained admittance. She was given a visitor's pass and asked to wait briefly in the lobby, which she did. Less than five minutes passed before she was approached by a small sprite of a woman. She was about 5'2" tall and looked to be about thirty years old. Her hair was a shocking blend of platinum blonde and gray. Loose bangs hung over her forehead, while the area above her ears and the lower part of the back of her head were shaved close to the skull. She wore a black pantsuit. On her lapel she wore the gold pin identifying her as an agent with the DHS. She reached out her hand as she approached Trinity.

"Agent Glass?" she asked. Trinity nodded and shook the tiny woman's hand.

"Agent Andrews. I'm here to escort you to your meeting." She turned without another word and began walking rapidly away. Trinity lengthened her stride and caught up quickly. Neither woman spoke as they walked the length of the corridor. Agent Andrews paused at a bank of elevators and pushed the up arrow. The door opened with a soft ping and both women stepped inside. Andrews pushed the button for the third floor and the doors closed with a soft swoosh.

The ride to the third floor was swift and silent. After exiting the elevator, Andrews led Trinity down a carpeted hallway to a door on the far right. The young agent gave the door two quick raps with her knuckles, then opened the door and entered. Trinity followed. The room was a small conference room. Three men were seated at a rectangular table inside. All stood when Andrews and Trinity entered.

"Agent Glass, OSI," said Andrews by way of introduction. She then turned and left the room. One of the men stepped forward with his right hand extended. He was tall, Trinity guessed 6'3", with close cropped gray hair.

"Agent Glass," he said as they shook hands. "I'm agent Malone, Deputy Assistant Commissioner of Field Operations." He turned towards the other two men. Indicating the man on their left he said, "This is Agent Nash, Deputy Director of the Signals Intelligence Directorate, of the NSA." Agent Nash, a stern looking man who stood about 5'9", stepped forward and shook Trinity's hand. Agent Malone then indicated the man to their right. "This is Agent Park, also with the SID and specializing in China and Korea." Agent Park, a slim Asian man, stepped forward with a wide smile on his face. "Agent Glass," he said as they shook hands. Agent Malone indicated the table and chairs. "Please take a seat," he said. "We have much to discuss."

42

PATRICK O'KEEFE

P at stared at Captain Williams for a long moment before he responded.

"I was completely forthcoming yesterday Captain," he finally said. "I told you everything I know and left nothing out."

Captain William's eyes narrowed a bit. He remained silent. Pat filled the uncomfortable silence after another long pause. "Do you want me to reach out to him?"

Captain Williams nodded. "How about right now," he said, framing the words as a statement rather than a question. Pat reached for his phone. He pulled up Loyal's contact information, placed the call, put the phone on speaker, and placed his phone on the desk squarely between the Captain and himself. He was surprised, and slightly relieved, when the call went straight to voicemail. "Loyal," Pat said, "call me as soon as you can." He paused, then added, "It is important." Pat gave the Captain a questioning glance. The Captain shook his head, he had nothing to add. Pat terminated the call.

. . .

Captain Williams leaned back in the chair. He studied Pat for a long moment, the older man's eyes focusing directly on the younger man's. Pat did not look away or blink. Finally the Captain sighed and looked toward the ceiling. Pat watched as tension drained from his boss's body.

"Things look bad for him, O'Keefe," the Captain said. "Really bad." Slowly Captain Williams rose from the chair. He looked down at Pat. "If you hear from him I need to know immediately." Pat nodded. "Absolutely. I'll inform you the moment he calls."

43

LOYAL TRUESDALE

L oyal followed Brandi up the walkway and back to the campsite. Her clothes clung to her wet body and he found it hard to get the image of her rising from the steaming water in nothing but bra and underwear out of his mind. They settled at the small wooden table, sitting across from each other. Loyal reached in the cooler and removed two sandwiches and two bottles of water. He pushed a sandwich and water bottle across the table to Brandi. They ate in silence.

When Loyal had chewed and swallowed his last bite he looked at Brandi. "Before we rest I have two questions. What are those things in the backpack, and what did you get from the gym?"

Brandi swallowed the bite of sandwich in her mouth and took a long sip of water.

"I told you before, I don't know what they are. Jodi sent them to me and told me to keep them safe." She paused and took another sip of water. "I got a paper from a locker at the gym. It was Jodi's. It has strings of numbers and letters on it. I think they are passwords. She told me to keep it somewhere separate from the backpack."

Loyal reached out his hand. "Can I look in the backpack?"

Brandi's hesitation was brief, but noticeable to Loyal. She handed him the backpack without saying anything.

Loyal unzipped the small pack and spilled its contents onto the wooden table. He sorted the pile of black and silver devices by color and shape. He pushed a pile of short cords to one side. When he had organized the items he counted them. There were 17 small devices on the table. Next, he took some time to examine them each individually. They were all small, Loyal estimated less than 4" x 2". There were four silver, rectangular boxes with the logo of *Keepkey* on one side and a screen on the other. There were five that hinged open, revealing a small screen inside. Two of this type had the logo *Nano X*, three had the logo *Nano S*. The final seven were black and five sided, tapering at the bottom. All had the logo *Trezor* at the top and a small screen in the middle. Three of this type also had the words *My Trezor* beneath the screen. All 17 had ports where a cord could be plugged in.

"They look like external hard drives to me," said Loyal, his gaze locked firmly on Brandi's brown eyes. "What did your sister do for a living?"

"Something with computers," said Brandi. "She traveled a lot." Loyal looked at Brandi for a long moment, then scooped the boxes and cords back into the backpack. He zipped it closed and handed it back to her with a long exhale. "Let's get some sleep," he said. "I want to be down the mountain before dusk."

Brandi took the backpack from him, stood, and walked to one of the sleeping bags that Loyal had spread out under a palm tree. Loyal watched as she slipped into the bag still holding the backpack in her arms. His inner radar had been fine tuned during his many years of interviewing suspects and witnesses. That radar was beeping loudly at the moment. Something about Brandi was off.

44

TRINITY GLASS

Trinity left the DHS building just over two hours after she had entered. She walked to a Panera Bread that was several blocks away and ordered a salad and an iced tea. She sat at a table for two near the back and mentally reviewed the meeting she had just participated in. Agent Nash had taken the lead. Trinity had disliked the man from the moment they had met. She was sure he had not shared everything that he knew. There were two pieces of information that she was mulling over at the moment. The first, Chen Zhao and Tung Shen had been identified and the news was not good. The two men's real identities were unknown, but they had many false identities that were well known. Both were Chinese assets; men who killed. The fact that they were on United States soil was disturbing. The second piece of information was that there had been a shootout at Oceanside Harbor the previous evening. Witnesses' descriptions of the shooters were eerily similar to descriptions of Zhao and Shen.

. . .

Trinity tried calling Loyal again. The call went directly to voice-mail. She did not bother leaving a message. Her next call was to the Carlsbad Sheriff's Department. When the call was answered she asked to be connected with Detective O'Keefe, who she knew from Loyal to be a trustworthy friend. When he answered she identified herself and explained her connection to Loyal.

"I've been trying to reach him," O'Keefe said.

"So have I," said Trinity. "I'm getting a bad feeling about this. Can we meet? I'd like to talk to you in person."

There was a long moment of silence, then O'Keefe said, "I'm going to have to include the Captain on this."

Trinity paused. "I can be there in an hour," she said.

True to her word, Trinity pushed through the doors to the Sheriff's Department just under an hour later. She strode briskly to reception, identified herself, and asked for Detective O'Keefe. Fatima, the receptionist, lifted the phone and spoke briefly into it.

"He'll be right down," she said to Trinity.

O'Keefe came down the stairs a few moments later. He walked straight to Trinity, his hand outstretched and a genuine smile on his face.

"Agent Glass," he said as they shook hands, "it is nice to finally meet you. Loyal speaks very highly of you."

Trinity returned the smile. "He speaks highly of you as well. Very nice to meet you."

Fatima handed Trinity a visitor's badge, which she clipped to her jacket.

"Follow me," said O'Keefe as he turned towards the stairs. "The Captain is expecting you."

. . .

Captain Williams rose and stepped out from behind his desk to greet Trinity. They shook hands then he gestured for her to take a seat opposite his desk.

"Thank you for making time to see me," said Trinity as she sat.

"It's not often we get OSI agents in here," he said. "How can I help you?"

Trinity sat up straight and crossed her left leg over her right. She was aware of the confidence she exuded and planned to use it to her advantage. "First, I've been trying, without success, to contact retired Detective Loyal Truesdale. I was wondering if you could help me on that front. Second, I'd like any information that you can give me about the shooting at Oceanside Harbor last night."

Captain Williams raised a single eyebrow. "I am also having difficulty locating Truesdale," he said. "And I'd think you would turn to Oceanside PD for information about the shooting."

"I'm working on a sensitive matter, Captain." Trinity said. "The less people involved, the better."

The Captain leaned back in his chair, his gaze never leaving Trinity's. It was O'Keefe who broke the silence.

"I think we should tell her what we know Sir," he said.

Trinity's eyes stayed locked on the Captain's. "That would be very much appreciated," she said.

45

TRINITY GLASS

I t was just past 2:30 when Trinity pushed through the doors and exited the Sheriff's Station. Her mind was buzzing with all the information the Captain and O'Keefe had provided. It had started with the missing person's report regarding Brandi Kendrick, then continued with Loyal snooping around Brandi's home. The field report stating he had been at the crime scene of a double murder and arson involving Brandi's sister didn't help. Then there had been Loyal's actions at the Jolly Roger. The shots fired at a man and woman whose descriptions fit Loyal's and Brandi's had topped everything off.

"Is he a suspect in her disappearance?" Trinity had asked.

"Let's call him a person of interest for now," the Captain had replied.

Trinity slid into the 4Runner and eased the car out of the parking lot. She drove straight to Loyal's apartment. No one answered the door and his Altima was in front of the garage. The buggy was nowhere to be seen. Trinity did not linger. She slid back into her vehicle and headed for Oceanside Harbor, a bartender named Ted Fogarty firmly in her sights.

Trinity glanced at her phone as she parked in front of the Jolly Roger. It was 3:22. She entered the restaurant and took a moment to let her eyes adjust to the dim light. A sign informed her that happy hour was from 3:00-7:00 daily. A quick look around the bar revealed that the usual crowd had not gathered yet. Trinity approached the man behind the bar. He was tall and thin, Trinity guessed him to be in his late fifties. His sandy brown hair was long and wavy, he wore a ball cap on his head. Trinity slid onto a bar stool and smiled as he approached.

"What can I get you?" he asked.

"You have Stone Ripper?" she asked.

He nodded. Moments later he set the glass of beer in front of her. Trinity took a long, appreciative sip, then set the glass down with a smile.

"Are you Ted?" she asked.

The bartender's eyes widened slightly. "I am," he said. "And who might you be?"

"Trinity Glass," she said. "I'm a friend of Loyal Truesdale's."

Ted's eyes narrowed.

"I'm a little worried about him," she said. "You are one of the last people to have seen him."

"Are you with the Sheriff's Department?" Ted asked.

Trinity reached into her jacket pocket and brought out her badge. "OSI," she said. "Federal agent."

Trinity's status as a Federal agent loosened Ted's lips. He

walked her though everything that had transpired between Loyal and himself. He was careful to include the fact that he had not known that Loyal was no longer on active duty. Trinity assured Ted that she was not interested in laying blame on anyone.

"Is the boat you directed him to still in the harbor?" she asked.

"Yes," said Ted. "I told the police about it. They've been through it. It has crime scene tape on it."

"I'd like to see it," said Trinity.

"It's at the tail end of J," said Ted. "Biggest boat in the harbor. You can't miss it."

Their conversation was interrupted by a group entering the bar. Ted excused himself and went to take their orders. Trinity sipped her beer and gazed out the window at the harbor. Boats of all sizes gently rolled on the water. Trinity drained the last of the beer, dropped some cash on the bar, and walked outside. She watched as a gray haired man in a bright Hawaiian shirt steered a dinghy into transient parking. He tied the small craft off, then held out his hand to the woman in the boat. Once she was safely on the pier, he slid his arm around the small of her back and they walked together into the Jolly Roger. Trinity glanced around. The pier was empty. She walked purposefully to the dinghy, stepped in, untied it, pulled the start, and motored into the harbor.

The boat Ted had told her about was easy to find. Not only was it the largest in the harbor, it was also draped with yellow crime scene tape. Trinity steered the dinghy to the back of the boat and tied the small craft to a hand rail. She pulled a pair of rubber gloves from her jacket pocket, stepped easily onto the boat and walked straight to the cabin. The door was unlocked. Trinity entered and stood still, taking in the scene. The boat had clearly been searched. Couch cushions were upended. Drawers and cabinets had been pulled out and emptied. She scanned the walls and ceiling, noting several tiny pinholes in the crease where the walls and ceiling met. Trinity selected a knife from one of the kitchen drawers and pulled a chair over to the wall. She climbed up and used the knife to create a larger hole around one of the pinholes, revealing a tiny lens connected to wires that snaked back into the moulding. She repeated the process with the second pinhole. Again she found a lens and wires. Trinity stepped off the chair. She walked down a short set of stairs and located the master stateroom. She stood just inside the door and surveyed the room. It held a bed, a television in a cabinet mounted to the wall, and a desk. The sheets and blankets were in a rumpled pile at the foot of the bed. The desk's single drawer was removed and had been emptied.

Trinity walked back to the main cabin, retrieved the chair, and went back to the stateroom. She placed the chair directly below the television cabinet and stepped onto it. She ran her hands along the edges of the cabinet. On the lower left side she found what she was looking for. Her fingers slid along a slight indent. She depressed it and the bottom of the cabinet slid open, revealing a slim drawer. Inside she found a remote control and two small plastic external hard drives, one still in its packaging. A USB port was also revealed. Trinity used the remote to power up the TV. The screen was divided into four sections, all showing the main cabin from different angles. Trinity opened the unused USB drive, inserted it, and downloaded all saved video recordings. She put both hard drives in her jacket pocket, depressed the button so that the small drawer slid back in place, took the chair back to the main cabin, and walked back to the dinghy. Five minutes later the dinghy was back in transient parking behind the Jolly Roger and Trinity was in the 4Runner on her way back to the condo and her computer.

46

BRANDI KENDRICK

Brandi was in that strange place between sleep and awareness. She lay quietly in the sleeping bag, eyes closed, and let her consciousness slowly swim to the surface. The sound of the palm fronds in the afternoon breeze was soothing, much like gentle ocean waves foaming quietly on the shore. Gradually her brain regained focus. She opened her eyes. The first thing she saw was Loyal in a sleeping bag about five feet away from her. His back was to her, he appeared to be sleeping. Brandi rolled onto her back and looked up at the palm fronds and the blue sky beyond them. The canyon was a romantic paradise. She glanced back at Loyal and found herself wondering if he and Maggie were romantically attached.

Brandi slid out of the sleeping bag, stood, and stretched her arms skyward. She plucked her still damp shirt and pants away from her skin. This gave her no relief, so she stripped out of the pants and shirt and laid them on a rock to dry. Remembering her suitcase, she walked to the buggy and retrieved it. She removed a denim miniskirt and a T-shirt and slid into them. She returned to Loyal and checked that he was still asleep, then walked the short distance to the man who had taken their money and directed them to the campsite. He was still on the stool. She pointed to the refrigerator beside him.

"Cerveza?" she asked.

He smiled."Si."

She held up two fingers and smiled. She turned and pointed towards their campsite. "He'll pay you."

The man smiled, opened the overturned refrigerator and removed two quart-sized bottles of Tecate. They started to sweat immediately. He held up a bottle opener with a questioning look. Brandi nodded and said, "Uno por favor." The man opened one, then handed her both. She took them and turned back towards the campsite.

47

LOYAL TRUESDALE

A cool feeling on his cheek woke Loyal from an uneasy sleep. He rolled to his back and saw Brandi kneeling next to him, a cold bottle of beer in her hand.

"Time to wake up," she said. Loyal closed his eyes for a long moment, then re-opened them and sat up. He turned towards Brandi and saw that she held an unopened beer in one hand, an opened one in the other.

"You owe the guy by the fridge some money for these," she said as she placed the unopened beer in his hand. Loyal watched as she stood and looked down at him.

"Do I have time for another dip in the hot tub?" she asked.

Loyal stood and walked to the buggy. He retrieved his phone and turned it on to check the time.

"I want to be on the road in an hour," he said.

Brandi approached Loyal and put her hand on his shoulder.

"Why don't you join me Loyal?" she asked. "The water feels amazing."

Loyal had to admit the invitation was tempting, for a variety of reasons, but he shook his head.

"You go ahead. I'm going to have some more food and review the maps Maggie gave us."

As Brandi walked away he added, "Thanks for the beer."

Loyal opened the beer with his car key and drank it while he ate another sandwich and reviewed Maggie's instructions and maps. According to her directions, they would head back down to Laguna Salada and continue South on the track. At the base of the lake bed they would travel on dirt roads for about an hour, then travel the length of a second dry lake, Laguna Del Diablo. Just Southeast of Laguna Del Diablo, they would crest a small mountain range and drop down into San Felipe. Maggie's friend's house was outside of town, about 17 miles to the South. Loyal studied everything until he felt fairly certain he understood the directions. He rolled the sleeping bags, added some gas to the tank, and repacked the buggy. When all preparations were complete he paused for a moment to take in the beauty of the canyon. Someday, he thought, he would bring Trinity here.

Just over an hour later, the beers paid for and Brandi properly soaked, they slid in the buggy and started down the mountain. The bumpy road smoothed and foliage disappeared as they neared the dry lake bed. Soon the smooth track across the silken sand appeared before them. Loyal downshifted, turned onto the track, and accelerated. The smoothness of the sand and the unchanging scenery were mesmerizing. Despite having gotten several hours of sleep, Loyal found himself fighting to stay focused. He supposed that drinking the beer hadn't been the best idea, but it sure had tasted good. Loyal felt something touch his shoulder and turned his head slightly to see that Brandi had scrunched herself up in the passenger seat and was resting her head on his shoulder. She appeared to be asleep.

Loyal turned his head back to a forward facing position. It felt almost dreamlike; the salty expanse before him, the hot July sun, and a beautiful woman's head on his shoulder. Despite the uncertainty of their situation, Loyal had to admit, he felt pretty damn good.

48

TRINITY GLASS

Trinity entered the condo and went straight to her lap top. She considered the two USB drives, and decided on the known rather than the unknown. She inserted the drive that she had downloaded the camera footage onto, tapped a few keys, and the split screen view of the boat's cabin came into view. The footage was date and time stamped and began on Saturday, July 13. The six Chinese Nationals from the file she had read on the plane entered the cabin at 6:45 pm. They carried duffel bags and appeared disheveled and out of breath. They were in the footage briefly, then walked out of camera range. Trinity fast forwarded until they reappeared just before 8:00. All had showered and changed clothes. The man identified as Keping Xie spoke briefly. There was no audio. Trinity made a mental note to get the footage to someone who spoke Chinese and could read lips as soon as she was done reviewing it. After a moment the men all exited the cabin, leaving the woman, Mei Hua, behind.

. . .

Trinity continued fast forwarding the footage. The woman smoked several cigarettes. At 8:45 the men returned. One handed a styrofoam container to Mei Hua. She moved out of view in the direction of the galley. Trinity continued fast forwarding. By 9:30 it appeared everyone had retired for the evening. The next action came at 8:17 the following morning, Sunday the 14th. Once again the group gathered in the cabin. There was some discussion, then Keping Xie and the two men identified as Chinese assets exited the boat. Trinity fast forwarded through all of Sunday. The two men and one woman left behind were rarely in the frame. The action began again at 10:23 Sunday evening when the three men returned. All six people were in the frame again, the conversation animated. The cabin was deserted by 11:42. Monday the 15th through Thursday the 18th passed in a blur. The six people did little except smoke. The men left for dinner at 7:55 each evening, leaving the woman behind and returning with a to-go- box for her. Friday afternoon Keping Xie and the two assets left. They did not return until Sunday morning. When they did return they had a woman with them.

Trinity slowed the footage and watched as Keping Xie entered, followed by a petite brown haired woman. The two assets entered behind her, one carrying a small suitcase. As soon as she was in the cabin the woman was bound with zip ties at her wrists and ankles. A bandana was tied around her head, covering her eyes, and she was pushed roughly onto the couch. Next Keping Xie opened the small suitcase and dumped everything onto the coffee table. He rooted through the pile, eventually coming up with a small black backpack. He pushed everything else off the coffee table, unzipped the backpack, and upended it over the table. A pile of small silver and black objects and some wires fell onto the table. Keping Xie picked up one of the silver objects, it looked like an external hard drive to Trinity, and a cord. He plugged one end of the cord into the small object and the other into a lap top that Mei Hua had placed on the table. Keping Xie hit a few keys. His face darkened and he said something to Mei Hua. She shook her head. Keping Xie went through the same process with the rest of the objects on the table. It was clear to Trinity that he was not having success with whatever he was attempting to do. Eventually he stood and walked to the woman on the couch. He grabbed her by the shoulders, shaking her and yelling at her. Even though the captive was blindfolded, Trinity could tell the woman was crying. She shook her head from side to side, her shoulders heaved. After a moment Keping Xie threw the woman back to the couch and stormed out of the frame. Trinity fast forwarded again. At 7:55 the men left for dinner and Mei Hua exited the frame. She returned about fifteen minutes later and sat down opposite her captive. Five minutes after that Trinity got the surprise of her life when a familiar face eased into the cabin.

49

LOYAL TRUESDALE

L oyal wasn't sure what time it was, but he could tell that several hours had passed by the angle of the sun's rays. They had reached the end of Laguna Salada, passed through a bit of rough road, and were now traversing Laguna Del Diablo. Brandi's head still lolled against his shoulder. The slant and position of her neck and head looked decidedly uncomfortable. Loyal wondered about the level of pain she would feel when she finally woke. In the distance he could see what appeared to be shrubs and small trees. According to Maggie, the lake bed would end and a handful of tracks would be laid out before them. He was to take one of the center tracks and ignore the tracks to the far left and right.

Loyal slowed as he approached the edge of Laguna Del Diablo. Much to his relief a large appliance of some type had been upended and spray painted in red across its bulk were the words **San Felipe** and a large red arrow indicating the correct track to take. Loyal had to slow and downshift as he entered the rough track. This action resulted in several bumps. These bumps, in turn, awakened his sleeping passenger. Brandi jerked upright. She looked around in apparent confusion, her posture stiff and seemingly ready for flight.

"You fell asleep," Loyal said as gently as possible. "The bumpy ground woke you. We just left Laguna Del Diablo."

Brandi's posture softened. She rolled her head and shoulders, then gently massaged her neck.

"How long was I out?" she asked.

"A few hours I'd guess," said Loyal. He looked at her for a moment. "You need a break?" he asked. "Want to get out and stretch?"

"Yeah," said Brandi, "I think I do."

Loyal stopped the buggy in the middle of the track. There was no need to pull over, the desert around them was devoid of any other vehicles. With the extinguishing of the engine came utter and complete silence. Loyal took a long breath in and slid out of the buggy, exhaling as he stood and stretched his arms towards the bright blue sky. He turned and saw Brandi rooting around in the back of the buggy. She was still wearing the backpack across her chest.

"Need help finding something?" Loyal asked.

"Did Maggie send any toilet paper?" Brandi asked.

"Yeah." Loyal reached behind his seat." It is tucked down here." He stood and handed Brandi a small roll of toilet paper. She took it from his hand, turned, and began walking away from the buggy. Loyal opened his mouth to remind her not to wander too far, then abruptly closed it. He simply turned so that his back was to her, leaned against the buggy, and waited.

50

TRINITY GLASS

T rinity watched in silent surprise as Loyal eased into the cabin, PM9 extended in front of him. She smiled as she watched him approach the captor with stealth. During their weekend together they had spared in Jiu Jitsu. She knew from experience that Loyal was lighter on his feet than he appeared. He slid his hand over the woman's mouth at the same moment that he placed the barrel of the gun against her temple. He spoke into her ear and she nodded silently. Loyal stepped to the couch and pulled the bandana off the woman's head. Keeping the gun trained on Mei Hua, he stepped to the galley and grabbed a knife. He used this to cut the zip ties from the woman's wrists and ankles. The woman, appearing to follow Loyal's instructions, bound Mei Hua's wrists and ankles with zip ties from a pile on the table. She took a moment to gather the electronics from the table and place them in the backpack, which she slipped over her shoulders. She scooped up her pile of belongings from beneath the table and stuffed it in the suitcase. Without a backwards glance she and Loyal exited the cabin.

. . .

As soon as they exited Mei Hua began struggling against her restraints. Trinity fast forwarded through this short portion. Less than three minutes passed before the five men returned. Seeing Mei Hua bound and their captive missing, they sprang into action. Keping Xie and the two assets exited the cabin. Trinity assumed to give chase in their own dinghy. She knew from Captain Williams that two dinghies had been beached on the South shore. One of the remaining men picked up the knife and cut Mei Hua's zip ties. All three disappeared, then reappeared minutes later carrying the duffels they had brought with them on the first day. No one spoke. They spent several minutes wiping down the cabin's interior, hoisted the duffels, and exited the boat. Trinity fast forwarded once more. The next group to enter the cabin were detectives from the Oceanside Police Department. They entered with guns drawn, quickly cleared the cabin, then disappeared from the frame as they cleared the rest of the boat. Trinity fast forwarded through the search and the forensics team. She already knew they wouldn't find much, if anything at all. The next person to enter the frame once the search was conducted and the scene processed and sealed, was Trinity herself. These frames she deleted.

Trinity pushed away from the table and stood. She walked to the kitchen and removed a Perrier from the fridge. She stood, leaning against the kitchen sink, and drained half the bottle in three large swigs. The burp that followed was surprisingly loud in the quiet condo. Trinity set the Perrier on the counter and returned to the fridge. This time she removed another pre-packaged salad, which she dumped into a large bowl and fluffed with a fork. Picking up both the salad and the water she returned to the table and the lap top. She ejected the USB with the camera footage on it and inserted the other USB. A prompt, written in what Trinity assumed to be Chinese, appeared on the screen with a small rectangular box beneath it. Although she could not read the prompt, Trinity was able to infer that this USB was password protected and most likely encrypted. With a sigh, she reached for her phone and placed a call to Doug Caldwell.

51

BRANDI KENDRICK

Brandi was adjusting the waist of her miniskirt when the thought hit her with the force of a tractor trailer.

"Shit!" She said out loud as she turned towards the buggy. It was about half a football field away from her. She could see Loyal leaning against the driver's side, his back to her.

"Shit, shit, shit, shit!" Brandi muttered as she ran across the uneven desert ground. The thought was about the paper she had stuffed in her pants pocket at the gym. She had forgotten about it when she had stripped down to go in the hot tub at the canyon. She had re-dressed when her body was still wet and slept in the still damp clothes. She said a silent prayer as she ran that the information on the paper was not ruined.

Loyal's back was still to her when she reached the buggy. She grabbed the small suitcase from the back seat and wrenched it open. Her belongings spilled out, partially in the buggy and partially onto the dry desert sand. Brandi picked up the pants she had been wearing and gently reached her hand into the front right pocket. She pulled the folded piece of paper out and, with trembling hands, slowly opened it up. A tidal wave of relief crashed through her when she saw the strings of numbers, letters, and symbols had not been compromised. With the relief came a second wave of bottled up emotions that she had been tamping down for the past week. This time Brandi could not hold back the stinging tears. She stood, the paper in her hands, and silently cried. Her shoulders shook and the warm tears flowed. Then, as suddenly as it had begun, the flood of tears stopped. Brandi looked up to see that Loyal had turned around and was looking at her, his expression a mixture of sympathy and confusion.

"I thought it got wet," Brandi said as she carefully refolded the paper and placed it in the backpack she still wore across her chest. She picked up and replaced the spilled contents of her suitcase and returned it to the back seat of the buggy. She then removed her sunglasses and used her sleeve to wipe her cheeks and eyes. She noticed that Loyal had a granola bar in one hand and a water bottle in the other. He set them both in the driver's seat, rummaged around in the cooler and the bag of dry goods, and reached across the buggy to hand Brandi a water bottle and a granola bar.

"You and your sister were close?" he asked.

Brandi nodded as she opened the water bottle and took a long sip.

"Best friends, really," she said.

"Tell me about her," said Loyal.

Brandi nodded, gave a small smile, and began.

52

LOYAL TRUESDALE

Loyal hadn't been sure of the best way to comfort Brandi, but thought talking about her sister might be helpful, so he had asked.

"She was two years older than me," said Brandi. "We didn't have the same Dad. Jodi's was totally out of the picture. Mine didn't see me much, but at least he paid child support." She paused, then continued. "My Mom tried, but she really wasn't cut out for motherhood. She had a string of loser boyfriends, but no more kids, thank God. Jodi and I were on our own a lot, we pretty much raised ourselves."

Loyal wasn't sure what to say to that, so he simply nodded.

"We lived in Seattle," continued Brandi. "When Jodi turned 18 she hopped on a bus for Southern California. Three weeks later I was on the bus too. We had a little one bedroom apartment in San Marcos, and both got jobs at Vons. It was a struggle, but at least we were together."

Brandi unwrapped her granola bar and took a bite. When she had chewed and swallowed she asked, "Do you have any brothers or sisters?"

"Nope," said Loyal. "I have a daughter." He thought about asking Brandi if she had any kids, but changed his mind before he spoke.

Brandi was quiet for a long moment. She gazed past Loyal, out into the vast desert, focused on something only she could see.

"Jodi saved up for a computer," she finally said. "She was on it all the time. On my twenty-first birthday she took me to the bank and added me on to a checking account she had. It had just over $10,000 in it. She told me she was making money on the Internet, lots of it. She said she could work anywhere there was an Internet connection."

Brandi brought her gaze back to Loyal.

"She left that day. Said she was becoming a nomad. Every month or so she would deposit money into the account. Eventually I bought my house in Carlsbad and quit working. Jodi kept depositing money and showed up every once in a while. It was just a few years ago that she bought the house on Morgan Road and started staying around more."

"What was she doing to earn so much money?" asked Loyal.

Brandi shook her head. "I truly don't know."

Loyal sensed that Brandi was done sharing for the moment. He packed their small bits of trash into the dry goods bag and checked to make sure everything was secure. He and Brandi each slid silently into the buggy. Loyal started it up and eased back onto the track. According to Maggie, once they left Laguna Del Diablo, they would have about an hour of travel left before they reached San Felipe. Loyal was ready for this part of the journey to be over. Although lower in the sky, the sun was hot and bright, the wind felt like a blowdryer on his face, and his back was tense from the long hours of driving. Loyal rolled his shoulders a few times and tried to distract himself by thinking about something positive. Trinity was his first choice, but his mind kept veering off course and landing on his parents. He supposed listening to Brandi talk about her own childhood had set his own mind on that course. Rather than fight it, Loyal gave in and let his mind wander down whatever path it chose.

Loyal's father, Walker Truesdale, was where his thoughts finally settled. He had not seen, nor communicated with, his father since he was eleven years old. In Loyal's mind his childhood was divided into two distinct segments. The first portion, up to age eleven, was the "Dad in his life" section. From age eleven until the present day was the "Dad gone" section. Neither of his parents had ever explained to Loyal why Walker Truesdale disappeared completely from their lives. Loyal's anger had cooled over the years, but still popped up on occasion. A long forgotten memory slipped into Loyal's head unbidden. Seven year old Loyal, asleep in his bed, was awakened by scratchy whiskers and coffee breath. His Dad was leaning over him whispering in his ear.

"Wake up buddy," his dad had said. "You are coming fishing with me today."

They had gone to Lake Wohlford, just above Escondido, and fished from shore. Loyal could see his father so clearly in his mind's eye. He could almost feel his father's strong arms and hands as he stood behind Loyal and patiently taught the young boy how to cast a line.

.   .   .

Loyal brought himself out of the reverie with a small shake of his head. He rarely thought of his father anymore. There had been no contact between father and son since the day Walker left. Loyal glanced to his right. Brandi was sitting casually in the passenger seat, her right arm extended out of the buggy, her hand seemingly caressing the dry desert wind. The expression on her face appeared neutral, all emotions set to the side for the time being. A vibration in his shirt pocket startled Loyal. He reached his hand up and felt the GPS he had placed there earlier. The vibration signaled that they were fast approaching another of Maggie's waypoints. He slowed the buggy and removed the GPS from his pocket. The waypoint was listed as Zoo Road. Loyal remembered now that he was to look for orange ribbons placed in the desert to guide off road racers. He scanned the area and saw some in the near distance. He put the buggy in gear and headed towards them.

53

TRINITY GLASS

Caldwell answered on the second ring.

"Glass, you have something?"

Trinity gave him an abbreviated summary of the day's events, being careful to leave any mention of Loyal out of her account. She detailed her meeting at Homeland Security, the discussion with Captain Williams, the talk with Ted, and the look around the boat.

" I found a USB by the monitor on the boat," she said. "It appears to be written in Chinese and encrypted. I was hoping to overnight it to you."

"Take it to the DHS guys you met today," said Caldwell. "That will be faster. Didn't you say one of them specialized in China and Korea?"

"Yes," said Trinity. "Agent Park."

"Reach out to him," said Caldwell. "And let me know as soon as you have something."

He disconnected before Trinity had a chance to respond.

Trinity pulled out the notes she had taken during the meeting that morning and located Agent Park's contact information. The call went to voicemail so she left a message asking him to call her at his earliest convenience. She tried Loyal again. The call went straight to voicemail. She did not leave a message.

Trinity finished the salad and the Perrier. She cleared her dishes and then went into the bedroom. She removed the business suit and slipped into sweatpants and a loose T-shirt. She picked out the pins holding her bun in place and let her hair hang loosely down her back. She then returned to her computer. She had decided that while she waited for Agent Park to return her call she would find out all she could about the woman Loyal had apparently rescued. Ms. Brandi Kendrick.

Being an agent with the Office of Strategic Investigations, or OSI, gave Trinity unique access to both domestic and foreign databases. Surprisingly, Trinity's search ended up taking her down both roads. She made notes as she researched, eventually filling two pages on a yellow notepad. She then typed everything up and sat down on the couch to read it.

Brandi Raven Kendrick

Born July 21, 1977 in Seattle Washington. Mother Alice Luise Strauss born January 18, 1952 in Boise, Idaho. Unemployed. Main source of income child support from Brandi's father. Father, Albert John Kendrick, born September 25, 1949 in Seattle Washington. Engineer with Boeing Industries. Sister Jodi Dawn Mahoney born August 8, 1975 in Seattle Washington. (Jodi's father Phoenix Mahoney, born March 6, 1951 in Twisp, Washington and out of picture) As per court order, Brandi was to spend alternate weekends and three weeks in the Summer with her father. Holiday's were to be rotated.

In 1993 both Jodi and Brandi relocated to San Marcos, California.

Both found employment at Vons grocery store and shared an apartment. In 1999 Brandi purchase a duplex in Carlsbad and quit her job at Vons. There was no employment history from that point up to the present. Her income came from deposits made by her sister to a shared account.

Jodi Mahoney quit her job at Vons in 1996 and dropped completely off the map. Her passport, and the occasional deposits, were the only evidence that she was still alive. She appeared to spend most of her time in Thailand. In 2017 she purchased a home on Morgan Road in Carlsbad, paying cash. She and her boyfriend, Travis Dewey, had died just over a week ago in an apparent home invasion. Autopsy showed evidence of torture and toxicology revealed traces of Sodium Pentothal in both their systems. No suspects had been apprehended.

Albert John Kendrick had strong ties to China and kept an apartment there. Brandi accompanied him on many occasions, even spending one semester during middle school at Shanghai American School. In 2001 Mr. Kendrick had been arrested on suspicion of spying for China and committing industrial espionage by selling Boeing's intellectual property and proprietary information to his Chinese contacts. Kendrick had agreed to a plea deal in exchange for his testimony. A private pilot, he owned a Cessna 337 Super Skymaster, the safest pressurized twin engine aircraft made. Riley Rocket, located in Carlsbad, Ca on McClellan Palomar Airport, was the only operation in the United States certified to work on this type of specialized plane. Riley held all the PMA's (parts manufacture authority) which are like patents. Kendrick took off from McClellan Palomar on June 18, 2001, after having some work done on the plane. As he was descending to land at Seattle Boeing Field Airport a pressure bomb exploded, killing him instantly. The pressure bomb was tied to the transponder, which gives information to air traffic control, and then tied to the encoder, which gives the altitude to the transpon-

der. When he ascended to 3,000 feet after take off in Carlsbad the bomb was armed. When he was on final approach and descended through 3,000 feet the encoder set off the bomb. While he never gave official testimony regarding his ties to the Chinese Military and Intelligence Services, he had given depositions regarding his contacts. Keping Xie and Mei Hua were both on the list.

Trinity read the information several times. The odds that those two names would be on Brandi's father's contact list and suspects in Jodi and Travis' murders were astronomical. What the connection was, Trinity did not yet know. Her thoughts went again to Loyal, who was likely still with Brandi, and possibly in more danger than he realized.

54

BRANDI KENDRICK

Brandi kept her eyes straight ahead as Loyal maneuvered the buggy along the bumpy track. They were ascending some low lying foothills. She glanced at Loyal. He appeared focused on the driving. She supposed that he was very tired. She thought about asking him how much farther it was to San Felipe, then changed her mind. Conversation in the buggy was difficult, and he likely didn't know how far away the seaside town actually was.

Her mind drifted back to the short conversation they had had about her childhood. She had given him the sanitized version. There was no point in going into great detail about her unconventional upbringing. The basic details had been correct. Jodi's father had been absent from her life. Their Mother had had a string of loser boyfriends who spent most of their time on the couch watching TV and drinking beer, their swollen bellies poking out from beneath the edges of tattered T-shirts. Most had been harmless moochers, staying until Alice got tired of them and kicked them out. Jodi and Brandi thought of them as extra pieces of furniture, lifeless lumps taking up space in the apartment. There had only been one boyfriend that had rung any alarm bells for either girl. Wayne Jolivette had entered their lives in the Summer of 1989, when Jodi was 14 and Brandi was just shy of her 12th birthday.

Wayne was different than any of the other men Alice had brought home. He worked, which was a first. His job was as a night shift utility clean up worker at a large lumber plant just outside of the city. He left the apartment just after 7:00 each evening and returned home around 5:00 am. He usually went into the bedroom and slept until around noon, then ate some food and lounged on the couch during the day. Wayne was lean and strong, he had narrow eyes, more like slits than actual eye sockets, a long pointed nose, and a slash of a mouth. He wore his dark brown hair just past his collar and a thin mustache perched on his upper lip. He was the first boyfriend that actually made Jodi and Brandi nervous. Neither girl wanted to be around him. They made sure they were out of the apartment before he woke, and tried to stay away until he left for work.

Brandi still spent every other weekend at her Father's house. When she mentioned to him that Wayne scared her, he acted immediately, quietly informing Alice that Brandi would be staying with him until Wayne was out of the house. He offered to take Jodi too, but Alice wasn't having that. Brandi had accompanied her father to China and lived there with him for over six months. She completed the first half of seventh grade at Shanghai American School. When she returned to America at

Christmas time Wayne was gone. Brandi could sense the change in Jodi and Alice's relationship, but when she pressed Jodi for details all her sister would say is "He's gone and he's not coming back."

Brandi shook herself loose from the web of complicated memories and focused on the landscape around them. Low lying scrub brush dotted the desert land around them. Brandi inhaled deeply, expecting the sharp scent of sage and creosote. Instead she was rewarded with the tangy scent of salty sea air. She took a few more deep breaths and sat up expectantly as they approached the crest of the foothills. Loyal slowed the buggy to a stop at the apex. When Brandi saw the view she felt a rush of adrenaline and relief. Visible below them was the small town of San Felipe. Beyond the town was the wide blue-green expanse of the Sea of Cortez. The wind, carrying the ocean on its wings, brushed cool against their sweaty faces. A wide smile appeared on Brandi's face, through it's own volition. She turned to see a similar expression on Loyal's dusty, sunburned face. He turned to her and said, "We made it."

55

TRINITY GLASS

Trinity's phone rang just as she was lacing her shoes for a run. She liked to be in motion, and all the sitting of the day had caused her muscles to contract and complain. She was stiff, sore, and worried about Loyal. She quickly tied the bow, then fetched her phone from the kitchen counter. The display informed her that it was Agent Park and she accepted the call.

"Glass," she said.

"Agent Park, returning your call." Came the reply.

"I have something that could potentially be of great use to both of us," said Trinity. "It is encrypted and in a foreign language, most likely Chinese. Doug Caldwell suggested I reach out to you rather than overnight it to Virginia."

"Can you give me context?" Agent Park asked.

"I'd rather have a face-to-face," said Trinity.

"Meet me tomorrow morning at Clayton's Coffee in Coronado," said Park. "It is on the corner of tenth and Orange. 7:00 am."

"I'll be there," said Trinity.

She disconnected and set the phone slowly on the counter. She was glad Park had called her back, but truly she had been hoping the caller ID would have said Loyal.

Trinity drove to Carlsbad and parked in Garfield Street Parking. She walked one block Southwest to Ocean Street and then began to jog South. Ocean Street merged with a walkway above the ocean. Trinity ran full out, savoring the feeling of her muscles working, feeling the surge of energy as endorphins were released into her blood stream. The sun dropped and then dipped into the ocean as she ran, the skies turning from blue to salmon. When half the sun was visible above the water, she turned and retraced her steps, arriving at her vehicle by the light of the full moon. She drove back to the condo, where she showered, dressed in shorts and a T-shirt, and prepared a light meal of tuna on sourdough. She paired the sandwich with a Stone Ripper and ate on the patio. She stayed out on the patio until nearly 10:00 pm. Her thoughts like ping pong balls, scattered and unpredictable. Eventually she went back inside, rinsed the plate and put the bottle in the recycling container. She set her alarm for 4:30 am, brushed her teeth and hair, and slid into the cool sheets. Sleep did not come easily, but when it finally did, it was deep and dreamless.

56

LOYAL TRUESDALE

L oyal was blown away by the view from the crest of the foothills. The sight and smell of the Sea of Cortez was almost more than he could bear. The word exhausted couldn't even begin to describe how he was feeling. The last few miles of driving it had taken everything he had to keep his eyes open and focused on the road. With the stunning view of the cerulean ocean and the scent of the crisp salty air, he felt a smidgen of energy return. He felt the corners of his mouth curl into a grateful smile. He turned to look at Brandi. She was smiling broadly too. When she turned her head toward his all he could think to say was, "We made it." Loyal let the buggy idle for a long moment while they both took in the view. The relief felt by the two occupants of the buggy was palpable. After a moment he shifted into first and began the descent into San Felipe.

Loyal and Brandi passed under San Felipe's iconic arches just as the sun was setting behind the mountains to the West.

Having lived in Southern California all his life, Loyal found it curious that the sun did not set over the ocean. He made a mental note to try and awaken early enough to watch the sun rise over the ocean in the morning. He turned towards Brandi and, in a voice loud enough to be heard over the engine noise said, "I think we should go straight to the house tonight. We have enough food to get through until tomorrow. We can go to breakfast and re-stock our supplies in the morning."

Brandi nodded. "That sounds good to me," she said. She glanced back at the road then added, "You should turn right at this Pemex station."

Loyal looked at her. "How do you know that?"

"You said the house was South of town," Brandi answered. "This road takes us South." She removed her sunglasses and looked directly in his eyes. "Trust me Loyal."

Loyal downshifted and turned at the corner as Brandi had suggested. He was tired and dirty, and found he didn't have the energy to question her accuracy. She was correct, the road did lead South. As to her suggestion that he trust her, he was not entirely sure he was ready to do that. He wasn't sure what to think about Brandi. His internal radar, he jokingly referred to it as a bullshit meter, was pinging. He thought about everything that had occurred since Sunday morning. None of it made sense.

When Maggie's GPS vibrated in his shirt Loyal slowed and looked for the sign to the house. It was called *Casa Junto al Mar* and the wooden sign was planted in a pile of red rocks. Loyal downshifted, turned, and traveled down the road which turned into a sand based circular driveway. He pulled the buggy up alongside the house and parked. The house was built into sand dunes that were about thirty feet above the Sea of Cortez. The tide was in at the moment, the water lapping peacefully at the base of the dunes. Old tires were built into the dunes creating a protective barrier against the sea, Loyal supposed for stormy times when the tide beat ferociously against the dunes. He found the key at the base of a cactus, just as Maggie had said he would. He opened the sliding glass door and stepped inside. The house was a long rectangle. The Eastern side was all glass, a true window to the sea. A quick look revealed a master bed and bath and a guest bed and bath to the right. A large living room dominated the center, the kitchen was to the left. Without speaking he and Brandi carried all their belongings into the house. They set everything in the living room, then stepped out onto the back deck. It faced the East and hovered above the sea.

Loyal turned to Brandi. "Let's put our stuff away, shower, and find something to eat. You take the master bedroom," he said. "I'll take the smaller one."

Brandi nodded and walked back into the house. Loyal followed. He watched as she picked up her suitcase and headed to the larger of the bedrooms. He grabbed his duffel and went to the smaller one. When he heard the shower start up, he slipped off his shoes and socks, walked back to the living room for the cooler, and took it into the kitchen. He did not receive a blast of cool air when he opened the refrigerator, and realized that it wasn't turned on. He checked behind and saw that it was plugged in. He stepped back and pivoted to look around the kitchen. He spotted a metal box on the back wall and went to open it up. There was a switch labeled *inverter*, but Loyal wasn't sure exactly what he was supposed to do. He closed the box and made a mental note to pick up ice the next morning.

When he heard the shower stop, Loyal headed into the guest bathroom, slipped off his dusty clothes, and stepped into the shower. The cool water was a shock at first, but Loyal acclimated quickly. After he had dried, he wrapped a towel around his waist and stepped back into his bedroom. He picked out some fairly clean clothes, dressed, and walked to the kitchen.

Loyal pulled the last two sandwiches out of the cooler and carried them to the living room. Brandi, bare foot, was standing at a bar built into the wall. He watched as she lifted bottles, inspected the labels, then replaced them. He cleared his throat and she turned to face him.

"I found some sandwiches," he said. "You hungry?"

Brandi nodded, then held out the bottle she was holding. "I found some tequila," she said with a smile. "When in Mexico...?" She looked at him with a question in her eyes.

"A shot?" Loyal asked. He paused a moment, then added, "Sure, why not?"

57

PATRICK O'KEEFE

Patrick O'Keefe sat on the couch in his darkened den. A beer sat open, but untouched, on the coffee table in front of him. The house was quiet, his family all asleep in their beds. Olive had tried to stay up with him, but as her due date neared, and with two young children to care for, she took rest when she could. Pat's eyes were open, but unseeing. He stared off into space and thought about Agent Glass' visit to the Sheriff's Department earlier in the day. He knew Loyal trusted her, but Pat wasn't entirely sure that he did. The circumstantial evidence against Loyal was mounting. Pat wanted to do something to mitigate things, but wasn't sure what that might be.

With a sigh Pat leaned forward and picked up the beer. He took a long sip, then swallowed and set the can back down. He looked at his phone, willing Loyal to return his many calls. He tried to put himself in Loyal's place, to think like the man he so admired. He knew there was no way Loyal was involved in something that would hurt the Kendrick woman. Of this he was quite sure. So why, then, had Loyal vanished with her? Protection was the only answer Pat's troubled mind could arrive at. He sat up straighter. Protection actually made sense. The next question was, protection from whom? Scenarios whirled around in his head, but nothing stood out. There were too many options.

Pat picked up the beer and took another long sip. He stood and walked to the kitchen sink. He upended the can and watched as the remnants of the amber liquid flowed down the drain. He tossed the can in the recycle than methodically made his rounds through the house checking doors and windows. He paused at each of his two children's rooms, pulling the blankets up under each child's chin and kissing each gently on their soft warm cheeks. He would do anything to protect his family. He thought about where he would take them if they were in danger and needed to hide away. Someplace remote, he decided. A place devoid of technology. With a sigh Pat turned and walked toward his bedroom. He wasn't sure if such a place existed.

58

BRANDI KENDRICK

B randi was surprised, and pleased, when Loyal agreed to the shot of tequila. He insisted that they get something in their stomachs, so they ate their sandwiches out on the deck, the bottle and two shot glasses just out of reach. When they had finished the sandwiches, she poured two healthy shots, handed one to him, and raised her glass to his. They clicked the small glasses together and each swallowed the fiery liquid in one gulp. The burn brought tears to Brandi's eyes. She looked at Loyal. He was standing and turned towards the sea. Brandi moved beside him. The full moon was low in the sky, just beginning it's nightly ascent. The moon's rays reflected off the white water at the crest of the tiny waves. The tide was halfway out. The white sands held specks of moonlight, a glowing expanse beneath the deck and down the shore.

"Let's take the buggy down the beach," said Loyal. Brandi looked at him in surprise. This was the last thing she had expected to hear him say.

"Ok," she said. "One more shot and I'm in."

He turned towards her. "That is what a buggy is built for," he said. "I bet Bruce and Winnie have driven down this very beach under a full moon. We should do it too."

Brandi poured the second shots, which they drained, then stood for a moment looking down the shoreline. It was a perfect night. The air was warm, the breeze off the ocean cool and refreshing. The moonlight was just bright enough to infuse the surroundings with an ethereal glow. The warmth of the tequila lit her from within. Despite having spent the bulk of the last twenty-four hours in the buggy, a drive down the beach seemed like the perfect thing to do.

Well into her later years Brandi would always remember that drive down the beach. The way the buggy floated on the soft sand. The ocean to their left, the moonlight lighting their smiling faces. In that moment Brandi felt truly free and unencumbered. She let her hair blow in the wind, raised her hands into the night air, and laughed out loud. She never looked at Loyal, but could hear his laugh above the engine and the wind. She hoped that he felt the same freedom that she did. It was truly exhilarating. When they arrived back at the house both Brandi and Loyal were windblown. When she looked at him she saw his eyes were watering just like hers and his face and hair were sandy. They each slid out of the buggy and walked to the house. It was dark inside, ambient light from the full moon providing gentle illumination.

"I'm not sure how to make the lights work," said Loyal.

"I saw candles and matches by the bar," said Brandi as she crossed the living room. She found what she was looking for, struck a match, and lit three candles. She turned and walked back to where Loyal stood.

"The drive was more fun than I've had in a long time, Loyal," she said, placing her hand gently on his forearm. "How about a night cap?"

Loyal said nothing for a long moment. Brandi thought she saw indecision in his brown eyes. Finally he smiled a small smile and said, "Thanks Brandi. I think I'm going to go ahead and turn in."

With that he turned and headed toward his bedroom. Brandi stayed where she was long after his door closed, staring at the wooden rectangle and wondering about Loyal Truesdale.

59

TRINITY GLASS

Trinity woke two minutes before her alarm was set to go off. She reached over and silenced it before it had the opportunity to make noise, then sat up and slid her feet off the edge of the bed. She sat quietly for a moment, savoring the quiet and the dark. She wasn't sure what would come of the meeting with Agent Park this morning. She wanted very much to trust the man. She was hoping that he could break the encryption and read the content of the USB she had found on the boat. Where that information would lead her she did not know.

Before she stood she tried calling Loyal. Once again the call went straight to voicemail. She hung up without leaving a message. He was somewhere in the wind with Brandi Kendrick. The how she knew, the why she did not, but intended to find out. Brandi's father's connection to China, his unsolved murder, and the presence of Keping Xie and Mei Hua on his list of contacts was too much to ignore. Something big was in play here.

Trinity stood and walked to the kitchen. She heated water and poured it over crushed beans in the French Press. She showered while the beans soaked. She drank her first cup of coffee while she blow dried her hair and slipped on a charcoal gray pantsuit for the meeting. She took her second cup of coffee out to the patio. Behind her and to the East, the sun had begun it's journey skyward, It's rays were not yet strong and bright. The space beyond the patio was gradually illuminated. Trinity sipped and considered everything she had learned. She had resisted looking into Loyal's call history, it felt as if she would be invading his privacy. She realized now that she needed to know if he had made any calls and to whom.

Trinity rose and went to her computer. She sent a message to a colleague in Virginia requesting Loyal's phone records from Sunday to the present. While she was on the computer she accessed a database and found Patrick O'Keefe's personal cell phone number. She added this contact information to her phone, shut down the computer, gathered her things, and walked out to the car. Once she was on the road she dialed O'Keefe's number. He answered on the third ring.

60

PATRICK O'KEEFE

Pat was just pulling into the Sheriff's Department parking lot when his phone rang. He glanced at the screen and saw an unfamiliar number. He usually did not answer calls outside of his contact list on his personal phone, but was worried enough about Loyal to chance a spam call. He hit accept and said, "Hello."

"Detective O'Keefe," a somewhat familiar voice said. "It is Agent Glass."

"How did you get this number Agent Glass?" he asked.

"That's not important right now," she replied. "I have definitive proof that Loyal rescued Brandi Kendrick from a boat anchored in Oceanside Harbor. She was being held by six Chinese Nationals who entered the United States with falsified passports over a period of three days several weeks ago. Homeland Security flagged the passports with the intention of tracking the six individuals." She paused and took a breath. "They lost them. That is why I'm here.

. . .

Agent Glass paused again. O'Keefe could hear engine noise in the background and assumed she was in her car. He waited, and when she did not continue he simply said, "I'm listening."

"We have identified four of the six Chinese Nationals. One is a former General, another is a scientist with ties to the U.S., two are assets." She paused again. "That means killers Detective."

O'Keefe remained quiet and when she spoke again he could hear the frustration in her voice.

"I understand your mistrust, Detective, as you don't really know me. I think it is safe to say that we both care about Loyal."

Pat thought about this for a moment, then said, "There have been a string of overdoses in our area over the past six months. All Fentanyl. I've been working with various technologies to try to work my way up the supply chain. There have been whispers recently about the drug coming from China through Mexican cartels and to the United States." He paused then added, "None of my information is admissible in court, Agent Glass."

Neither person spoke for a long moment. Eventually Trinity said. "You have any thoughts about where Loyal might go to lay low?"

"I was thinking about that last night," Pat said. "I don't know."

"Don't lose this number," said Trinity. "Call if you think of anything."

"Will you do the same?" he asked.

There was another very long pause, then Trinity said, "Yes."

61

LOYAL TRUESDALE

Despite his exhausted state, Loyal slept fitfully. The bedroom had a wall clock that ticked very loudly. When Loyal did manage to fall asleep he dreamt that he was a bomb disposal technician. The blast suit was very heavy. His body was hot, sweat poured down his face and into his eyes. The bomb was in a vest that was secured to a woman he thought was Trinity. He couldn't be sure, everything was blurred and in slow motion. His hands shook as he tried to decide which wires to cut. His dream self made the choice and cut the green wire. The bomb exploded and Loyal woke up.

He sat up in the dark. His heart was racing and his breaths came in short, abrupt gasps. He swung his legs over the side of the bed and sat for a moment, letting the dream fade from his memory. His heart calmed and his breathing normalized. As he sat in the dark he remembered his plan to watch the sun rise over the ocean. He was certainly up early enough to accomplish that. Loyal stood and slipped on a pair of shorts and his

Big Bear Bash T-shirt. A look around the house last night had revealed no washer or dryer. He had only worn the T-shirt from the buggy run for a short period of time and it was the cleanest thing he had. Loyal walked quietly through the house and out the side door. He skirted the edge of the house and walked through the sand dunes towards the sea. The moon was dipping down in the West, providing just enough ambient light for him to see. He found a nice spot about fifteen feet from the water and settled himself on the soft sand.

Loyal had no idea how much time passed before the sun began it's daily ascent into the heavens. The quiet of the pre dawn hours and the soft, rhythmical sound of the waves combined to put him in an almost trancelike state. He was aware of himself and his surroundings, but at the same time separate from them somehow. It was the gentle illumination on the Eastern horizon that brought him back to reality. The sky and ocean gradually lightened from black to blue. The wispy clouds in the sky caught the gentle rays and slowly became tinged with pink and orange. A pelican flew through his field of view just as the sun made an appearance, a ball of fire rising out of the inky blue water, yellow on top and a red reflection cast across the sea. The exact opposite of the sunsets he had watched for most of his adult life. The sea giving birth to the light. Loyal did not consider himself to be poetic or whimsical, but in that moment with the soft sand beneath him and the glory of the sky above him, he longed for Trinity.

Loyal sat on the sand until the sun was fully in the sky. At last he rose, dusted off his shorts, and returned to the house. It was quiet and still. He checked the loud clock in the bedroom and saw that it was nearly 7:00 am. He peeked in the master bedroom. Brandi was still sleeping. He unpacked his duffel and tossed his clothes into the bathtub. He ran cool water until the tub was about half way full, then lathered the bar of soap from the sink, and swished his clothes around in the soapy water. He drained the tub, then refilled it with clean water and repeated the swishing without soap. He twisted each item to wring the water out as much as possible, then took everything out to the back deck and laid it all out to dry. He then went back inside and knocked on the doorframe of the master bedroom. When Brandi stirred he said, "I'm heading to town in about twenty minutes if you want to go."

62

TRINITY GLASS

Trinity arrived to the coffee shop a few minutes after 7:00 and found street parking in front of Clayton's. She entered the coffee shop and saw Agent Park already seated at a table for two. She crossed the small shop and sat down opposite him.

"Thank you for meeting me," she said.

"You piqued my curiosity Agent Glass," said Park.

Trinity smiled. "Please call me Trinity."

Park returned the smile. "Ok Trinity, then you call me Lee."

A waitress appeared beside the table. "What can I get you?" she asked.

Trinity took a moment to glance through the menu. "I'll have the veggie scramble and a decaf please," she said.

"I'll have the same," said Lee

"You got it," said the waitress as she turned away.

Trinity leaned across the small table towards Lee. "I found where the six Nationals were staying," she said. "They are gone, but I found this." She opened her hand to reveal the USB, then re-closed her fingers around it.

"I could use your help breaking the encryption and reading the contents." She paused. "I need to know you are willing to share everything that you find."

Lee leaned back in his chair and folded his arms across his chest. "You really have no idea what is on there?"

Trinity maintained her position leaning across the table. "I do not. The more I dig into this situation though, the more complex it gets. This could be about anything from industrial espionage, to drug running, to a list of U.S. contacts. Two lives may hang in the balance, Lee. I need to know I can trust you."

The waitress returned with their coffee, carefully placing each mug on the table. Trinity leaned back to make space, never breaking eye contact with Lee.

"Be right back with your eggs," said the waitress. As she turned away Lee said, "You can trust me."

Trinity paid for breakfast then followed Lee outside to their cars. They agreed to drive to Homeland Security and meet in front of the building. Lee would escort Trinity in and she would be present for the initial analysis of the USB. If it was easily opened, she would remain on site and see the results at the same moment as Lee. If the encryption turned out to be more difficult to break, she would leave the USB with him and count on him contacting her the moment he had something to share. Trinity parked in the same parking garage as she had on her previous trip and walked briskly to the office of Homeland Security. Lee was waiting for her as promised. He escorted her in, saw that she was issued a visitor's badge, then walked her down the hallway to the bank of elevators. They rode to the second floor then walked to an office at the far end of the hall-way. Lee knocked on the closed door. A small sign identified it as the Data Analytics Control Center.

Just over an hour later Trinity was back in the 4Runner and heading back to her condo. The USB encryption had not taken too long to break. The contents of the USB had been a list of 17 names. Trinity recognized only one name. Number five, Jodi Mahoney. Although she was not normally in the habit of sharing information, Trinity did tell Lee that Jodi Mahoney was a recent homicide victim in Carlsbad. She left out the Brandi Kendrick kidnapping and Loyal Truesdale rescuing informa-tion. Lee had put his team to work tracing the other names and promised to share any results with Trinity. She had a copy of the list and was planning on emailing it to Doug Caldwell as soon as she was back at the condo.

Trinity parked and entered the condo. She sent the email containing the names to Doug and received a reply immedi-ately. He would get a group on it right away. Trinity checked the rest of her emails and saw that her colleague had responded to her request for Loyal's call list. At 1:40 pm on Sunday he had called a Verne Cooper. At 1:49 he had called Phil Gillespie, and at 2:05 he had received a call from Phil Gillespie. None of theses calls lasted longer than three minutes. At 9:18 Loyal had called Maggie Macphearson. This call had been short, lasting only 18 seconds. It didn't take Trinity long to find out that Verne Cooper was the man who had reported Brandi Kendrick missing in Big Bear. His Facebook and Instagram were both filled with pictures of him in a buggy, he was clearly a member of the club. Phil Gillespie was a firefighter in Carlsbad. He had recently married a woman named Elsie Davenport. Trinity remembered the wedding that Loyal had attended in April, she was sure these were the same people. Maggie, she knew, was Loyal's friend from Valley Center. Since he had called Maggie after the rescue of Brandi Kendrick, this was the person Trinity called first.

63

LOYAL TRUESDALE

L oyal was just about to knock on the door of the master bedroom when it opened and Brandi breezed out. She was wearing a low cut spaghetti strap floral print dress and sandals. The black backpack dangled loosely from her left hand.

"I'm ready," she said.

Loyal looked at her for a long moment, then turned towards the front door without saying anything. He was feeling frustrated with Brandi. The woman acted like they were on some kind of vacation. All Loyal wanted was to see her to safety and return home. He was thinking of Trinity and wondered how long her business would be keeping her in Southern California. Loyal locked the front door after Brandi passed through and pocketed the key. He slid into the buggy and started the engine. He let it idle for a moment, then shifted into gear. He turned towards Brandi and said, "If you don't mind, I'd like to take the beach."

. . .

Loyal's mood lightened as soon as they hit the smooth sand. He felt much the same way he had on a long ago birthday when he had found a Yamaha YZ 125 parked in front of the fireplace. All he had wanted to do was get outside and ride. All he wanted to do now was drive. The tide was on its way out, revealing a flat and featureless pathway for the buggy. As he accelerated and the wind caressed his face and ruffled his hair, he found himself smiling again. It was amazing how much of a mood elevator the buggy was. He glanced at Brandi. Her loose hair was blowing around her head, a wide smile on her face. As Loyal turned back towards the front he felt his worries and frustration blow away with the wind.

About five minutes into the drive Loyal noticed what looked like a checkpoint in front of them. Three men dressed in camouflage and carrying M16 rifles blocked their forward progress. Loyal slowed as he approached, stopping completely about ten feet away from the men. He killed the engine and held his hands up above the steering wheel so that they were visible. The three men surged forward, guns at the ready, giving rapid fire directions in Spanish. Loyal opened his mouth to say something, but Brandi beat him to it. When she spoke Loyal was shocked to hear her speaking to the men in what sounded like perfectly fluent Spanish. He turned to look at her. Her posture mimicked his own, her hands raised up above the dashboard, the black backpack strung across her chest.

"They want us to get out of the car," said Brandi quietly. "Move slowly."

Loyal slid carefully out of the buggy and stood next to it. Brandi slid out as well, keeping up a stream of rapid fire Spanish the entire time. Loyal looked across the buggy at her.

"You never told me you spoke Spanish," he said.

Brandi glanced at him. "It never came up," she said. "I can handle this Loyal." She paused, then added, "Trust me."

Loyal definitely did not trust Brandi. The woman was full of contradictions and surprises. Rather than trust, Loyal felt mistrust. The men, Loyal assumed they were soldiers of some kind, herded Loyal and Brandi up the sand dunes towards a Humvee parked at the top. A man stood by the passenger door, binoculars raised to his eyes, the lenses facing towards the sea. He lowered the binoculars as they approached. Loyal could see immediately that this man held a higher rank in the military. He wore an olive green uniform and when he turned fully towards them Loyal could see three stars prominently displayed on his right shoulder. Loyal was not familiar with the ranking system of the Mexican Army, but was fairly sure three stars meant a high rank in any country. When they were about five feet away from him Brandi launched into rapid fire Spanish once again.

Loyal had no idea what she was saying. He simply watched as the officer approached her. He pointed to the backpack, which she removed and handed to him. He opened it, looked inside, then removed one of the objects which he held up to Brandi. Loyal watched the back and forth conversation between Brandi and the officer in much the same way one watches a tennis match. The officer lobbed a question and Brandi lobbed an answer. The officer replaced the item in the backpack, zipped it closed, and tossed it into the Humvee through the open passenger window. He then turned to the soldiers, but just as he began to talk engine noise from the North interrupted him. A tan Ford Ranger came barreling up the dunes and screeched to a stop in front of the Humvee. A soldier slid out of the truck, saluted the officer in charge, and began speaking rapidly while gesturing towards the truck. Voices from behind him drew Loyal's attention back towards the water. A Panga boat had arrived on shore. Two soldiers were pulling it towards shore. A third sat in the boat, his M16 pointed at two men who were in handcuffs. The next five minutes were chaos and confusion. The handcuffed men from the Panga were escorted to the Humvee. Another Humvee arrived and two more handcuffed men were removed from the Ranger and escorted to it. The officer in charge, who seemed to have forgotten about Loyal and Brandi, was barking orders at everyone. He was about to get in his Humvee when Brandi approached him and put her hand on his arm. They spoke quietly for a moment. Brandi stood close to him and kept her hand on his arm. It looked to Loyal like she was actually flirting with the man. After a few moments the officer reached into the Humvee and, with a smile, handed Brandi's backpack to her. She smiled that slow sexy smile right back at him, gave a quick salute, then turned and walked back towards Loyal.

64

TRINITY GLASS

rinity was not surprised when Maggie's phone went to voicemail. Nobody answered unknown calls these days. She left a brief message stating her name, her concern about Loyal, and her contact information. Her next call was to Phil Gillespie who, surprisingly, answered on the second ring. Trinity explained who she was and her reason for calling. Phil explained that Loyal had wanted information about the house fire on Morgan Road, and that he had briefly met him there. He had no idea where Loyal currently was. Trinity rattled off her contact information and thanked him for his time. She disconnected and then called the last person on Loyal's call list, Verne Cooper.

Verne did not answer. Trinity left a message explaining who she was and asking him to please call her. She re-checked her emails, finding nothing from Caldwell or Lee Park. Trinity sat down on the couch with a deep sigh. She felt stalled. She had lots of information to work with, but none of it seemed to fit together. She found herself wondering abut Loyal. They enjoyed each other, she knew that much to be true. They both had enjoyed the time they had spent together and wanted it to continue. She couldn't help but wonder, though, how he managed to get himself involved in these crazy situations. He still hadn't shared the entire truth of the previous Summer with her. How had a low key homicide detective redirected a satellite toward Las Vegas? A smile she couldn't stop graced her lips at that thought. Loyal was definitely an interesting guy.

Trinity was brought out of her thoughts by the ringing of her phone. She stood quickly and picked it up off the counter. The caller ID informed her that Douglass Caldwell was calling. She answered in her usual way.

"Glass."

"I still don't know the link between the people on your list, but seven out of the seventeen are dead," Caldwell said.

Trinity drew in a slow breath. "How did they die Doug?"

"Home invasions," he said.

"Send me the names of the dead," Trinity said. "And find that connection Doug."

"You will know as soon as I do," said Caldwell, who then, in his typical fashion, ended the call abruptly.

Trinity turned and leaned against the counter. It seemed that the list was a hit list. That explained the presence of the Chinese assets. What could the connection between all those names possibly be? Trinity thought again about the footage of Loyal rescuing Brandi Kendrick. She retrieved the USB and reinserted it in her computer. She fast-forwarded to the moment Loyal entered the screen, and watched as he freed Brandi and had her zip tie her captor. She slowed the footage when Brandi scooped the contents of the coffee table into the backpack. She froze the frame and attempted to zoom in on the objects. Perhaps she had underestimated their importance. The more she zoomed the less in focus the objects became. Trinity was working on adjusting the focus when her phone rang again. She turned away from the computer and picked up her phone. Caller ID indicated a call from Patrick O'Keefe. Trinity answered.

"Glass," she said.

"Agent," said O'Keefe, "I'm hearing chatter on Stingray that I'm pretty confidant involves Loyal."

"I'm listening," said Trinity.

"There is definitely a connection between the Chinese and the cartels," said O'Keefe. "They are working together to get drugs, specifically Fentanyl, into the U.S."

"What does that have to do with Loyal?" asked Trinity impatiently.

"The Chinese know that Loyal is with Brandi. They believe they are in Mexico." O'Keefe paused. "They have enlisted the cartel to find them."

Trinity was silent for a long moment, then said, "You are sure about this?"

"Yes," said O'Keefe.

"You have included Captain Williams in this chain of information?"

"Yes," said O'Keefe. "To be honest, he's still on the fence about Loyal being on the right side of the law on this one."

"We need to find them. I've discovered a hit list. Brandi's sister, Jodi, was on it. Seven of the seventeen on the list have died in home invasions," Trinity said. "Those Chinese assets are here for a reason, and I can't think of any that could possibly be good."

65

LOYAL TRUESDALE

L oyal drove the buggy about a mile North on the beach, then pulled up on a sand dune and stopped. He quieted the ignition and turned to Brandi.

"I want to know everything that just happened," he said. "Everything. Do not leave out one single word." His voice was hoarse with anger and frustration. "Every fucking thing, Brandi. I'm serious." His eyes were laser focused on Brandi's. The calm way she was looking back at him just angered him more. He realized in that moment that she frustrated him in much the same way his daughter had during her teenage years. Stella would look at him with those calm, brown eyes and tell him half truths and misdirections. Brandi was a grown woman, but seemed to still be operating in that teenage way, obscuring the truth, distracting and confusing him, making him question his own version of reality. He forced himself to calm and be focused.

. . .

Brandi stared into his eyes and said nothing for a long moment. Then she began to talk.

"They were set up to bust up a drug buy. The drugs were coming from a shrimp boat out in the sea. The buyers were to be waiting somewhere on shore. When they saw us, they assumed we were the buyers. The man by the Humvee was a General in the army. When they figured out I spoke Spanish the soldiers took me to him. He wanted to know what we were doing on the beach. I told him we were vacationing in a house just South of here."

"What about the backpack?" Loyal asked. "He took it from you. Why?"

"He wanted to know what the devices were," said Brandi. "He thought they were some kind of money."

"What did you tell him about them?" asked Loyal.

"I told him we were doing a lot of filming and that they were hard drives containing the footage."

"What else?" asked Loyal.

Brandi looked away for a moment, then returned her gaze to Loyal."He wanted to know if you were my husband." She paused again. "I think he liked me."

"Who were the people in handcuffs?" asked Loyal.

"The two off the Panga were the drug sellers," said Brandi. "The two in the truck were the buyers. They had a duffel full of cash." She paused again. "American dollars."

Loyal finally looked away from Brandi. He stared out at the unbelievably brilliant blue waters of the Sea of Cortez and ran her commentary through his filter. He decided she was probably being fairly truthful, though he doubted he would ever get anything close to the full truth out of her. He didn't think it was in her nature to be completely forthcoming, even in the best of situations.

"Ok," he said, "let's go into town and get something to eat and buy some supplies."

"Bar Miramar is good," said Brandi.

Loyal looked at her again. "Have you been to San Felipe before?" he asked.

"Yeah," she said.

"And you never thought to tell me that during the entire trip?" Loyal asked.

"I never got here the way we came," said Brandi. "What would it have mattered?"

Loyal had nothing to say to that. He simply shook his head, started the buggy, shifted into first, and took off down the beach.

Loyal followed Brandi's directions and was soon parked just down the street from Bar Miramar. They slid out of the buggy and walked in silence to the restaurant. They found a table on the patio, the ocean just a stone's throw away. Both ordered Huevos Rancheros. Brandi ordered a Bloody Mary, and on impulse Loyal ordered one as well. The bartender delivered both food and drinks. Loyal took his first bite of the eggs and felt the tension start to drain out of him. He followed the bite with a long sip of his drink. He leaned back in his chair and closed his eyes. The salty air was warm against his face and the sun was warm on his body. The first taste of food and drink warmed him from the inside. He sat like that for a moment, then slowly opened his eyes to find Brandi looking at him with an amused expression.

"You finally going to start to relax?" she asked.

Loyal looked around the restaurant. There were a handful of diners enjoying breakfast. He looked out towards the water. Lazy waves broke on the shore. He could see a few kids playing out in the water, an older couple walked along the sand holding hands. He looked back at Brandi. "Yeah," he said, "I guess I am."

Both finished their food and drinks. When the bartender came to clear their dishes Brandi asked for two more Bloody Marys. Loyal opened his mouth to protest, then realized that there really wasn't any reason not to have another drink. They were in an exotic vacation locale and had no pressing plans for the day. "Why not?" he thought. The bartender delivered the second round. Loyal and Brandi sipped their drinks in comfortable silence, each seemingly lost in their own thoughts. Loyal's drifted, as they often did these past four months, to Trinity. On impulse, he pushed his chair back and stood. He told Brandi he would be right back, then turned and walked towards the water. As he neared the shore he removed his phone from his pocket and turned it on. It responded by emitting a torrent of pings and beeps, indicating missed calls, voicemails, and text messages. Loyal tapped the phone icon and scrolled through the list of missed calls. O'Keefe, Captain Williams, and Trinity topped the list. He tapped on Trinity's name and raised the phone to his ear.

"Loyal," she said when she answered, "where the hell are you?"

"San Felipe," he answered.

"Loyal," she said, "I need you to listen to me. Please. You are in real danger."

66

TRINITY GLASS

W hen her phone had rung immediately upon
ending the phone call with O'Keefe, Trinity had
assumed it was him calling back with some piece
of information he had forgotten to pass along. Her heart literally skipped a beat when she saw that the caller was Loyal.

"Loyal," she had said when she answered, "where the hell
are you?"

"San Felipe," he had answered.

She paused a moment. He sounded so happy and relaxed.
Trinity wondered for a brief moment about that fact. She had,
after all, seen pictures of Brandi Kendrick. Trinity re-focused
and said, "Loyal, I need you to listen to me. Please. You are in
real danger."

When he remained quiet she continued.

"I was sent to San Diego to track six Chinese Nationals who
entered the U.S. on falsified passports via Mexico. It seems that
once again our cases intersect. The people I am looking for are
the same people from whom you rescued Brandi Kendrick. I've
been on the boat, Loyal. I found footage. I've identified four of

the six. One is a former General, the woman is a scientist, and two are assets."

"Killers," Loyal said quietly.

"Yes," said Trinity. "I also found an encrypted USB. We've broken the encryption. We still don't know the common thread, but it is a list of 17 people. Seven are dead, Loyal. Jodi Mahoney was one of them. All died in home invasions, and all had traces of Sodium Pentathol in their systems. You have also caught the attention of local law enforcement, meaning your former Captain, who considers you a person of interest in Ms. Kendrick's disappearance."

"She vanished from Big Bear," said Loyal. "It was lucky I found her."

"I'm assuming she is still with you?" Trinity asked.

"Yep," said Loyal.

"It seems that the Chinese are in bed with the cartels," Trinity said. "They are moving some serious quantities of drugs from China, through Mexico, and into the U.S. The Chinese know who you are Loyal, and they have tapped the cartels to find you."

Trinity heard Loyal take a quick breath in, but he remained silent.

"I'm going to come get you both," she said. "I'm looking at a map. I think the best airport that I can safely land at is in Mulege. Leave now, Loyal," she said. "You should be able to get there by Thursday. I'll arrange to fly in that day." She paused, then added, "And destroy your phone. They can track you with it."

There was silence on the line for so long that Trinity thought perhaps the connection had been broken.

"Loyal?" she said.

"I'm here," he said. "Call O'Keefe. Tell him he has permission to enter my apartment by any means necessary. There are some ziplock bags on the counter containing evidence I collected near Brandi and Jodi's homes. Call the Captain. Tell him as much as you can. I have maps and a GPS, I'll make sure we are in Mulege by Thursday." He paused. "Can you call Stella and just tell her I went to Mexico for a few days?"

"Yes," said Trinity.

"Thanks," said Loyal.

There was another long pause, then he said, "It is really good to hear your voice." With that he terminated the call.

Trinity remained motionless after Loyal disconnected the call. She stood, phone in hand, simply staring at the screen. Her relief at finally speaking to him was tangible. She actually felt it cloaking her body. She tapped the photos icon on her phone and scrolled through the pictures. It didn't take long to locate the one she wanted to see. It was of the two of them at Stone Brewery. They sat close together at an outside table. The background was all foliage. The waiter, who had been standing, had taken the picture of them as they sat. Trinity and Loyal, both with wide smiles on their faces, looked up at the camera. Their heads were tilted towards one another in that way that shows familiarity and closeness. She used her fingers to zoom in. Loyal's face filled the screen. The depth of her affection for him had caught her off guard. She took one last look at his brown eyes, his impossibly white teeth, and his happy smile. Then she closed the photo, opened her contacts list, and started making calls.

67

LOYAL TRUESDALE

L oyal disconnected the call and stood completely still, phone in hand, mentally processing all that Trinity had just told him. She was absolutely correct that if the cartel was after them they were in grave danger. Loyal had seen crime scene photos of cartel murders. He did not frighten easily, but those guys scared him. The ruthless brutality of their crimes was beyond anything he had experienced in his tenure as a homicide detective. He did not intend to become one of their victims.

On impulse Loyal opened the photos app on his phone. He scrolled through until he found the latest picture Stella had sent him. She was just over six months into her pregnancy. She was turned to the side and had pulled her blouse against her belly to further highlight the growing bulge. Her brown hair was loose around her face and midway down her back, her eyes and smile shining. She and Mitch had opted not to find out the gender of the baby until he or she was born. Loyal felt his throat tighten as he thought about the fact that he might never meet his grandchild. He scrolled through a few more pictures and found another that brought a smile to his face. He and Trinity at Stone Brewery. Both faces so relaxed and content. He vowed in that moment that he would make it back for all of them.

Loyal moved back towards Bar Miramar, his eyes scanning the ground. Just before he reached the patio he saw what he was looking for. He leaned down and picked up the gray brick. He set his phone on the low wall of Bar miramar, raised the brick, and brought it down on the phone. The screen shattered. He repeated this action two more times. The phone was obliterated. He walked back towards the shore, pulled his arm back, and threw the phone as far into the Sea of Cortez as he could. He watched its trajectory, its descent, and the small splash that followed its landing in the ocean. He then turned and headed back into the bar.

Brandi was where he had left her. It looked to him as if she was on her third drink, it was too full to have still been the second. He walked up to her, leaned down, and said very quietly, "We have to go. Now."

She looked up at him.

"Come on Loyal. We were just starting to have fun."

"Fun's over," said Loyal. He glanced at the bartender and saw that the man was keeping a watchful eye on the two of them. Loyal forced a smile onto his face and attempted to keep his tone light, despite the seriousness of his words.

"We are in big danger," he said. "I'm leaving now. If you want to stay that is your choice, but it would be a very bad one."

Loyal straightened. He reached in his pocket, removed some money, and tossed some bills onto the table.

"Last chance, Brandi," he said quietly. He turned and began to walk out of the bar. When he glanced back he saw that she was up and following him.

As soon as they were in the buggy and driving down the smooth sand Brandi began peppering him with questions. Loyal remained silent, his face blank, his focus on the driving. He parked in front of the house and turned off the ignition. As he began to slide out of the buggy, Brandi placed a hand on his forearm. He turned to look at her.

"Aren't you going to answer my questions?" she said.

"Why should I?' asked Loyal. "You never answer any of mine."

He slid out of the buggy with out another word, unlocked the door, and entered the house. He cleared all the rooms, completely aware of how naked he felt without his gun. Once the rooms were cleared, he went out on the deck and gathered his clothes. He repacked his duffel and placed it in the buggy. When he passed by the master bedroom he saw that Brandi was quickly and quietly repacking her own suitcase. The black backpack, as always, worn backwards across her chest. She had changed out of the dress and into slacks and a T-shirt. Her hair was gathered into a pony tail. He supposed he owed her some explanation, but was so tired of dealing with her half truths and manipulations that he remained silent. Once they were packed up, he replaced the house key, and slid into the buggy. He turned to her then and said, "The people who had you on the boat know where we are and have connections to the cartel. I don't have time to explain everything." He paused, then added, "You are just going to have to trust me on this."

Despite feeling an overwhelming urge to travel South, Loyal headed North towards San Felipe. He gassed up the buggy and refilled the gas cans at the Pemex. He stopped at Mercado La Vaquita and stocked up on food, water, and ice for the cooler. Brandi's contribution to the cart was a bottle of rum, two six packs of Tecate, and a bag of Mexican candy. Loyal gave a mental eye roll, but said nothing about her additions. He simply paid and they left.

Loyal wanted to look at the maps and GPS, but felt exposed in the parking lot of the market. He drove South on the highway until he found some empty sand dunes and parked the buggy overlooking the ocean. He pulled out Maggie's maps and the GPS and studied them. In order to reach Mulege, they would have to travel South along the coast, then turn West and head inland a bit to connect with Highway 1. They would actually be crossing the Baja peninsula, reaching the Pacific Ocean, then re-crossing back to Mulege which was located on the Gulf side. It seemed to Loyal a very round-about way to get there, but Mexico had limited highways and this appeared to be the only way to go. Loyal estimated the entire trip would take 12-14 hours.

Maggie had highlighted a place called Coco's Corner. It was located just past a tiny town called Punta Final, where they would be making the turn West and leaving the coast behind. Loyal decided to make Coco's corner their first stop. It looked to be about three hours from their current location, and he was sure both he and Brandi would be ready for a rest stop at that point. He did not think they would be able to travel to Mulege in one day, so locating a safe stopping point was going to be important. Loyal did not share any of his decisions with Brandi. She sat quietly in the passenger seat. She had opened a beer and the bag of Mexican candy. She sipped and nibbled, saying nothing. For this, Loyal was grateful. Although their conversation had been rushed, it was Trinity's voice that he wanted echoing in his mind.

PATRICK O'KEEFE

Pat was walking down the hall to a meeting with Vice and Narcotics when his personal cell phone rang. He paused in the hallway and fished it out of his pants pocket. Caller ID identified the caller as Agent Glass. Pat accepted the call. She wasted no time with niceties.

"I've spoken to Loyal," she said. "He's in Mexico with Kendrick. I'm working on an extraction plan. He has some evidence that he gathered near Jodi Mahoney and Brandi Kendrick's houses in his apartment. He said to tell you to use whatever means necessary to get into the apartment and start analyzing the evidence."

"Got it," said Pat.

"I'd like to know the results of whatever you find," said Trinity.

"Absolutely," said Pat. "I'm on my way to a meeting. Can't skip it. I'll get on it immediately afterwards."

"I'll just remind you that time is of the essence here," said Trinity.

"I'm aware of that."

"I'll be reaching out to Captain Williams as per Loyal's request," said Trinity.

"Understood," said O'Keefe. He waited a moment for her response, but when he looked at his phone, it appeared that Agent Glass had already broken the connection.

The meeting with Vice and Narcotics lasted just over an hour. Stingray was proving to be a valuable resource in tracking the drug supply. Pat made sure to remind everyone that none of it was admissible in court. The detectives didn't care. It was information they were after, they would find admissible evidence to provide to the court. After the meeting, Pat went to reception and notified Fatima that he would be out of the office for a few hours. He crossed the parking lot rapidly, slid into his car, and headed towards Loyal's apartment.

Pat parked in front of Loyal's apartment and walked to the manager's apartment/office. The complex was small, comprised of just six units. The manager's apartment was across a small courtyard, his front door facing Loyal's. Pat mounted the stairs and knocked on the office door. It opened in less than a minute, revealing a man who appeared to be in his mid seventies. He was slender, his hair short and gray, and he wore a short sleeve button down shirt and blue jeans. His blue eyes peered at Pat through thick glasses.

"Can I help you?" he said.

Pat removed his badge from his pocket and held it up so the man could see it.

"I'm Detective O'Keefe with the Carlsbad Sheriff's Department. I was wondering if I could have a minute of your time,

Mister...?" He let the sentence trail off and the Manager did just as he was hoping saying,

"Wilson, Tom Wilson. What is this about Detective?"

"I need to get into the apartment of Loyal Truesdale," said Pat. "It is an urgent matter."

"Do you have a warrant?" asked Wilson.

"I have Loyal's express permission to enter and retrieve several evidence bags that relate to an ongoing murder investigation," said Pat. "I can certainly obtain a warrant, but time is of the essence Mr. Wilson."

Wilson was quiet for a moment then said, "I'll need to enter with you."

"I wouldn't have it any other way," said Pat. "According to Loyal the bags are on the counter."

Wilson excused himself for a moment, leaving the front door open and Pat at the door. He came back moments later holding a key ring in his hand.

"I've seen you at Mr. Truesdale's apartment before," he said to Pat. "That is the only reason I'm opening it for you."

"We were colleagues and remain friends," said Pat. "I do appreciate this Mr. Wilson."

Wilson was spry for his age and moved down his own steps and back up Loyal's easily. Pat kept the pace behind him. The older man knocked, waited a full minute, then inserted a key in Loyal's front door and opened it slowly.

"Mr. Truesdale?" he called. "It's Mr. Wilson, the manager." He waited another full minute, then turned to Pat. "Doesn't look like he's here," he said.

Pat gave Mr. Wilson a smile. "Nope," he said. He gestured towards the interior of the apartment. "May I?" he asked.

Wilson stepped inside the apartment. He stopped in the entry way. "Help yourself," he said. "I'll just wait here."

Pat stepped to the counter. Five ziplock bags sat squarely in the center. Pat could see at a glance that two contained cigarette butts, one contained a lime green disposable lighter, and two contained matchbooks from the Jolly Roger. Written on the front of each in Loyal's blocky printing were the time, date, and location where he had found them. Pat gathered all five into his hand and turned to find Mr. Wilson standing directly behind him.

"You find what you need?" he asked.

"I did," said Pat. "I'm all done here." He and Wilson exited the apartment. Pat watched while Wilson re-locked the door, then followed the older man down the stairs. At the bottom Pat reached his right hand out towards Wilson. They shook hands briefly.

"Thanks again Mr. Wilson," Pat said. "I'm hoping Loyal will be home soon."

69

TRINITY GLASS

Trinity had placed a call to Captain Williams immediately after disconnecting with O'Keefe only to be informed that the man was in a meeting and would have to return her call. Trinity left her contact information and, without giving the receptionist details, stressed her urgent need to speak with the Captain. She was assured the message would be passed on in a timely manner. The next person Loyal had requested that she contact was his daughter, Stella. Trinity accessed Stella's contact information and saw that she lived in Encinitas, which was about fifteen minutes from her current location. She had not yet met Stella, but knew that Loyal and his daughter were very close. Perhaps, she thought, this conversation would be better conducted in person.

Just under twenty minutes later Trinity stood in front of the locked gates surrounding Stella's condo complex. There was no buzzer system for Trinity to announce herself, so she pulled out her phone and called Stella's number. To her relief, Stella answered.

"Hello?"

"Stella," Trinity said, "my name is Trinity Glass. I'm actually at your gate. I'm a friend of your Dad's. He's fine, he just asked me to pass a message along to you."

"He's mentioned you," said Stella. "Give me just a moment and I'll be out to open the gate."

Trinity disconnected and put her phone away. Just over a minute later she saw Stella approaching the gate. Her resemblance to her father was uncanny. She was about Trinity's height, had long brown hair, and was slender with the exception of her pregnant belly. She wore a loose sleeveless dress and was barefoot. She opened the gate and held it for Trinity.

"Come on in," she said.

Trinity followed Stella past a pool on their right which overlooked the ocean. The condo was the second one on the left. Stella entered and Trinity followed. They walked down a short hall and into the living room. Stella indicated a couch and Trinity sat. Stella sat beside her, elbows on knees and leaning towards Trinity.

"Is he ok?" she asked.

"Yes," said Trinity. "He's gone to Mexico for a few days. His phone doesn't work where he is."

Stella held Trinity's blue eyes in her brown eyed gaze.

"What aren't you telling me?" she said. "My Dad wouldn't just leave like that."

Trinity thought about her own family. Her parents and brother were all gone, passed away many years ago. If she was in Stella's position she would want to know the truth. She mentally sorted through everything that she knew and made her decision.

"He's helping someone," she said. "A woman who is in a tight spot and needed to lay low for a few days."

"He's really in Mexico?" Stella asked.

Trinity nodded.

"I don't suppose you are going to give me any details?" Stella asked.

Trinity shook her head.

Stella leaned back. She looked at Trinity for a long moment.

"He likes you a lot, you know," she said.

"I like him a lot too," said Trinity.

"He hasn't told me much about you," said Stella.

"No," said Trinity, "I don't suppose he would have."

"Do you have time for a glass of iced tea?" Stella asked.

Trinity paused. She was on a tight schedule and still had lots to do before Thursday. Still, she thought, perhaps she could spare half an hour. She nodded.

"I'd love a glass," she said.

70

BRANDI KENDRICK

Brandi, not feeling the urge for conversation, simply sipped her beer and nibbled on her candy. She had been feeling so relaxed and safe in Bar Miramar. Then Loyal had stepped out and made a phone call. She had watched the whole thing. He had casually pulled his phone out and made the call. His body had stiffened. He had listened to whomever was on the other end of the phone call, spoken briefly, then disconnected. Brandi had been surprised when he had picked up a brick, destroyed his phone, then flung it out to sea. His expression when he re-entered the bar had been grim. His brief explanation, when he had finally given it to her, was truly frightening. Brandi was dealing with her anxiety as she always did, with booze and sweets.

The scenery outside the buggy was unchanging. The sparkling blue of the Sea of Cortez to their left, dry rocky earth to their right. The wind was constant and, despite their proximity to the water, quite hot and dry. Brandi ran her finger over her lips, they were chapped and starting to crack. She drained the beer, crumpled the can, and opened another. She felt Loyal's eyes on her and turned to see him looking at her. She held the beer out towards him. He shook his head and faced forward again.

After some time, Brandi wasn't sure how long they had been driving, the road veered towards the right and they left the Sea of Cortez behind them. Now the desert stretched out on both sides of the buggy. The land was rocky, barren, and unforgiving. The two lane road carved its way into the desert, they were the only vehicle traveling its length. The deceleration of the buggy brought Brandi out of what must have been sleep. She looked around in confusion, then remembered where they were and why. The bag of candy lay in her lap, the unfinished beer remained upright in her right hand. She smiled at the thought that even in sleep she had not spilled a drop. She saw the wooden sign just as Loyal veered off the highway onto a dirt road. **Coco's Corner. Free camping.** They traveled down the bumpy dirt road for a time. Brandi found it hard to believe that anyone lived around here, much less ran a campground. Everything was so desolate. Then, just like a mirage, Coco's Corner appeared before them. Ramshackle fencing surrounded what looked to Brandi like an outbuilding. Another sign, this one on the fencing read **Coco's Corner Info Touristica.** Loyal pulled the buggy through the open gate and parked near the building. He turned off the engine and turned to Brandi saying, "Looks like this is it."

Brandi unstrapped and slid out of the buggy. She stretched her arms skyward for a moment, then lowered them and turned in a slow circle. Besides the building they were parked in front of, there was a trailer in the distance, a small boat with the words *Coco Cold Beer* painted on the side, a white Dodge truck with a *Coco's Corner* decal on the driver's door and a pair of red panties flying from the antenna like a flag, and a strange assortment of toilets arranged in a circle. Brandi supposed they were intended to be some sort of strange art installation. Movement to her right caught her eye and she turned to see a man in a wheel-chair approaching them. He was very tan, with white close cropped hair and a neatly trimmed white mustache and beard. Her first impression of the tan, shirtless man was "round". His smiling eyes were round, his face was round, and his pudgy belly was round. His legs were both amputated at the knee. He rolled up with a wide smile on his face and said, "Hola. Welcome."

It didn't take Brandi long to warm up to Coco. He had taken them into the building and gotten them each a beer. A large wooden circular table dominated the room. He had sat with them as they sipped their beers and told them the history of Coco's Corner. He had lived there, alone, for the past 35 years. Born in Tijuana, he had grown up in Ensenada, then moved out to this barren, windswept spot. He had become something of a celebrity over the years. People came from all over the world to meet him. He had shown them the signature books he kept, then had them sign as well. Now, the beer empty, Brandi stood and walked around the room. Postcards, stickers, and photographs filled the walls. The oldest pictures showed Coco with one of his own legs and what looked to Brandi to be a prosthetic. Gradually the pictures showed him with no legs, both having been amputated at the knee. He had explained that an accident and diabetes had robbed him of both legs, but that he could still walk. He wore special leather coverings to protect the stumps. Brandi tilted her head towards the ceiling. Bras and panties, blowing in the breeze, covered the entire space. They had been donated by visitors over the last three decades. Brandi supposed she should leave something as well. Loyal came and stood beside her.

"I think we should stay here tonight," he said. "We can leave tomorrow for Mulege."

71

PATRICK O'KEEFE

Pat called the Sheriff's Station as he drove back towards it. He asked to be connected with Captain Williams and was informed that the man was in a meeting, but that it should be wrapping up fairly soon. He continued to the station, parked in the back, and entered through the back door. He went straight up to William's office. The door was open and the Captain was just settling into his chair behind his desk, his office phone in his hand. Pat gave a quick knock and Williams raised his eyes.

"O'Keefe," he said, covering the mouthpiece briefly, and waving Pat in. "I'm just returning Agent Glass' call."

Pat entered and sat in one of the two chairs that faced the Captain's desk. Williams spoke into the receiver.

"Agent Glass," he said. "Captain Williams returning your call."

Pat watched as the Captain listened to what Glass said.

"Yes, he's here," said the Captain, his eyes resting briefly on Pat.

"Ok. See you then," said the Captain and he hung up the phone. He turned back to Pat.

"She'll be here in fifteen minutes," he said. "She asked me to have you wait."

Pat waited, and true to her word, Agent Glass showed up within fifteen minutes. She sat down in the other available chair and started talking. She told the Captain about Loyal's call, the hit list, the connection between the Chinese and the cartel, and her plan to get both Loyal and Brandi out of Mexico.

"You can take him off your suspicious persons list, Captain," she said. "We are dealing with much bigger fish than Loyal Truesdale." She turned to O'Keefe. "Did you get into the apartment?"

"Yes," said O'Keefe. He held out the five ziplock bags.

"What are these?" Williams asked.

Pat lay the bags on the Captain's desk oriented towards his supervisor. Williams leaned forward and examined them. Trinity did the same from her side of the desk.

"Let me take them to Homeland Security, Captain," she said. "I'll be able to get results faster."

The Captain sighed. "Fill out the forms O'Keefe. Keep the chain of custody in order."

Pat stood. "Absolutely Captain." He picked up the bags and turned to Trinity. "Let's make this official Agent Glass."

72

LOYAL TRUESDALE

Loyal was impressed by Coco. The man lived in the middle of nowhere, had lost the first leg in a taxi cab accident in Tijuana, and the second leg to diabetes, and yet, somehow, had managed to keep a positive outlook and sunny disposition. He had actually become a celebrity of sorts. People came from all over the world to meet him. He kept books full of well wishes and signatures to which Loyal and Brandi happily added their names. Coco loved to share stories of the people he had met over the years. He sat with Loyal and Brandi, sipping beer and pouring through the books, sharing stories of travelers who had passed through his little camp. The time passed quickly, the sun arching through the sky to the West, and gradually sinking below the mountains. On this particular day Loyal and Brandi were the only campers. They shared a dinner with Coco, sitting at the round table until the moon and stars were bright in the sky.

Loyal's first yawn came when Coco was in the middle of a story

about a woman from Europe who had been riding her motorcycle around the world for over six years. She had circumnavi-
gated the globe once and was on her second go-round when
she stopped in Coco's corner. He paged through the latest book
until he found her signature, then turned the book so Loyal
and Brandi could see. Loyal struggled unsuccessfully to contain
the second yawn that came close on the heels of the first.

"I'm sorry," he said. He picked up his beer and drained the
last drops. "I think this is going to do it for me."

"You go ahead, Loyal," said Brandi. "I'm going to stay up for
a bit more." She turned to Coco. "That is, if you are up for one
more?" she added.

Coco smiled and nodded.

Loyal stood. "I'll see you guys in the morning. Thanks again
Coco."

Loyal used the restroom and brushed his teeth with water from
a water bottle. He unrolled his sleeping bag in an area with soft
sand, removed his shoes, puffed up a sweatshirt for a pillow,
and crawled in. He lay on his back and looked up at the skies
above him. The moon was just a hair past full, slightly flat on
the bottom curve, but providing plenty of ambient light. The
stars were bright as well, Loyal could not remember the last
time he had seen so many this clearly. Southern California was
full of light pollution. Here in the desert of Baja, with the
exception of Coco's single light, there were no other lights to
compete with the stars. Loyal lay on his back and looked up at
the sky. He wondered what Trinity was doing at this moment.
He found himself hoping, in a strangely unfamiliar way, that
she was looking at this sky as well. Imagining that she was, he
felt a connection to her.

. . .

Loyal lay this way for a long time. He drifted in and out of sleep. Although he had chosen a spot with soft sand, the ground still felt hard beneath him. Even in semi-sleep he heard the wind rattling the tin cans that Coco had strung up along his fences, coyotes howling in the far distance, the gentle hum of the generator, and Coco and Brandi's quiet conversation. They had switched to Spanish and spoke in low tones. Brandi's giggles punctuated the conversation now and then. Loyal drifted and dreamed. In his dream he was young, maybe nine or ten years old. He was laying in bed in his family home in Fallbrook. He could hear his Mom and Dad in the kitchen. They were talking quietly. He couldn't hear the content of their conversation, just the rhythm of it. His Dad's voice, deep and low, alternating with his Mom's higher voice. Her quiet laughter sprinkled into their exchange. Loyal felt so safe in that moment, yet at the same time his dream self seemed to realize that his Dad would soon be gone; vanished from their lives with no explanation. Loyal slid out of bed and walked to the kitchen. His parents stood, arms around each other, looking out the window above the sink. His Mom leaned her head on his Dad's shoulder. His Dad tightened his arm around her waist. They both seemed to sense Loyal approaching and turned at the same moment to face him. As they turned it seemed as if Loyal's vision became hazy. His parents faces began to soften and blur, their features liquefying as he watched. Loyal attempted to walk toward them but his feet refused to move. He looked down and saw that he, too, was melting. His feet dissolved into the kitchen floor. He felt his torso flowing downward and watched helplessly as his parents dissolved into nothing.

. . .

Loyal woke with a start and for a moment was unsure about where he was. The sleeping bag was twisted around his body, his arms trapped tightly against his torso. He struggled for a moment, then managed to free his arms. He lay on his back for a minute as he reoriented himself. He focused on the moon, now far to the West, beginning its nightly descent. He glanced to his left and saw that Brandi had gone to bed. She lay on her side in her sleeping bag, her back toward him. He listened to the sounds of the night. The wind and the tin cans tinkled like a poor man's wind chime. The generator no longer hummed. Coco's lights were off. Loyal lay still and thought about the dream. His parents voices had sounded so real, so alive. He had come to terms with his Mom's death. They had had many years together. He hated to admit it to himself, but on rare occasions, Loyal missed his Dad. He shook his head and dismissed these thoughts. He had more important things to consider at the moment. The trip to Mulege would take about nine hours. After studying the maps and talking to Coco, Loyal had decided that they would camp outside the town's perimeter and drive to the airport in the morning. Trinity had not specified a time and he wanted to make sure they were there and ready when she arrived. He had realized earlier that he would have to leave the buggy in Mulege. He wasn't sure how it would happen, but he made a silent promise that he would be back for it someday.

73

TRINITY GLASS

T rinity lay in her bed and stared at the ceiling. She needed the sleep, but was finding it impossible to drop off. She mentally reviewed her day. After getting Loyal's evidence bags from Pat she had returned to Homeland Security in San Diego and dropped them off to Lee Park. She had returned to her condo, gone for a run along the beach, and stopped at Pizza Port for dinner and a beer. As she was driving back to the condo she had received a call from Doug Caldwell. Laying in bed now, she replayed their conversation in her mind. Caldwell, as usual, had gotten right to the point.

"Glass," he had said, "we've located two of the people on the list, number nine and number ten. Both are in Northern California. Number nine lives Southeast of Tahoe, number ten is a married couple on the coast. I'll email you the details. You need to get up there. I've got a King Air 350 set for you out of McClellan Palomar tomorrow morning. 7:00 am."

"You have an agent to go with me?" Trinity had asked.

"Rodger Stuart," said Doug.

"He can fly," said Trinity. "But I'd like another agent."

"He is a former agent," said Caldwell, "and a good one. You can trust him. He started flying for us after his retirement from the field." Caldwell had paused for a moment and when Trinity did not respond had simply said, "Keep me informed Glass." Then he had disconnected.

Trinity rolled onto her side and thought about the fact that Rodger was a former agent. She had traveled with him on so many occasions and he had never mentioned it. Trinity rolled this information around in her mind for a bit. She had not yet requested a plane to fly her to Mulege, or an agent to accompany her. She was trying to come up with a scenario that would convince Caldwell to approve such a mission. Her new information about Rodger could come in very handy in that regard. As she contemplated different strategies regarding Rodger Stuart, Trinity finally drifted into sleep.

Trinity was deep into a dreamless sleep when her alarm woke her at 5:00. Her body gave an involuntary jerk at the sound. She rolled to her side and silenced the alarm, then lay back on her back, eyes towards the ceiling. She figured she had gotten just over four hours of sleep. Not much, but it would have to do. Trinity gave herself a long stretch, then sat up in bed. The condo was dark and quiet, the sun still hiding in the East. She swung her legs off the edge of the bed and stood. She raised her arms towards the ceiling and stretched again, then headed to the bathroom for a shower. Once she was showered, dried, and dressed for the day she made her way to the kitchen for coffee and breakfast. Trinity did not know what the day was going to bring. Starting off with a full stomach was a priority.

By 6:50 Trinity had parked in the Western Flight parking lot and was inside the building with Rodger. They walked together to the hangar where the Beechcraft 350i was fueled up and waiting for them. Rodger led Trinity up the four steps and into the plane. He settled himself in the pilot's seat and gestured towards the co-pilot's seat with a smile and a question in his eyes. Trinity nodded, dropped her briefcase on a passenger seat, and settled herself in the co-pilot's seat. A tug was hooked up to the King Air and they were towed out to the ramp. Trinity could count on one hand the number of times she was able to sit in the co-pilot's seat during take off. This was the first time she had been given the opportunity at McClellan Palomar where planes took off over the ocean. Adrenaline flooded her system as Rodger accelerated down the runway and eased the plane into the air. The land disappeared below them and, as Rodger banked the plane into an Alpha North departure, the ocean appeared beneath them. The morning sun sparkled and danced on the blue expanse. Rodger brought the plane around and they were over land again. He turned his face towards Trinity. "Once we are at altitude you can move around the cabin," he said.

Trinity stayed in the co-pilot's seat for nearly half an hour. She and Rodger did not converse. The quiet was comfortable, each of them lost in their own thoughts. Eventually Trinity unstrapped and moved back into the passenger area of the plane. She settled into one of the plush leather seats and removed her computer from her briefcase. Earlier, while she was eating breakfast, she had opened her email and downloaded a file Doug Caldwell had sent to her. She sat back in the chair, computer on her lap, and opened it now. The file contained the names and brief bios on the people she was heading to see.

Regina Krause, their first interviewee, was number ten on the list. Caldwell had included a picture from her passport. Regina was a thirty-eight year old African American woman. The picture, which Caldwell indicated was eight years old, revealed little. Her hair was short, cropped close to her skull, her eyes wide, her mouth unsmiling. Her bio was short. She had been born and raised in Monroeville, Alabama. In 2005, at the age of eighteen, she had joined the army. When her four year commitment ended she opted not to re-enlist. At this point Regina dropped off the map. She had used her passport in 2011 on what appeared to be an extended trip to Thailand. She had re-entered the United States in 2016 and purchased land in California. Caldwell had noted that she had paid cash for the property, a twelve acre parcel just off Highway 89 Southeast of Lake Tahoe. Trinity and Roger would be landing at South Lake Tahoe Airport. Caldwell's secretary had arranged a rental car for them. The drive to Regina Krause's property would take just under an hour.

Joel and Corinne Amos were the second interviewees. They owned 18 acres in Hales Grove, an unincorporated community in Mendocino, California, about an hour South of Eureka and just West of the 101. Both had been born and raised in Cannon

Beach, Oregon. They had married when Joel was 20 and Corinne was 18. Noting the date of their wedding, Trinity calculated that they had just celebrated their forty-first wedding anniversary a month ago. The young couple had relocated after marrying, moving nearly 300 miles South of their hometown. Joel had worked at Indian Creek Fish Hatchery in Gold Beach, Oregon from 1977 to 2009. The couple had two children, boys, born in 1978 and 1980. Tax records showed that the family lived modestly on Joel's single income. They had purchased a three bedroom home on Ocean Way in 1979 for $85,000. In 2009, after Joel's retirement, they sold the home for nearly $400,000. From passport activity it appeared that they traveled for the better part of a year, spending 4 months in Thailand. In 2012 they purchased the property in Hales Grove, paying cash.

Trinity opened the fold away table next to her seat and set the computer on it. She stood and stretched, then opened the slide out fridge and removed a water bottle. She sat back in the chair, took a long sip, gazed out the window, and thought about the similarities in Regina Krause and Joel and Corinne Amos' stories. The most glaring were extended stays in Thailand and purchasing expensive properties with cash. Joel and Corinne Amos had paid just shy of one million dollars for their land. Regina Krause had paid nearly $600,000. A thought occurred to Trinity. She sat up, turned back to her computer, and opened the file on Brandi Kendrick. She skimmed the information until she found what she was looking for. Brandi's sister, Jodi, had also spent time in Thailand and had paid cash for her home on Morgan Road. Jodi had also been Brandi's only source of income for years. Trinity reached for the SAT phone and called Caldwell. The call went to voicemail.

"Doug," Trinity said, "I need to know if you have found anything else out about the people on the list, specifically if they spent time in Thailand and what their source of income is." She paused, then added, "I'm calling from the SAT phone in the King Air. We should be landing in Tahoe soon. I'll have my cell when I'm on the ground."

74

BRANDI KENDRICK

The tinkling of the tin cans brought Brandi out of sleep just as the sun was coming up in the East. She lay, unmoving, in her sleeping bag. The desert breeze, warm and dry, caressed her face. She inhaled deeply through her nose. The aroma of the desert was becoming familiar. She found that she was enjoying the smells, so different from the coastal scents that she was used to. Brandi rolled over to look at Loyal. He was on his side in his sleeping bag, his face turned towards her. He looked peaceful. As she gazed at his sleeping form, Brandi realized that she was getting used to Loyal as well. What kind of man risked so much for someone they hardly knew? Three days ago Brandi wouldn't have paid much attention to a guy like Loyal. This morning, however, watching him sleep she found herself thinking about him a little differently. After a lifetime of counting on no one but Jodi and herself, Brandi had a hard time trusting anyone. It was an unfamiliar feeling, and took her a moment to recognize, but as she lay there, she realized that she trusted Loyal.

. . .

After a while, Brandi slid out of the sleeping bag. She had slept in yesterday's clothes and didn't really see the point in changing. The majority of their day would be spent in the buggy anyways. She slipped her shoes on her feet and walked towards Coco's house. The door was closed. It appeared he was still asleep as well. Brandi returned to the buggy, pulled a water out of the cooler, then walked back to sit on Coco's covered patio. She thought about their conversation last night, after Loyal had gone to sleep. She had told him about the drug bust in San Felipe and her exchange with General Javier Salvador Zepeda. Coco had warned her about the man.

"He's hooked up with one of the cartels." He had said. "The Jalisco. They are the most aggressive and violent of all. He protects them and works to defeat their main competitor, the Sinaloa." Coco had paused for a moment, then said, "It is very lucky for you that he didn't detain you. He has a reputation with beautiful women, and it is not a good one."

Brandi sipped the water and watched the sun move higher in the sky. The desert brightened as the sun rose, the sand reflected its rays, the mountains in the distance became clearer and more distinct. Brandi sat quietly, not really thinking about anything. "Just coasting" is what Jodi would have called it. She let an image of Jodi form in her mind. She imagined her as she was at 18 years old, when they had first moved to San Marcos. Their apartment had been a dump, they had eaten macaroni and cheese and ramen for months, but they had been happy despite the struggles. Finally free from their Mom and her endless stream of boyfriends, they had been content. The jobs at Vons paid the bills and they were not dependent on anyone except themselves. They had finally felt free.

. . .

Her thoughts moved to her father, Al Kendrick. The image that
formed in her mind was of the last time she had seen her
father. He had flown his Sky Master down to Carlsbad to have
some work done at Riley Rocket. He had stayed with her for a
few days. She had known something was on his mind, but he
had refused to talk about it until the last day. She was driving
him to McClellan Palomar when he had said, "I'm done playing
the game Brandi. I should have quit while I was ahead. With
any luck I'll avoid prison time and manage to stay alive."

Brandi had suspected that her father sometimes skirted the
edges of the law, but these words had confirmed it. She had
dropped him at Riley, stepped out of the car and hugged him
tightly, then driven towards the exit. At the stop sign she had
turned and seen him standing there, watching her. His right
hand shaded his eyes, his brown hair was tousled by the wind.
It was the last image she had of her father. He had died
descending to the airport in Seattle. She thought again about
how she had told Loyal she didn't really know her father. The
lie had flowed so easily from her lips.

She was considering this when she heard the door to Coco's
house open behind her. She turned and saw him stepping out.
She was amazed at his agility, he walked on the stumps so
easily. He smiled and waved a good morning to her. She smiled
and waved back at him. At the same moment Loyal rounded
the corner and entered the patio area. His light brown hair was
disheveled. He was rubbing his face with his hands. He looked
very tired. Brandi stood and walked over to him. She placed her
hand lightly on his forearm.

"Morning," she said, looking up at him. "What's the plan?"

He looked down at her hand on his arm, then in her eyes. "Breakfast, then hit the road," he said.

Coco walked up to them. "You leaving so soon?" he said.

Loyal nodded. "Thanks for letting us stay, Coco," he said.

"Yes, Coco, thanks." Brandi added. "It was great to meet you."

Coco looked at Brandi for a long moment. "You are welcome," he said, then added in Spanish, "Remember what I told you about the General, Senorita."

Brandi leaned down and gave him a hug. "I will," she said.

75

TRINITY GLASS

R odger's landing in Tahoe was smooth, as usual. Trinity barely felt the wheels touch down, just felt the familiar tug in her stomach as the plane decelerated. She waited in the passenger seat until Rodger had taxied and parked. They had not closed the door between the cockpit and the cabin. When she saw him unstrapping, she did the same. He entered the cabin, actuated the handle that released the stairs, and allowed them to slide into place. Trinity followed him down the stairs and waited as he closed the door to the plane. There was a white Range Rover Sport waiting for them at Global Air. When the attendant held out the keys, Roger raised his sunglasses and looked at Trinity with a question in his eyes. She reached for the keys.

"You fly, I'll drive," she said.

Rodger lowered his sunglasses and walked around to the passenger side.

"Works for me," he said.

. . .

The drive to Regina Krause's property took 49 minutes. On the way Trinity told Rodger the little that she had learned about the woman. She also received a callback from Caldwell. Trinity had explained the connections she had found regarding Thailand and unexplained income. He had promised to get the team working on that angle right away. The last twenty minutes of the drive Trinity remained silent. The road they were traveling on was extremely steep and windy. Concentration on the road was essential. It was a two lane and lined with trees. There was no room for error.

At the base of a steep straightaway the road and surrounding land flattened out into a large grass filled meadow. Trinity almost missed the small wooden sign with Regina Krause's address on it. She braked hard and turned onto the narrow dirt track that led straight into the meadow. About 50 yards ahead of them she could see chain link fencing. As they drew nearer she saw the razor wire on top of the fence. Cameras were mounted on the fence as well in what looked like fifteen foot intervals.

"Not your average security system," said Rodger.

"A little over the top," said Trinity.

She pulled up next to a wooden post with a small keypad attached and looked for any type of intercom system. Seeing nothing, she turned to Rodger.

"Any thoughts?" she asked.

"Someone who is this security conscious probably has motion detectors," he said. "Let's give it a few minutes. See if she comes to us."

Trinity nodded. She checked her phone.

"No signal here," she said. She unconsciously ran her hand over the Sig Sauer on her hip, finding comfort in its presence. Roger watched this action, but said nothing. Nearly five minutes passed. The tall grasses in the meadow swayed peacefully in the breeze. In the far distance Trinity could see a large stand of trees. She had brought her gyro-stabilized binoculars with her, but had left them on the plane. She wished now that she had brought them in the car.

Rodger sat up a little straighter and pointed towards the stand of trees.

"Looks like we got her attention," he said. Trinity followed his finger and saw the small dust cloud. Some type of vehicle, she couldn't yet make out what it was, was coming towards them. She sat up straighter and adjusted her jacket.

"How do you want to play this?" Roger asked.

"Let me do the talking," she said.

He nodded. Trinity took a deep breath, let it out slowly, and opened the car door.

76

LOYAL TRUESDALE

Loyal thought it odd that Brandi placed her hand on his forearm like she did. It felt inappropriate and oddly intimate. He made no comment, simply suggested food and then departure. His curiosity was raised when Brandi and Coco slipped into Spanish briefly. He made no comment at the time, but asked her about it when they were loading up the buggy.

"He told me to take good care of you," said Brandi. "I told him I would."

Loyal looked across the buggy at her for a long moment. She held his gaze. Finally he looked down at the sleeping bag he was stashing in the back seat. While it was true that he did not speak the language, many Spanish words were similar to English. He was quite sure he had heard Coco say *General*. He was quite sure that it was not himself that Coco was referring to.

Loyal and Brandi were ready to go by 10:00 am. A group of ten

motorcycle riders arrived to Coco's Corner just as they were
sliding into the buggy. They rumbled up to the fence and
parked just to the left of the buggy. The one nearest Loyal slid
off the bike and removed his helmet. He looked to be in his
early forties. His cheeks were dusty in the spots that the helmet
did not cover. He hung the helmet on his handlebars and
turned towards Loyal.

"Where you guys heading?" he asked.

"Mulege," said Loyal. "Where are you guys coming from?"

"San Felipe," said the rider. "We're spending the night here.
Came early to drink beer with Coco."

Loyal smiled. "We did that last night," he said. "We came
through San Felipe too. Drove down on the dry lake beds."

"Bet that was fun in the buggy," said the rider. "I've done it
on a bike."

"Yeah," said Loyal, "I grew up on bikes. This is my first
buggy. Just did my first buggy run last weekend." He waved his
arm towards Brandi who was surprisingly quiet. "Met her
there."

The rider raised a hand in greeting to Brandi. "Buggies have
a lot of history down here," he said to Loyal.

"Yep," said Loyal. "I'm lucky to know Bruce and Winnie
Meyers. They actually helped me find this." He patted the side
of the buggy.

"That's cool man," said the rider. He raised his hand again.
"Stay safe guys."

Loyal had studied the map earlier while they ate their breakfast
of turkey sandwiches. The route to Mulege was both straight-
forward and circuitous. They would travel Southwest for about
thirteen miles on Highway 5, then transition onto Highway 1,

which would take them South across the entire peninsula. At Guerrero Negro, which nearly kissed the Pacific, they would transition from Baja Norte to Baja Sur. At that point Highway 1 would turn Southeast and cross the peninsula once again. Loyal figured they would take a rest stop in Guerrero Negro, then stop for the night in a town called San Ignacio. The trip from San Ignacio to Mulege the next morning would take just under two hours. Loyal planned on getting a very early start.

The drive across the peninsula to Guerrero Negro was monotonous and very hot. Desert stretched out in all directions around them. Tall cactus, Loyal couldn't remember their proper name, stretched spiny arms toward the light blue sky. Wisps of clouds floated overhead, occasionally providing a brief respite from the scorching sun when they floated in front of it. Neither Loyal nor Brandi attempted conversation. They stopped only once so that Loyal could add fuel from one of the gas cans to the buggy's tank. Loyal was happy to admit to himself that he felt a giant ripple of relief when they passed beneath a sign which read *Bienvenidos a Baja California Sur*. The air cooled slightly as they neared Guerrero Negro. When they entered the town, Loyal pulled abruptly to the right on the main drag. He stopped in front of a food truck that was painted like a whale. An awning covered an open space on one side of the truck. The words **Fish Taco** were painted just to the right of the opening. He turned towards Brandi. "Maggie had a note on one of her maps that these are some of the best fish tacos in Baja," he said. "It is called Tacos El Muelle. Sound good?" Brandi smiled and nodded. "Hell yeah," she said.

. . .

Loyal and Brandi left Tacos El Muelle with full stomachs. The tacos had been delicious and the owner, Tony, had remembered Maggie and Ed. He had been sad to hear of Ed's passing, but asked them to please give Maggie his best. On the way out of town Loyal pulled into Auto Servicio Guerrero Negro. An attendant came out to pump the gas for him, which was a pleasant surprise. The young man spoke English quite well, which Loyal also appreciated. He wasn't real comfortable with Brandi as a translator.

The attendant topped off the buggy's tank and refilled the gas can. He took Loyal's money then leaned against the pump, arms crossed in front of him, and seemed to study Loyal, Brandi, and the buggy.

"Don't see many tourists here this time of year," he said. "Most come to see the whales in the Spring. Where are you heading?"

"North," said Loyal. "Back to the U.S."

He slid back into the buggy and exited the station. Looking in the rearview mirror he saw that the attendant was back in the building. He couldn't be sure, due to distance and glare, but it looked as if the kid was holding a phone.

77

TRINITY GLASS

Trinity stood ramrod straight and watched the approaching vehicle. As it neared she saw that it was a side by side. Through the dust it was stirring up she could make out oversized tires and an enhanced suspension. The engine was loud and, Trinity assumed, powerful. The side-by-side pulled up and stopped about ten feet from the fence. As the dust settled Trinity could see that it was a Polaris. From experience she knew these vehicles were powerful, agile, and expensive. Regina Krause turned off the vehicle and slid off. She looked enough like the passport photo that Trinity thought she would have recognized her. She was a small woman, 5'3" at the most, lean and strong. She was wearing a white tank top, camouflage cargo pants, and heavy boots. The muscles in her arms were well defined. She looked like she spent time lifting weights. She removed her sunglasses, revealing her wide set brown eyes. She was not smiling.

Trinity held her badge up and said, "Regina Krause? I'm Agent

Glass, Office of Strategic Investigations." She indicated Rodger with a wave of her hand. "This is Agent Stuart."

Regina stepped a bit closer and inspected the badge through the chain link fence. She looked up at Trinity, her brown eyes meeting Trinity's blue eyes with a palpable intensity. Much to her dismay, Trinity blinked first.

"What is this about?" asked Regina.

"Can we come in?" asked Trinity. "We have some questions for you."

"Right here is fine," said Regina.

Trinity sighed. "Ok Ms. Krause," she said, "we will play it your way for now. I'm in possession of a list of seventeen names. One of them is yours. I'm looking for a connection between the people."

"What kind of list?" Regina asked.

"Well," said Trinity, "considering seven of the seventeen are dead, I'd probably call it a hit list."

Regina said nothing for a long moment, her face remained expressionless.

"You gonna read me the names?" she asked.

Trinity pulled out her phone and brought up a picture of the list. She read each name out loud. She spoke slowly and clearly, the names dropping into the silence of the meadow like rocks dropping into a pond. She studied Regina's face for any ripples the rocks might create. A glance at Rodger indicated he too was watching the woman's reactions carefully.

No one spoke for a full minute after Trinity finished reading the list. Once again, her eyes were locked onto Regina's. This time the brown eyes blinked first. Regina shook her head.

"I don't know any of them," she said.

"Should I read it again just to be sure?" asked Trinity.

"I've given you all the time I'm going to," said Regina.

"I can call local law enforcement to come detain you," said Trinity. "We can finish talking at the police station."

"You do that," said Regina.

She replaced her sunglasses and strode back to the Polaris. The engine roared to life and Regina Krause disappeared in a cloud of dust. Trinity and Roger slid back into the Range Rover and began the drive back to Tahoe.

"You catch the micro expression?" Rodger said about ten minutes into the drive.

"Yes," said Trinity, "a flick of the eyes. Barely there, but I caught it." She paused a moment, then added, "She knew Jodi Mahoney."

Trinity and Rodger arrived back at South Lake Tahoe, boarded the King Air, and were in the sky on their way to Eureka by 11:45. The flight time from Tahoe to Eureka was just over an hour and a half. The drive from the airport to the Amos' house in Hales Grove would take just under two hours. If everything went smoothly they should arrive in Hales Grove by 3:30. Trinity sat in the cabin during this flight. She re-read the small amount of information she had on the Amos family. It wasn't much. She hoped they would be more open to talking to her. Regina Krause's reluctance to talk hadn't really been a surprise. Trinity was used to people not wanting to talk to her in an official capacity. Once she was done reviewing the information that she had, Trinity picked up the SAT phone and called Caldwell. She relayed the details of the interview with Regina Krause, including both her and Rodger's belief that Regina knew Jodi. Caldwell promised to look at that angle. Trinity ended the call and leaned back in her seat. She closed her eyes and brought up the image of Regina Krause. She replayed that tiny flick she had seen at the mention of Jodi Mahoney. Trinity was well trained in the art of reading facial expressions. She was fairly confidant that she had seen more than recognition in those brown eyes at the mention of Jodi Mahoney's name. The second thing she had seen was fear.

78

BRANDI KENDRICK

B randi dangled her right arm out of the buggy, letting the hot breeze blow against her hand and through her fingers. The highway was a two lane road that cut through some of the most barren land she had ever seen. The desert stretched out in all directions around them. There were small hills, more like mesas she supposed, rising out of the land in the far distance. Low growing brush covered much of the land. Brandi found herself thinking about people from long ago who had likely traversed this desert on foot or in a wagon. Although she was tiring of being in the buggy for such long sections of time, she found herself grateful for the nimble little vehicle.

When they left Guerrero Negro Loyal had told her that the drive to San Ignacio, where he had decided they would spend the night, would take approximately two hours. She had no idea how long they had been driving thus far, but was hoping the day's trip was nearing the end. She turned in her seat and reached her left hand into the cooler. She had been drinking beer and eating candy for most of the drive. She hadn't offered any to Loyal, and he had not asked for anything. Her hand finally located what she was looking for in the cooler, the last beer. She pulled it out and let the cooler lid drop back in place, then turned to face forward again. She cracked the beer and took a long sip, then glanced down at the nearly empty bag of candy in her lap. Hopefully this town had a good bar and a market. It was time for her to stock up on necessities.

Brandi finished the beer, crumpled the can, and tossed it out of the buggy. The first time she had done that, just outside of Guerrero Negro, Loyal had been shocked.

"Hey," he had said above the wind and engine noise. "What was that? I've seen the *no tire basura* signs all day long." She had just given him a long look. "I know basura means trash, Brandi," he had said. "I'm assuming the signs are telling people not to throw it out of their cars."

Brandi had looked at him for a moment, then said, "No one keeps their empties, Loyal." He had just shaken his head and turned back towards the front. Now, with her beer all gone and her bladder full, she peered ahead of them searching for any sign of a town in the distance.

When she first saw the smudge of green far off in front of them, Brandi thought it must be a mirage. She removed her sunglasses, rubbed her eyes, then replaced the glasses. It was still there. She placed her hand on Loyal's forearm. When he turned to her she pointed and said, "Do you see that? The green in the distance?"

Loyal followed her finger's trajectory. He squinted, then rubbed his eyes and looked again. He nodded and smiled.

"Maggie's notes referred to San Ignacio as the "oasis of the desert", he said. "I guess we know why."

The closer they got, the larger and more distinct the green blob became. Brandi could see now that the green was palm trees, hundreds of them. She supposed the town was in the center of the palm forest. Loyal turned off the highway onto the narrow two lane that led into town. The road curved through stands of palm trees. The scorching wind that had buffeted them through the desert was nonexistent here. The shade provided by the trees lowered the temperature noticeably. They passed a body of water on the way into the town's center. Brandi wasn't sure if it was a lake or a river. She didn't care, she was just so happy to see water. She glanced at Loyal. He was smiling, apparently as happy as she was to have reached their destination. They passed a sign that read **El Padrino Campground and Rooms. Hot Showers.** Loyal pulled the buggy to the side of the road. He glanced around, then put the buggy in reverse and backed up to the road that branched off at the sign. He turned and drove into the campground. He looked at Brandi and said, "I don't know about you, but a shower sounds pretty damn good to me."

Loyal secured them a yurt, which was a tent-like structure, that had two cots, a chair, a small desk, and a wall mirror. The showers were about a football field away. Brandi watched as Loyal checked out the area. He deemed it safe enough and sent Brandi to the showers first. The water was like heaven. She stood under the stream of water, just letting it pour over her body like a waterfall. She dried off, re-dressed, and returned to the yurt. While Loyal headed to the showers for his turn, she changed into her dress and sandals, brushed her wet hair out, and applied a bit of makeup. The town was within walking distance and she was ready to check it out with Loyal.

When Loyal returned he was wearing a wrinkly Tommy Bahama and blue jeans. Brandi was amused by Loyal's attempts to smooth the shirt. He kept running his hands down the front, with no success. Eventually he gave a sigh and stopped the attempts.

"It's ok," said Brandi, "you look nice."

He looked at her. "You too," he said. "Let's move everything from the buggy into the yurt. We can lock it up and go to town."

Brandi nodded her agreement and soon the buggy was empty. She kept the black backpack on, and noticed that Loyal put the GPS in his front shirt pocket.

"I doubt we are going to need that," Brandi said.

"Maggie asked me to keep it safe," said Loyal.

They locked the yurt and began the walk to town. The streets were narrow and very old. Brandi suspected they were the original streets that were built for donkeys and carts long ago. There was very little traffic in San Ignacio. Two cars passed them in the ten minutes it took to walk to the town square. A few people, likely tourists, milled around the center of town. The square was beautiful, full of huge trees and stone benches. Sculptures, in the shape of crosses, were placed strategically around the square. Small lanterns, unlit, hung from one arm of each cross. Brandi imagined it was lovely in the evening when the lanterns were shining.

"So, what's the deal with you and Maggie?" she asked Loyal.

He stopped his forward motion and looked at her.

"I told you," he said, "we are friends."

Brandi paused a moment, then asked the real question that was on her mind.

"Is there someone in your life?"

Loyal looked at her for a long moment, then said, "Yes, Brandi. There is."

79

TRINITY GLASS

Trinity sat in the co pilot's seat for the landing at Arcata-Eureka Airport. The scenery as they approached was stunning. The lush green landscape of Northern California, so different from parched Southern California, stretched out below them in all directions. The sparkling blue Pacific Ocean lay directly in front of them. As they approached Trinity saw that the airport was small, with just one runway, a long gray stripe punctuating the green. Rodger executed yet another perfectly smooth landing, the arrows and the number 32 that were painted on the runway sliding neatly beneath the plane as they touched down. Rodger taxied to transient parking. The small airport had no jet center, but tie downs were available for a nominal fee. Trinity removed both her briefcase and her gyro-stabilized binoculars from the cabin and placed them in the rental car. Rodger handled the tie down fee and arranged to have the King Air re-fueled while they were in Hales Grove, then joined her in the black Camry. As per their previous discussion, Trinity was in the driver's seat.

· · ·

The drive to Hales Grove took them South on Highway 101. The highway curved inland, carving its way through Redwood forests. They exited the 101 for the 1, California's iconic coastal highway, just past the town of Leggett. They passed the famous Drive Through Tree Park, something Trinity had always wanted to do. For a brief moment a small part of her considered pulling over and exploring the park. She gave her head a small shake and continued past the entrance. Highway 1 was a windy road that meandered through forests towards the West. Trinity rolled down the Camry's windows and let the cool breeze flow through the car. The breeze carried a scent that took her a moment to place. She turned to Rodger. "You smell that?" she asked.

He nodded. "It's legal now," he said.

As the road began to rise in elevation Trinity noticed a new smell on the breeze. "I smell the ocean," she said.

Rodger nodded. "Me too."

Less than five minutes later they crested the hill and the Pacific Ocean lay before them once again. The turn onto the dirt road that led to the Amos' property was on the left. A small wooden arch, with the single word *Amos* on it spanned the entrance to their property.

"Looks a little more welcoming," said Rodger.

Trinity nodded her agreement.

Joel and Corinne Amos owned 18 acres in the shape of a square, and their house was in the very center of the property. The dirt road snaked through the land in a seemingly random way. The hillside property was filled with large redwood trees, ferns, and assorted other plants Trinity could not identify. Vines climbed the branches of the trees, all the plant life struggling for rays of sunlight. The terrain was uneven. Trinity drove cautiously, wishing they had been given a four wheel drive vehicle rather than the Camry. Eventually the house came into view. Trinity actually stopped the car to take in the view. The house was a huge two story A frame, with an extended rectangular addition to the right. A front porch ran the entire length of the lower story. Two chairs, facing a large cement fire pit, sat on the front lawn. Trees surrounded the sides and back of the house.

"Wow," said Rodger.

Trinity eased the car forward into the circular drive. As they got closer she could see that the front porch turned the corner and continued on the side of the house. She also saw a large, two story garage to the right of the house, partially hidden by the thick stands of trees. Parked in front of the garage was a Yukon with an airstream trailer attached.

Trinity parked and she and Rodger slid out. She looked at him over the roof of the car.

"You taking the lead again?" he asked.

"Let's start that way," said Trinity. She paused a moment then added, "I trust your instincts Rodger."

He nodded. They both turned, walked towards the house, and mounted the stairs. The front door was massive and obviously custom made. Trinity rang the bell and listened as it echoed through the house. After a brief moment the front door opened and a man looked out at them. Trinity recognized him at once as Joel Amos. He still looked like his passport picture taken in 2009. His face was tan and lined with deep wrinkles around his eyes, which were an unusual shade of light green. His hair was thick, shoulder length, and shockingly white. He stood about 5'9", was dressed in shorts and a T-shirt, and was thin and wiry. He looked strong despite his size. He stepped partway out of the doorway and said "Yes?"

"Agent Glass," Trinity said as she held up her badge for him to see. "Office of Strategic Investigations." She waved a hand towards Rodger. This is Agent Stuart. We need a moment of your time Mr. Amos."

Joel Amos leaned his face toward the badge that she held in front of him. He peered at it for a long moment, then leaned back and looked in her eyes.

"What's this about Agent Glass?" he asked.

Trinity was just about to speak when another head popped through the door. It was Corinne Amos. She was about 5'5" and slender, her shoulder length sandy brown hair was loose around her face. She wore white capris and a loose sleeveless blue blouse. Her eyes matched the blouse perfectly.

"Who is it Joel?" she asked as she leaned out. Her husband stepped protectively in front of her.

"Federal agents," he said. "They want to speak with us."

"Well, are you going to stand out here all day Joel?" she asked. "Let them in, honey. Let them in."

The inside of the Amos house was as stunning as the outside. The floor plan was open, the living room quite large. The wooden ceiling was vaulted, with real wooden crossbeams, and recessed lighting. Floor to ceiling windows dominated the front and rear walls. Trinity turned as she walked in. The view out the front windows was a true "million dollar" view. The green hillside sloped down and away from the house. The great expanse of the Pacific Ocean just beyond it. The sun, still high in the sky, was just starting to edge towards the West. She imagined the sunsets were spectacular.

"Come sit in the dining room," said Corinne.

Trinity, Rodger, and Joel all followed her through the living room and into the dining room. A small oval shaped table filled the breakfast nook, the windows behind it faced a side of the hill that had less trees growing on it. The meadow grasses between the stand of trees were tall and waving gently in the breeze. They all sat at the table. Corinne and Joel's eyes were focused on Trinity. She began with the list, explaining that the Amos' names both appeared on it, and asking if she could read the names to them to see if they were familiar with anyone else on the list. They nodded and she read the names. She watched both their faces carefully, looking for any sign of recognition. She was sure Rodger was doing the same.

Silence filled the room upon the completion of the reading of the list. Corinne and Joel looked at each other for a long moment, then turned to Trinity in unison and shook their heads.

"Sorry," said Joel.

"Nope," said Corinne.

Trinity and Rodger shared a long look as well. Rodger gave a nearly imperceptible nod, then pushed back from the table and stood. Trinity turned back to Joel and Corinne.

'Tell me about your time in Thailand," she said. She saw that Joel's eyes stayed on Rodger as he moved towards the windows and stood looking out of them at the hillside.

"Oh," said Corinne, "Thailand is amazing."

At the same time Joel turned his attention to Trinity and said, "How did you know we spent time there?"

"Passport activity is easily accessed," Trinity said. "And it is a common thread connecting people on the list."

"Joel," Rodger interrupted the conversation, "do you have any buildings or workers on this slope?" He was pointing towards a grassy area with one small stand of trees.

"No," said Joel.

Rodger looked at Trinity. "We have guests."

80

PATRICK O'KEEFE

Wednesday was Pat's day off. He spent the morning with Olive. They dropped their oldest, a boy named Sullivan, at school, then spent the morning with their one year old, a girl named Piper. Olive had a doctor appointment at 11:30. Pat and Piper accompanied her. Olive's due date was early November. They had opted not to learn the gender of their third child. The appointment was routine and everything looked good. Pat took Olive and Piper to lunch after the appointment, picked up Sullivan from school, then dropped everyone at home. Although it was his day off, he still wanted to check in at the station. Olive understood this and did not voice any objections.

Pat arrived to the station just before 2:30. He entered through the back door and went straight to his office. He swapped his car keys for the keys for the department's mobile surveillance van. He stopped by narcotics and asked Detective Schreiber to go with him, then headed back to the parking lot and got in the van. To say Pat was proud of the van was an understatement. He had spent many hours applying for a grant from Homeland Security, and had been both surprised and elated when he had received one. The van was a Mercedes Benz Sprinter, black in color, and equipped with unique high tech features. The van had four cameras mounted with durable BASH camera enclosures. Made by Dotworkz, BASH was an amphibious, extreme off-road, and all-environment-ready camera protection. It was designed to work flawlessly with all mini-dome, HD, megapixel, micro PTZ, action, and specialty cameras. The portable stingray unit was inside and at the ready as well. The van even featured a "smoke cloak". This was a security system that could be activated to produce tons of blinding smoke. It deployed within seconds, instantly blocking vision and effectively deterring potential intruders. The Smoke Cloak also had an added option that marked the intruders with a site specific DNA that could be used to link them to the crime scene.

Pat and Schreiber headed out of the parking lot. They drove randomly for a while, Schreiber at the wheel, and Pat monitoring Stingray. There were half a dozen numbers that he was monitoring. All he got was silence. It was just past 5:00 when Pat heard some chatter. The number belonged to a high level drug dealer out of Mexico. Through Stingray, they had massive amounts of evidence on the man but none of it was admissible in court. The first voice was a heavily accented Mexican one, the second clearly Chinese.

"We have had a sighting in Guerrero Negro," said the Mexican voice.

"Did you engage with them?" asked the Chinese voice.

KATHLEEN HELMS

"No, but they are heading North," Said the Mexican voice. "To the border. I've alerted my men. They won't get that far."

"Call me when you have them," Said the Chinese voice. "Don't harm the woman."

"Understood," said the Mexican voice, and the call ended.

Pat pulled out his personal cell and called Trinity Glass.

81

TRINITY GLASS

Trinity's phone rang just as she was standing to look where Rodger was pointing. She silenced it without looking at the caller ID. She followed Rodger's extended finger and saw it moments later, a flicker of light in the distance; a reflection off glass. She turned towards Joel and Corinne.

"Move into the living room," she said as she moved to usher them that direction. Corinne went into the kitchen, opened a drawer, and removed something. Trinity caught a glance before the woman pocketed it.

"What is that?" Trinity asked. Corinne turned away. Trinity moved with surprising speed and caught the woman by the arm.

"Show me," she said.

Corinne removed the object from her pant's pocket and held it out for Trinity to see. It looked remarkably similar to the objects she had seen on the video from the boat.

"What is it?" she asked.

Corinne, looking like a deer caught in headlights, was silent.

"Mrs. Amos," said Trinity, "seven of the seventeen people on that list are dead. Thailand, large cash purchases, and those," she pointed at the object, "are the only common threads."

Corinne held Trinity's eyes for a moment. Finally she said, "It is a hard drive. It contains all our financial information."

At that moment Joel appeared at her side.

"We are leaving Agent Glass," he said. "Come on Corinne." Trinity followed Joel and Corinne to their front door and watched as they crossed the driveway to the Yukon that had the airstream hooked to it. Joel slid in the driver's seat and Corinne slid in the passenger seat. Trinity strode across the driveway and leaned in the open passenger window.

"Give me five minutes to get behind whoever is on the hill," she said. "If you leave now, they will likely follow you." She paused, then added, "I'm pretty sure they are after your financial information."

Trinity turned and walked back to Rodger, who was waiting for her on the front porch. She reached in her pocket, removed the car keys, and tossed them to him.

"You drive," she said. "They are giving us five minutes before they take off. When we round that big curve, let me out and I'll double back and come at whoever is up there from behind."

Rodger nodded and headed to the Camry. Trinity slid into the passenger seat, removed her Sig Sauer, and and racked the slide.

"You armed?" she asked Rodger.

"Always," he said.

When they had rounded the large curve in the r(
pulled the car to the side and shifted into park.
perfect spot to stop. The trees were thick and the'
invisible to the watchers.

"How do you want to do this?" he asked Trinity.

"Let me see if I can get a look from higher up," she said. She
holstered the Sig Sauer, looped her gyro stabilized binoculars
around her neck, and slid out of the car. She took a moment to
study the trees, then picked what looked like an Oak, and
started climbing.

Trinity paused on one of the higher branches and took a
moment to orient herself. The Ocean was the most obvious
marker. She could see the roof of the Amos' house below her
and to the left. She swiveled a bit, located the grassy meadow,
then the stand of trees just above it. Trinity brought her left leg
over the branch and settled herself on it, one leg on each side to
secure her position. She leaned her back against the trunk and
brought her binoculars to her eyes. As always the Fraser Volpe
performed spectacularly. The lenses brought the stand of trees
so close, it was as if Trinity was standing right in front of them.
The trees were thick and heavy with leaves. Trinity strained to
see another light flash or movement. The leaves blew softly in
the breeze. Trinity stayed still, her breathing soft, her eyes
focused. After a moment she saw what looked like a puff of
smoke. It dissipated in the air, then another one appeared,
floating gently out of the leaves and disappearing in the breeze.
When the third puff appeared she realized what it was.
Whoever was hidden in the trees was smoking. Her mind
flashed back to Loyal's evidence bags. They had contained cigarettes. Trinity raised the binoculars so that they were focused

.bove the trees. She widened the field of view and searched for a vehicle. Whoever was in those trees had not walked to this remote location. She found it about three hundred yards to the Northwest of the trees, and zoomed in. A late model dark green 4Runner was parked to the side of what looked like an old fire road. Trinity zoomed in on the license plate and took a picture, grateful as always for the binocular's many capabilities.

Trinity followed the same route as she descended the tree, looking down rather than up, and placing her feet with care and deliberation. She dropped to the ground when she was about six feet above it and landed with a slight thump. She walked to the Camry, bent down, and looked in the open passenger door.

"There is at least one in the stand of trees. I saw cigarette smoke. Their car is a late model 4Runner, dark green, and parked about three hundred yards Northwest of the trees. Looks like an old fire road."

"You want to come at them from that point?" Rodger asked.

"You do that," Trinity said. "I'm going to hike up and over. There is lots of cover. I'll come at them from above."

Trinity saw Rodger glance at her shoes. She was wearing low heeled pumps. Trinity smiled. "I can handle the terrain, Rodger. Just get yourself up to their car and come at them from that direction."

"Copy," said Rodger as Trinity closed the car door. He put the car in gear and drove away from her. As the engine noise faded, silence filled the void.

82

LOYAL TRUESDALE

L oyal wasn't sure why Brandi had asked if there was someone in his life, but he had answered honestly. He didn't ask her the same question. He found, when he thought about it, that he didn't really care one way or another. His goal was to get her to safety, not become friends. He reminded himself that by this time tomorrow they would be safely back in the United States and his part in this drama would be over. That thought brought a smile to his face.

Brandi's hand on his arm brought him out of his thoughts.

"Loyal," she said. "Look at that church."

His eyes followed her pointing finger. Across the street from the town square was an old church. Stone steps led up to the square white building. A taller tower-like section was behind the square building and to the left. A large arched doorway, flanked by alcoves containing statues provided entry.

"You want to go check it out?" asked Loyal.

"Can we?" asked Brandi. "I love churches."

"That," thought Loyal sarcastically, "is truly surprising." Out loud he simply said, "Let's go."

They crossed the street and walked up the stone stairs toward the door. Loyal was impressed with the size of the church. His original impression, from across the street, had not been one of size, but up close he could see the church was quite large. The arched doorway led into a long narrow building. The first thing Loyal noticed was the temperature. It was cool inside. He estimated that the temperature had dropped by about ten degrees. A single row of wooden pews ran along each interior wall. The walkway between them led to a huge gilded altar. Loyal gazed up. The ceiling was extremely high and domed. He followed Brandi towards the altar. She stopped in front of it and stood, still as stone, her eyes fixed on a nearly life sized statue of Jesus on the cross. Loyal turned and looked back towards the entrance. He saw now that there was a balcony above the huge door.

Loyal turned around and saw that Brandi was walking towards him.

"Let's look outside," she said.

They walked through the giant doors and turned towards the left. They rounded the corner of the building and found themselves in a courtyard. The walkway was dirt, and carefully placed stones created a barrier of sorts for a group of fruit trees planted in the center. Brandi pointed at two wooden benches placed against the wall of the church and said, "Let's sit."

Loyal couldn't see any harm in that, so he followed her to the benches and sat down beside her. They sat in silence for several minutes and Loyal was just about to suggest that they get up and go look for food when Brandi spoke. Her voice was quiet, yet it had a rough edge to it, almost as if she had been crying.

"It is so beautiful," she said.

Loyal turned to look at her. She had removed her sunglasses when they had first entered the church and had yet to replace them. Her brown eyes were damp. She turned so that her knees were touching his. She took his hands in hers. "I haven't been completely honest with you," she said. "When I told you about my childhood I said I didn't know my Dad." She blinked a few times. "I did know him Loyal," she said. "He's the one who brought me to San Felipe." She swallowed once. "He died some years ago, but I still find it hard to talk about him."

Loyal looked at her for a long moment, untangled his hands from hers, and stood.

"Let's go find some food," he said.

Brandi stood, replaced the sunglasses, and walked out of the courtyard.

On the corner of the Plaza, across from the church they found Restaurant Bar Victor's. It was a small place, with dining inside and out. Brandi chose a table outside, facing the town square. A couple sitting a few tables away from them had plates of food and oversized margaritas.

"I'm getting one of those," said Brandi.

"Yeah," Loyal said, "me too."

A waiter came and took their orders. Loyal chose scallops in a garlic sauce, while Brandi opted for the chile relleno. Both ordered margaritas, which were delivered swiftly. They sat in silence for a bit, sipping their drinks and thinking their own thoughts. Eventually Loyal spoke.

"I'm sorry about your Dad," he said. "It is fine that you didn't mention him. Your relationships with your parents are none of my business."

"Thanks," said Brandi. "I think it was just being in that church. It made me feel guilty about not being totally truthful."

Loyal looked at her for a long moment.

"Is there anything else, something that might matter to our safety, that you have neglected to share with me?"

"No," said Brandi. "I've told you everything I know." She paused, then smiled, before adding, "Trust me."

83

TRINITY GLASS

Trinity stood still in the silence for a moment to get her bearings, then started up the densely wooded hillside. The foliage was thick and wild. Low lying branches caught on her jacket and the binocular strap. As she raised her right foot to step over a dead branch, it caught on an exposed root and she went down on her hands and knees, hard.

"Damn," she muttered under her breath.

She stood, inspected the binoculars, then her hands and knees. The palm of her left hand was scraped and oozing thin lines of blood. Her pants were torn just below her right knee, dirt mixing with blood. Ignoring the pain in her knee, Trinity stepped over the branch and continued on.

After several minutes, she climbed another Oak and scanned the hillside. She could see the Amos' house to her left. The Yukon and Airstream were still in the driveway. Apparently Joel Amos had decided to give her more than five minutes. "Smart man," she said out loud. She scanned for the stand of trees and saw that she was now above and behind it. She raised the binoculars to her eyes and studied the trees. Smoke still wafted out of them. From this height she could see that the forest which had been providing excellent cover was ending soon. The meadow, with its tall grass was laid out before her. She calculated the distance from the forest's edge to the stand of trees to be about 50-60 yards. She focused the binoculars on the stand of trees. From this angle and distance she could see the shapes of two men sitting on the ground. One held binoculars, trained on the house below them, the other held a cigarette in one hand and a phone in the other.

Trinity turned the binoculars so that they were hanging down her back rather than her chest, knelt down in the grass, then lay flat on her front. She raised up for a moment to orient herself, then began to army crawl towards the stand of trees. The grass was tall enough to hide her approach, should either of the men turn in her direction. When she was close enough to smell the cigarette smoke, she paused her forward motion and risked a peek above the grass. She was close and could see the men without the aid of the binoculars. They were standing now. The man who had been holding the binoculars walked out of the trees and stood scanning the meadow. Trinity dropped to the ground, pressing herself as flat as she could. When nothing happened, she risked a peek. The man had turned and was walking up the slight hill towards the car. She hoped Rodger was in place and ready. The second man emerged from the trees. He held the phone up to his ear with his left hand. His back was to Trinity. She stood in one fluid motion, gun in her right hand and extended.

"Federal Agent," she said. "Freeze. Hands in the air."

The man stopped and held his hands out to his sides. Trinity had taken two steps towards him when he moved. In a blur of motion his right hand dropped to his waist and he began to spin. Time slowed for Trinity. She saw the motion and reacted with two shots, one to the torso and one to the head. In the moment before the man crumpled to the ground she saw the gun in his right hand.

Trinity, gun in both hands in front of her, approached the man cautiously. She kicked the gun away from his body, although the chance of him ever using it again was zero. His face was familiar, she recognized him as one of the Chinese assets. She entered the trees and cleared the area. With the exception of a small pile of cigarette butts, the area was empty. Trinity turned and looked up the hill in the direction the other man had gone. Certainly both he and Rodger had heard her two gunshots. Her position on the lower part of the hill left her vulnerable if the other man returned. Still, Rodger was up there somewhere. He had been out of the field for years. Trinity hoped he had kept his skills sharp. With her gun in front of her she started up the hill. The silence of the meadow was broken again by three shots, fired in quick succession. Trinity stopped for a brief moment, then began to run up the hill towards the sound.

Trinity reached the top of the rise and scanned the area. She saw the 4Runner in the distance, about a football field away from her. From her vantage point she could see the passenger side of the vehicle. She didn't see Rodger or the other man. Trinity moved to her left so that the rear of the vehicle was visible to her as well. Still no sign of either man. She moved towards the car, gun still extended, eyes sweeping the area. She moved with both caution and speed, her many years of training and experience providing muscle memory. She approached from the rear of the car. The gunshots had frightened the birds away. The silence in the meadow was complete. Trinity knelt by the rear bumper and risked a peek around the driver's side of the car. Two feet, clad in black shoes, extended out from the front of the vehicle. Whoever they belonged to was laying on the ground in front of the car. They were not moving. Trinity brought an image of Rodger up in her mind's eye. She tried to remember what shoes he had been wearing, but could not. She remained in a crouch and eased herself towards the front of the 4Runner. When she was at the wheel well, and within touching distance of the dead, she supposed, man's feet, she stood with her gun raised in front of her. She stepped around the front bumper and saw Rodger. He was kneeling down over the definitely dead man and going through his pockets. He sensed her motion, looked up with his gun at the ready, then lowered it and stood.

"You good?" he said.

She nodded. "There were only two," she said. "The other one is by the trees." She paused and looked at the dead man's face. "I recognize both of them Rodger. These are some of the people I've been looking for."

84

BRANDI KENDRICK

Brandi was almost embarrassed by how quickly she finished her entire meal. A day in the buggy, ingesting only beer and candy, had left her hungry and dehydrated. She finished her margarita quickly too, and ordered another round when the waiter came to check on them. The couple at the other table had ordered another round as well. They were all delivered at the same time, and the man caught Brandi's eye as he raised his glass.

"Good margaritas, yes?" he said with a smile. His accent was European, German perhaps. Brandi raised her glass.

"The best," she said. She glanced at Loyal, then added, "Would you like to join us?"

The man, who looked to be in his early thirties, glanced at his companion, a twenty something woman, who nodded her assent. Both couples stood and maneuvered the tables together.

"My name is Berndt," said the man as he sat. He gestured to his partner. "This is Claudia." The woman smiled.

She was pretty, thought Brandi, taking in the woman's blue

eyes, blonde hair, and white smile. The man was handsome as well, his blue eyes matching Claudia's, his hair a shade darker, stubble on his chin and cheeks.

"American?" Berndt asked.

"Yep," said Brandi. "And you are German I'm guessing?"

"Yes," said Claudia. "We are following the mission trail. We started in Loreto and just came from Mulege and Santa Rosalia."

"Did you see the mission church yet?" Berndt pointed across the street.

"Oh yes," said Brandi, "it is beautiful. Is there one in Mulege?"

"Yes," said Claudia. "There is also a church in Santa Rosalia that was designed by Gustave Eiffel, the same man who designed the Eiffel Tower."

Loyal, Brandi, Berndt, and Claudia spent about half an hour talking and drinking margaritas. Brandi had a third, while Loyal switched to water after the second. On the walk back to the campsite Brandi asked if they could stop and look at the church and the mission before meeting the airplane. Loyal actually stopped his forward progress and turned to look at her. The sun was setting, but she could still make out his impatient expression.

"We aren't on vacation Brandi," he said. "We need to be at the airport early."

"Please Loyal," she said. "I'll get up as early as I have to."

Loyal was silent for a bit, then said, "Pick one. I'm not stopping at both."

Brandi thought about this then said, "The Eiffel. In Santa Rosalia."

Loyal started walking again. "I'll give you ten minutes in the church," he said. "No more."

85

TRINITY GLASS

Trinity placed a call to Doug Caldwell, who placed a call to local FBI, who placed a call to local sheriffs. The FBI satellite office that covered Mendocino County was located in Santa Rosa which was 122 miles away. The director of that office agreed to send eight agents by helicopter, which would be a forty-five minute flight. The Mendocino County Sheriff's office would be sending some detectives as well. The nearest field office was in Fort Bragg, just under an hour away. The detectives would be arriving by car. After she disconnected the call to Caldwell, Trinity raised the binoculars and looked down at the Amos house. The Yukon and Airstream were no longer in front of the garage. She followed the long track from the house to the road. Some places were obscured by trees, but she was fairly sure they were not on the property. They had likely driven away when the first shots rang out.

Trinity left Rodger by the 4Runner and went back down the hill to the stand of trees. The man lay just as he had when she had left him. She walked to his side, leaned down, and went through his pockets. He had no identification, only a pack of cigarettes, a cheap lighter, and the phone that had dropped from his hand when he had fallen. She attempted to check for a previous number, but it was password protected. She took the cellophane off the cigarette pack, put the phone in it, and slipped it in her pocket. Flies were starting to buzz above the dead man's still form. Trinity took off her jacket and covered his face and as much of his chest as she could. The suit was ruined from her fall and the crawl across the meadow anyway. She wouldn't be wearing it again. She inspected the palm of her left hand. The small amount of blood that had seeped from the scratches was dried now. Thin, dark red, lines trailed across her hand. She sat down on the ground and looked at her right knee through the hole in her pants. She pulled the fabric a bit to widen the gap. The skin had split when she had hit the branch. Here, too, the blood had dried. She picked at some debris that was embedded in the cut, causing a bit of fresh red blood to flow. Trinity decided to leave the clean up of her knee for later. She stood, then glanced at her phone. It had been twenty minutes since her call with Caldwell. Reinforcements would be arriving in the next half hour. Not wanting to disturb the scene any more than she already had, Trinity walked up the hill. She stopped about ten yards from the dead man and the stand of trees. She turned, so that she was facing the vast Pacific, and sat down. When talking to Caldwell, she had seen that she had a voicemail from Detective O'Keefe. She taped the icon and raised the phone to her ear. She listened as he highlighted the latest chatter. She knew that Loyal was heading to Mulege, not the border. His misdirection would hopefully buy them enough time to remove both Loyal and Brandi from Mexico. She did not call

O'Keefe back. Instead she stared at the blue ocean and waited.

Trinity heard the sirens just as her phone beeped, indicating an incoming text message. She stood, then glanced down at the phone and saw it was from Rodger.

Three unmarked and four marked vehicles. One crime scene van. Be ready.

Trinity pocketed the phone, pulled out her badge, and turned towards the hill. In less than two minutes two figures appeared at the top of the rise and began to make their way down to her. Trinity stood still, hands at her sides, as they approached. As they neared she saw that there was one man and one woman. They stopped about two feet from her.

"Agent Glass," she said, holding the badge in front of her so they could see. "Office of Strategic Investigations." They both looked at the badge, then the woman spoke.

"Detective Caldera," she said, "Mendocino County Sheriff's Office."

"Detective Armstrong," said the man. "We have limited details, agent. Want to fill us in?"

Trinity took a moment to brief the detectives on the situation. She explained about the list, the Amos' who were in the wind, and the two Chinese Nationals. Detective Caldera raised a radio and gave a series of directions to whomever was on the receiving end. She instructed them to leave a marked unit at the beginning of the fire road, to secure the scene by the 4Runner, to send some officers down to secure the scene by the stand of trees, and to send another marked unit to the Amos' house. She had lowered the radio and turned to say something to Trinity when they heard the rumble of the helicopter.

They all heard the rotors of the helicopter moments before the large beast appeared above them. Trinity turned and looked to the East. It took just a moment for the Bell 430 to come into view. The pilot spotted them and brought the helicopter down in the field about fifty yards away from where they stood. Trinity covered her eyes to protect them from the debris that was stirred up by the rotor wash. When the air had stilled she looked up at the two detectives.

"I'm assuming that you were informed that the FBI was coming," she said.

86

TRINITY GLASS

A s soon as their feet touched the ground the eight FBI agents took over the scene. The agent in charge, Stephen O'Shea, who looked to be in his mid forties, was clearly used to running the show. He assigned two agents to the scene by the 4Runner and two agents to the area by the stand of trees. Two agents were dispatched to take control of the search of the Amos' house, and two remained with him to conduct field interviews with Trinity and Rodger.

"Caldwell explained that you are in the middle of an investigation," he said to Trinity. "I'm not happy about it, but I'm going to conduct field interviews and let you both go." He paused, looking her in the eye, and added, "I'll be keeping both your guns, and you are both going to need to return to my office for official interviews."

"Understood," said Trinity.

Trinity and Rodger were kept separate for the field interviews, which lasted about half an hour. When O'Shea was satisfied with the information that they supplied he cut them loose. They returned to the Camry and headed North to the airport. Both were exhausted and were quiet for the majority of the drive. The sun was just dropping into the Pacific when they taxied to the runway. Trinity opted to sit in the co pilot's seat for takeoff. Rodger accelerated down the runway and the King Air rose smoothly into the air. The sunset was brilliant, rich tones of red, orange, and purple were painted across the sky and reflecting on the ocean. To Trinity it seemed as if they were ascending into heaven itself. Rodger banked and turned South. The sun, on Trinity's right, dipped lower and lower until it was swallowed by the sea. The vibrant colors faded, replaced by the evening sky. Trinity leaned her head against the window and drifted off to sleep.

She was awakened by the jolt of the wheels on the runway and the gentle pressure of deceleration. She was quiet while Rodger taxied to Western Flight. They both deplaned and walked through the building and toward their vehicles.

"I spoke with Caldwell earlier," said Rodger. "While we were waiting for the Sheriff and FBI. He has instructed me to fly you to Mulege tomorrow morning."

Trinity nodded. "I was hoping it would be you."

"Meet me back here at 5:30," he said. "We will have to stop in Calexico for an inspection and paperwork required in Mexico. San Felipe is an official point of entry, so we will stop there as well. Should be in Mulege by 10:00 if everything goes smoothly."

Trinity drove to the condo and showered. She heated a can of tomato soup and ate it on the patio. The sky was clear and the gentle breeze was cool. When she had finished her soup, she returned to the condo and sat at the table with her computer in front of her. She typed up a detailed report about the events of the day. When she was satisfied she saved the document to her computer and to an external hard drive she kept in a hidden pocket in her briefcase. She stood, stretched, then looked at the kitchen clock. It was nearly midnight. She thought about O'Keefe and Stingray, then texted him the SAT phone's number and explained her itinerary for the following day. That done, she brushed her teeth, set her alarm for 4:00 am, and slid into bed. She lay her still damp head on the pillow and drifted into a fitful sleep.

87

BRANDI KENDRICK

Brandi was sleeping soundly when a hand on her shoulder forced her consciousness to swim to the surface. She rolled away from the pressure of the hand and snuggled deeper into the sleeping bag. She was struggling to find her way back to that deep sleep when a voice said, "Time to wake up." She lay still for another moment, then pulled the sleeping bag off her head and rolled onto her back. When she opened her eyes she saw Loyal's face above hers.

"We need to be on the road in twenty minutes," he said. "I let you sleep as long as I could. The buggy is packed, except for your stuff."

Brandi sat up on the cot and stretched her arms toward the ceiling. She slid out of the sleeping bag and hung her legs over the side of the cot. Her head was pounding.

True to his word, Loyal had them completely packed and ready to go within twenty minutes. Brandi watched as he did all the work, rolling her sleeping bag up and loading it and her suit-case into the buggy. She had walked to the showers to use the bathroom and dress in pants and a loose T-shirt. She slid into the passenger seat of the buggy when he announced their departure, sunglasses on despite the gentle light of the early morning. The streets of San Ignacio were quiet. Loyal drove slowly toward the highway. He pulled into a Pemex located just before the entrance to the highway.

"I'm going to top off the tank," he said. "You need anything?"

Brandi nodded and slid out of the seat. Loyal reached into his pocket and pulled out some cash. He peeled off a few bills and handed them to her.

"Grab some waters?" he asked. Brandi nodded again and went into the gas station's small market. An older man, about the same height as her, smiled at her from behind the counter. His smile grew wider when Brandi spoke to him in Spanish. He happily found her the things she wanted; candy, beer, ice, and a pain reliever for her head. She was almost out the door when she remembered Loyal's request for water.

Loyal was waiting for her beside the buggy. She saw the look on his face when he saw the beer and candy, but ignored it. He had his way of dealing with things, and she had hers. She had no intention of apologizing for her actions. Loyal dumped the ice in the cooler and nestled several water bottles and beers into it. After removing two pills from the bottle, Brandi stashed the pain meds, one beer, and the candy in her footwell. Loyal started the buggy and drove onto Highway 1. It would take about an hour to get to Santa Rosalia. Brandi reached down and grabbed the beer, She cracked it open, tossed the two pills in her mouth, and swallowed them with a large swig of beer. She slouched down in the seat, sunglasses on, hair loose and blowing in the wind, and, as always, the black backpack across her chest.

88

PATRICK O'KEEFE

Pat woke three minutes before his alarm was set to go off, silenced it, and lay in bed next to Olive savoring the warmth of her body next to his. She was lying facing away from him, her hair feathered across her pillow. He could just make out the rise and fall of her chest in the dim morning light. He slid carefully out of bed, hoping not to wake her. They had talked late into the night. She knew he was going in to work early, there was no reason to disturb her sleep. Pat stepped into the bathroom and closed the door before turning on the light. He had placed his clothes in the small room the previous evening, another safeguard against waking his sleeping family. He dressed, brushed his teeth and hair, and turned off the light before opening the door. He walked down the dark hallway to the kitchen and filled his soft-sided cooler by the light of the fridge. He brewed coffee, and filled two travel mugs when the coffee maker beeped. When everything was ready he exited the house and walked to his car by the light of the rising sun.

. . .

Detective Schreiber was waiting in the Sheriff's Department rear parking lot when Pat arrived. He had already retrieved the keys for the surveillance van and had it unlocked and idling. Pat parked, transferred the cooler and the coffee mugs to the van, and settled into the rear portion of the vehicle. Schreiber slid into the driver's seat. He drove the van to an area off Melrose Drive, just Northwest of Carillo Way. This was a location where they had had some success in capturing conversations with Stingray. Schreiber parked, then joined Pat in the back of the van.

"Thanks for coming out early with me," said Pat as he handed Schreiber one of the breakfast burritos that Olive had prepared for them the previous evening.

"You bet," said Schreiber. "I want to get a line on these guys, Pat."

Time passed in that strange way that is unique to surveillance. They ate their burritos and sipped their coffees, neither much in the mood for smalltalk. It was just past 8:00 when Stingray crackled to life. The number was the same one they had heard conversation on the previous evening. The Mexican voice spoke first.

"They couldn't have gone North. We would have seen them by now. There are only three ways to go from Guerrero Negro, North, East, or Southeast."

"They must be found," said the Chinese voice. "Saturate the area."

"It is already being done," said the Mexican voice.

"Cover the airports," said the Chinese man. "I don't care about the man, but I want the woman alive."

· · ·

The connection broke without any further conversation. Pat pulled out his phone to call Trinity and realized that he had silenced it the previous evening when he and Olive were talking. He saw now, that he had a text message from Trinity, sent late the previous evening. He dialed the number she had provided for the SAT phone and listened as it rang.

89

TRINITY GLASS

Trinity's alarm brought her abruptly from deep sleep to wide awake. She sat up with a jolt, then turned to silence it. 4:00 am had come early. She supposed she had gotten only four hours of sleep, and she didn't feel rested. Rodger had instructed her to be at Western Flight by 5:30. She knew he would get there earlier than that, and was determined to do the same. She loosened her body with about twenty minutes of stretches. Her right knee was stiff, and her palms were sore from her fall in Hales Grove. As she stretched she thought about the events of the previous day. It was unfortunate that she and Rodger had been forced to kill the Chinese Nationals. They would have been much more valuable alive. She wondered abut Loyal and his companion, Ms. Kendrick, and whether he had been able to get any useful information out of her.

Stretching complete, and feeling a bit more centered, Trinity dressed in army green cargo pants, a black T-shirt, a black

windbreaker, and tennis shoes. She placed her Federal ID in
one of the pants' pocket, and her passport and turned off phone
in the other. She braided her long hair in a single braid down
her back. She applied sunscreen, but no makeup. She placed
some granola bars, two apples, two bananas, and a few water
bottles into a small cooler. By 5:00 she was in her car and on
her way to meet Rodger. The pre-dawn air was cool and clear.
The sun was still hidden in the East, but the Moon was visible
to the West. It hung in the sky, still round, but for a sliver
shaved off the bottom curve. Trinity could tell the day was
going to be clear and bright. She thought abut Loyal and
wondered where he was and if he had started his day yet.
Trinity did not have a strong religious belief, but she did believe
in positive energy. As she drove she sent positive thoughts
Loyal's way.

Rodger was waiting for her at Western Flight. They repeated
their actions of the previous day and were soon airborne. From
this height and angle Trinity could just see the line of light to
the East. The Sun was making an appearance. Once they were
at altitude Rodger explained the hoops they would be jumping
through in order to land in Mulege.

"Our first landing will be in Calexico," he explained. "Our
paperwork will be checked and we will receive a declaration
that we will need to show when we land in Mexico. They will
probably check the plane for large amounts of cash. Last time I
went they had cash sniffing dogs."

"And then straight to Mulege?" Trinity asked.

"Nope," Rodger said. "Remember I told you we will be
landing in San Felipe. That is an official port of entry."

"That's right," said Trinity. "San Felipe, then Mulege."

"Yep," said Rodger. "That's where the Mexican officials will collect their "fees"."

He put air quotes around the word fees. Trinity smiled. "I guess some things never change," she said.

The landing and inspection in Calexico went just as Rodger had described. Once their paperwork was in order and the officials were satisfied that they were not carrying unusually large amounts of cash, they were airborne again. Trinity remained in the co-pilot's seat. Just as they were descending into San Felipe the SAT phone rang. Trinity unstrapped and moved to the cabin to answer it. Expecting to hear Caldwell's voice, Trinity was surprised to hear O'Keefe's voice come through the handset.

"Agent Glass," he said, "I have some more chatter. It's not good. They figured out that Loyal didn't head towards the border. They are saturating the peninsula with men. They have been told, specifically, to look at airports."

"Copy," she said. "Call back if you hear anything else." Trinity replaced the SAT phone, moved back to the cockpit, and strapped in.

"We are approaching San Felipe," said Rodger.

Not wanting to disrupt his concentration, she decided she would wait until they were in the air again to tell him about O'Keefe's warning.

90

LOYAL TRUESDALE

L oyal wasn't thrilled with Brandi's choice of beverage, but he said nothing. He was almost to the point where he could hand her off, and it didn't really seem worth the hassle. Her request to stop at the church still rankled, but he was worried that if he started an argument with her he wouldn't be able to stop it. He glanced over at her. She was slouched in the passenger seat, the candy in her lap and a beer in her left hand. She wore that damn black backpack backwards across her chest. The sunglasses hid her eyes.

The drive to Santa Rosalia was uneventful. Brandi ate candy and drank beer. Loyal drove and let his thoughts wander where they chose. He thought about Stella, and the grandchild she would soon be having. When he first had learned of the impending birth he had thought that it meant he was now an old man. His opinion on that had changed, however. He was looking forward to this new chapter in his life. His thoughts moved from Stella to Trinity. Their relationship, much like his grandchild, was in its infant stage. She intrigued him, and he hoped it would continue. Trinity was so different from Michelle, his first wife, and Angela, his second. After his second divorce Loyal had sworn that he would never marry again. When he was with Trinity he wasn't sure about that. She was younger, and still deep into her career. They were both enjoying their stolen moments together, the future had never been discussed.

The streets of Santa Rosalia were wider than those of San Ignacio. The buildings were brightly colored, mostly painted blue and yellow. The Church was easy to find. Loyal found parking in front. He turned to Brandi.

"Ten minutes," he said.

"Aren't you coming with me?" she asked.

Loyal sighed and slid out. "I'll walk you to the door," he said. "I want to keep an eye on the buggy."

Brandi slid out of the buggy and they walked towards the large building. It was made of steel and painted white. The German couple had explained that Gustave Eiffel had designed it in 1884. In 1889 it had been entered into the Paris World's Exposition, and had won first place for design. In 1897 it had been purchased by the French Boleo Mining Company, disassembled, and shipped to Santa Rosalia where it was reassembled. Loyal thought it looked like a huge barn. It had a large wooden door and stained glass windows. He peeked inside. The light in the church had a different quality than the light outside. The stained glass windows gave it a yellow hue, almost a glow. The ceilings were tall and pews lined each side wall, as well as a row down the center aisle. Loyal remained at the door

so he could keep an eye on the buggy. Brandi went inside for
her ten minute tour.

Loyal did not wear a watch. He waited for what he guessed to
be ten minutes, and was just about to lean in and call Brandi,
when she stepped out the door.

"It is beautiful Loyal," she said. "Do you want me to watch
the buggy so you can go in and look?"

Loyal shook his head. "We need to get to the airport," he
said.

They returned to the buggy and slid in. The town of
Mulege, and the airport he was referring to, were South of
Santa Rosalia. Loyal turned East on Alvaro Obregon. This
street would take them back to Highway 1, where they would
turn South toward Mulege. They had gone about half a block
when Brandi grabbed his arm.

"Loyal," she said, "stop."

He saw a space ahead on the right and pulled the buggy
over. He suspected the beers were not sitting well in her stomach. Perhaps she was going to be sick.

"Do you smell that?" she said.

Loyal sniffed the air, then shook his head.

"There's a bakery near here," she said as she slid out of the
buggy. She turned toward him and leaned across the passenger
seat, her hand outstretched. "Can I have some cash?"

Loyal tamped down the words that came to mind, forcing
himself to remember that Brandi was almost someone else's
problem. He pulled some bills from his pocket and handed
them over.

"Five minutes, Brandi," he said. "I'm not kidding."

"I'll bring you something," she said. "Maybe some sweets will lighten your mood," she added with a smile and a wink.

Loyal sat in the buggy silently counting. Five minutes was three hundred seconds, so that was what he was counting to. The position of the buggy afforded Loyal a view of the round-about that connected to the highway. It was less than one block away. The highway was not busy. When his count reached 83 he saw two armored vehicles pass by heading South on the highway. He sat up a little straighter and kept counting. At 242 two Suburbans, both black with tinted windows, passed heading South as well. Loyal felt a small adrenaline spike. Those vehicles, heading in the same direction as he was, made him uncomfortable. He looked over his left shoulder to see if Brandi was approaching, then jumped at the sound of her voice to his right. He turned to see her sliding into the buggy. She handed him some kind of pink bread.

"It's a concha Loyal," she said. "Try it. You should always eat when you can in Mexico," she added with a smile. "You can't always be sure when you will have the chance again."

91

TRINITY GLASS

Trinity watched as the town of San Felipe slid beneath the plane. The Sea of Cortez, blue and sparkling in the morning sun, was visible to the left. Barren desert and the mountains of the Coastal Range filled the window to her right.

"There," said Rodger as he pointed his finger out the windshield.

It took Trinity a moment to see what he was pointing at. A single runway lay before them, like a stripe in the desert sand.

"That's it?" she asked. "I thought you said this was an International Airport."

"It is," he said.

As they descended towards the runway the tiny airport became more clear. Trinity was able to make out a small building, a parking area, and a white tower that reminded her of a lighthouse somehow. Rodger brought the plane down with ease and taxied to the short arm inspection area alongside the runway and in front of the building. The words **Aeropuerto Interna-cional San Felipe B.C.** were painted on the white structure. Rodger turned to her and said, "I'm going to need to fill out some paperwork with the officials. I'll let them know that we are taking off again. They might want you to wait at Customs and Immigration, we will just have to see." He picked up their declaration from Calexico, a folder with all their documents, and his wallet, then unstrapped and eased into the cabin. He opened the door and the stairs descended. Trinity unstrapped and joined him in the doorway, standing slightly behind him and to his left. The warm breeze entered the cabin and swirled around her.

"Wait here," Rodger said, then he walked down the stairs where four men dressed in fatigues were waiting for him. He spoke to them briefly, then turned to Trinity.

"Stay in the plane," he said.

She nodded and took a seat in one of the passenger seats.

Rodger spent over twenty minutes in the offices of the airport. Trinity waited patiently in the King Air. Armed military boarded the craft and spent about five minutes looking through everything. Leashed dogs were brought out to sniff around the outside of the plane. Trinity wasn't sure what they were smelling for, and she knew better than to ask. When Rodger returned to the plane she looked at him with a question in her eyes. He just smiled, raised the stairs and closed the door.

"All set," he said as he slid into the pilot's seat. Trinity joined him in the cockpit. She slid into the co-pilot's seat and strapped herself in.

"We'll be in Mulege in about an hour," he said as he taxied back to the runway, brought the engines to full power, and moved the King Air down the runway. The nose of the sleek aircraft tilted slightly up and Trinity felt them leave the ground. She looked out the small window to her right and watched as they left the airport behind.

They had been in the air about fifteen minutes when Trinity relayed her conversation with O'Keefe to Rodger. He shook his head as he listened.

"Mulege is going to be a hot stop, Glass," he said. 'I've had trouble in Mexico before. I'm going to leave the left engine running in Mulege. Open the door, get your people, then get back in and we take off." He paused, then added, "We can land in Ensenada on the way back and get the paperwork sorted out there."

Trinity nodded. "Understood," she said. "I'll deplane and locate Truesdale and Kendrick, then get back on. They will be looking for us and should be ready to go."

"I don't want trouble Glass," said Rodger. "Get it done quickly."

92

BRANDI KENDRICK

Brandi nibbled on her concha and watched Loyal out of her peripheral vision. He maneuvered them through the roundabout and onto the highway heading South, then ate his concha in four large bites. He radiated tension, and she couldn't help but wonder if something had happened while she was in the bakery. She thought about asking him, but by the set of his jaw and the way his hands were gripping the steering wheel, she decided it best if she did not say anything. Instead she focused her attention on the road in front of them. Brandi thought highway was a bit of a fancy of a name for the paved two lane road, but had to admit the scenery was spectacular. The desert stretched out to her right, the Sea of Cortez was visible on the left. At times the highway veered inland a bit and the blue expanse disappeared from view. Brandi could tell it was still close by the salty scent of the air.

When she couldn't stand the uncomfortable silence any longer, she turned to Loyal. "Did something happen while I was in the bakery?" she asked loudly over the engine noise. Loyal pulled the buggy to the side of the road with a jerk of the steering wheel. Dust rose up around the buggy as he skidded to a stop. Brandi just stared at him, saying nothing. When the dust had settled he turned to her.

"You need to stop acting like this is some damn vacation," he said. "There are very bad people after you. And, honestly, I think you know a hell of a lot more than you are letting on."

He looked at her for a long moment as if he was expecting a response from her. She figured she owed him something.

"Loyal," Brandi said, removing her sunglasses and laying her hand on his forearm. "I truly don't know why they are after me. I'm assuming it is because of what is in this backpack." She patted the backpack that lay across her chest. "But I don't know what they are."

Loyal was silent for a long moment. Then he shook his head and said,

"We are heading into an unknown and potentially dangerous situation here," he said. "I don't know the layout of the airport, what kind of plane to be watching for, or who else might be waiting there."

He faced front for a moment, then added, "I'm sick of your bullshit. If you aren't going to tell me the truth then just don't talk."

Brandi was surprised by the forcefulness of Loyal's words. Her first instinct was to grab a beer, but she decided that was not the best idea at the moment. Instead she replaced her sunglasses and slouched down in the seat, turning her head to her right. She watched the desert landscape flow by and thought about what he had said. She wasn't going to lie to herself, his words had stung. She was realizing more and more that she wanted Loyal to like her. Right now she was pretty sure he didn't. She tried to think of something that might elicit sympathy from him. It didn't take her long to decide on tears. Brandi brought the images of her father and Jodi into her mind. They truly were the only people in this world to whom she had been close. Tears followed pretty quickly in the footsteps of the images. Brandi left her sunglasses on and let the tears slide gently down her cheeks, the drops darkening her T-shirt where they fell. After a moment she looked at Loyal out of the corner of her eye. He had both hands on the steering wheel and his eyes were focused straight ahead. He had not even noticed the tears.

As they approached the entrance to the airport, which Brandi could see now was really just a dirt strip with an office to one side, Loyal pulled the buggy to the side of the road and turned off the ignition.

"This looks wrong," he said. He turned to her. "Get out and help me push the buggy into that stand of trees."

Brandi said nothing, just slid out of the buggy and helped push. Loyal steered it into the stand of trees, then slid back in. Brandi did the same.

"What is it?" she asked in a whisper.

Loyal pointed at the runway.

"The army is here," he said. "I think that is normal. But I don't like the look of those two Suburbans over there."

Brandi followed his pointing finger and saw, through the leaves, two black Suburbans, parked to the side of the office, facing South. A jolt of adrenaline shot through her. She forced herself to be calm and watched as Loyal pulled the GPS out of his shirt pocket, and some paper maps out of a pocket on the inside of the driver's side where a door would be on a standard car.

"What are you doing?" she asked him.

"Shh," he said. "I need to focus. If everything falls apart we are going to need a way out of here."

93

TRINITY GLASS

The approach to Mulege was beautiful. Although she was anxious to get Loyal and Kendrick safely on the plane and back in the air, Trinity couldn't help but admire the view. The Sea of Cortez, to her left, sparkled in the mid morning sun. The desert and mountains beyond, stretched out to her right. A small inlet allowed ocean water in towards the small town. Rodger flew past the town, turned, and approached the airport from the South. Trinity saw what she assumed was the paved runway in front of them, then Rodger adjusted his approach and she saw that the paved stretch was actually a road. The runway, now directly in front of them, was dirt.

"This landing will be a bit rougher than usual," Rodger said. "Be ready for some bumps."

Trinity nodded. As they approached she noticed a few army vehicles, which she was getting used to. It was the two black vehicles, they looked to her like Suburbans as the King Air descended from the skies, that caused her concern. She pointed at them.

"I see them," said Rodger. "Remember what I said Glass. If things go to shit, we are out of here."

Trinity nodded. "I remember."

As they dropped towards the dirt strip, Trinity scanned for any sign of Loyal and his buggy. She saw nothing.

"Come on Truesdale," she whispered under her breath, "where are you?" She could see that the army officers had exited their vehicles and were approaching the edge of the runway. Rodger touched down with a jolt, and they bounced a bit as they hit uneven patches on the dirt runway. Trinity braced herself with her right hand against the wall of the cockpit. The King Air decelerated and Rodger brought it to a stop just in front of the office, near the army vehicles. The officers were waiting by the side of the plane.

"Remember Glass," he said, "it's a hot stop. Make it fast."

Trinity unstrapped and slid out of the co-pilot's seat. She moved to the door and opened it, actuating the stairs to drop gently to the ground. With one last look at Roger she moved towards the open door.

94

PATRICK O'KEEFE

Detective Schreiber had agreed to remain with O'Keefe and the van until noon. They had a small list of phones they were tracking with Stingray, and had heard some conversations and captured some text messages throughout the morning. It was just before 10:00 that they got a hit on the phone that O'Keefe was most concerned about. Again, the conversation was between the Chinese and Mexican male voices that were becoming uncomfortably familiar to both men.

"I found a connection between Truesdale and a Federal agent named Glass. A woman," the Mexican man said. "I have a source at DHS. He's low level or we would have had this information sooner."

"Continue," said the Chinese voice.

"I just received a call from an informant in San Felipe, at the airport. This Agent Glass just landed, then took off again for Mulege." He paused. "It cannot be a coincidence."

"Do you have anyone in Mulege?"

"Yes," said the Mexican. "Two cars at the airport. How do you want to proceed?"

"No more wasted time," said the Chinese man. "Take out any army that might be there, this agent and her pilot, and Truesdale. I want the woman alive."

"Understood."

"No mistakes," said the Chinese man.

"The Sinaloa do not make mistakes."

There was a pause in the conversation. O'Keefe thought perhaps the connection might have been broken, then the Chinese man said, "A source at DHS? That is impressive."

"Addicts are everywhere Senor," said the Mexican man. "You would be surprised."

"Nothing surprises me," said the Chinese man. "Call when you have the woman."

This time O'Keefe heard the snip of the connection being disconnected. He turned to Schreiber. "I have to warn them," he said as he picked up his phone. He went to recent calls and tapped on Trinity's SAT phone number. O'Keefe's heart was racing, he could feel the adrenaline surging through his veins. Trinity had said she would be landing in Mulege around 10:00. As he heard the phone begin to ring, he prayed silently that he was not too late.

95

TRINITY GLASS

J ust as she was about to step out of the plane, the SAT phone rang. Trinity leaned to her right to pick it up. As her hand picked up the receiver, she heard a whoosh and a bullet sped past her shoulder and embedded itself in the thick cushion of a passenger seat. Trinity dropped into a crouch. Time slowed down for a brief moment, then everything sped up. Several things happened at once. She heard more gunshots outside the plane. She heard thumps as the army personell hit the ground. Rodger appeared on the other side of the doorway. He hit the actuator for the stairs and turned back towards the cockpit. At the same time she heard O'Keefe's voice coming out of the SAT phone.

"It's the Sinaloa," he was yelling. "They have someone at DHS."

This was as much as Trinity heard. The stairs were starting to come up. There was no way she was leaving Loyal behind. She slipped through the small space and dropped to the ground. She landed, rolled towards one of the fallen army men and plucked his M16 out of his hand. She continued the roll and ended up back upright, in a crouch, her left knee and right foot on the ground.

Trinity felt the King Air ease away from her. She fired towards the Suburbans. She could see now that the front passenger side of each vehicle was open. The shooters legs, from the knees down, were visible beneath each door. Trinity took the only shot she had. She placed a bullet into the knee of each man and watched as they dropped to the ground with a yelp. She stood and sprinted towards the Suburbans. She covered the ground in seconds. She kicked the gun away from the first man she had shot, leaned into the Suburban and shot the driver in the head. She rounded the back of the vehicle, heading for the other open door. That driver pulled away with a screech, leaving his injured comrade on the ground. The man was struggling to sit up. Trinity shot him again, this time in the head. She then went around the back of the remaining Suburban, and shot the remaining gunman in the head as well.

She stood still for a moment, considering her options. Two men were peering cautiously out of the office door, one of them held a phone to his ear. The King Air was roaring down the runway, she would get no help there. She heard an engine coming from behind her and turned, ready to fire. It was Loyal. He was coming towards her fast. He swung the buggy around just as he reached her, bringing the backseat right in front of her. Trinity flung her body into the backseat, grunting as she hit something hard. Loyal did not waste a moment. He gunned the engine and sped away from the airport. At the entrance he turned left, towards the desert. Trinity tossed the M16 out of the buggy then held onto the back of the passenger seat as they roared towards the desert.

96

LOYAL TRUESDALE

Loyal let his eyes, by looking in the rearview mirror, rest on Trinity for a brief moment. She was sprawled across their luggage and supplies. Her eyes met his. Despite everything she smiled. He knew it was cheesy, but couldn't help winking at her. He held her gaze for a moment, then refocused on the road in front of him. He pulled the GPS out of his shirt pocket and handed it to Brandi.

"Hold this on your leg until it vibrates," he said over the engine noise and wind. "When it vibrates lift it up so I can see."

She took the GPS and nodded at him. Maggie's maps were detailed. She and Ed had traveled in Baja extensively, much of their travels taking them off road. Loyal had found a track that would take them through the desert, avoiding the main roads, at least until Guerrero Negro. Brandi lifted the GPS. Loyal slowed and kept his eyes on the right side of the road. In less than fifty feet he saw it. The track was narrow, barely wide enough for the buggy. Loyal slowed, turned onto the track, and headed into the vast desert.

.   .   .

Every mile further from the main road that they traveled, the more Loyal felt himself relax. They were far from safety, but with Trinity aboard the odds of survival were dramatically greater. He drove carefully on the narrow track, an accident at this point would mean certain death. Occasionally the track would split and branch off in several directions. Loyal would stop the forward motion, consult Maggie's maps, then make a choice and continue on. The track became rougher and more rocky as they got closer to the mountains. On his right Loyal caught sight of a small hill with a rocky outcropping that would provide some shade and protection. He veered off the track and made his way there. He parked the buggy as close to the wall of the rock as he could and turned the engine off. The silence of the desert enveloped them.

For a moment no one moved. Then Loyal twisted his torso to the right as much as the confines of the buggy would allow and looked back at Trinity.

"Are you hurt?" he asked.

She sat up. She was perched on top of all their supplies. "No," she said.

"That was kick-ass." This came from Brandi, who had completely turned in her seat and was on her knees facing backwards. "Who the hell are you?"

Loyal grimaced, and watched several emotions play over Trinity's face. Finally she simply said, "I'm a Federal Agent, Ms. Kendrick. I'm here to get you home."

97

TRINITY GLASS

Trinity identified herself to Brandi, then slid out of the buggy. She stretched her arms toward the bright blue sky. Her body was in pain. Her right knee throbbed and her shoulders were sore from her roll on the ground at the airport. The adrenaline that had surged through her veins had ebbed now, leaving her drained and fatigued. She watched as Loyal slid out of the buggy and walked around it to where she stood. He opened his arms and she allowed herself to drop into them. They stood like that, enjoying the comfort and closeness, until they heard the *psssch* of a can opening. They parted and both turned to look at Brandi. She stood beside the buggy, beer can in hand.

"You guys want one?" Brandi asked.

"No thanks," said Loyal.

Trinity remained silent. She looked at Brandi, standing there in a T-shirt and pants, sunglasses on and beer in hand like they were on some kind of vacation. If Loyal hadn't been there, she thought she might have decked the woman. Loyal must have sensed Trinity's feelings because he turned back to her. "Can you tell me what you know?" he asked. "What the hell happened back there?"

Trinity glanced back at Brandi, then turned to Loyal.

"Some of it is classified. I need to talk to you privately."

Loyal turned back to Brandi. "We need to talk," he said. "You stay here."

Loyal and Trinity walked about twenty feet away from Brandi. This brought them out from under the outcropping and into the hot desert sun. Trinity felt a trickle of sweat slide down her spine. She was angry, and when she turned toward Loyal she could see that he could read the anger in her eyes. "I just risked my life for you, and you two are down here partying like teenagers. What the hell Loyal?"

Loyal waited a beat before answering. "She's down here partying like a teenager, Trinity, not me. I've just been trying to stay alive." He paused, then leaned towards her and added in a harsh whisper, "You think I want to be down here with her?"

"It's hard to tell," said Trinity.

There was a long moment of silence, then Trinity took a deep breath. She exhaled slowly, struggling to find a place of calm inside of her.

"We aren't out of danger Loyal," she said. "And I have no way of calling for help."

"What happened back there?" Loyal asked.

"The Chinese want her." She nodded her head in Brandi's direction. "They are working with a cartel. I think the Sinaloa. O'Keefe called on the SAT phone just as I was about to deplane." She paused. "His call saved my life. All I heard him say was that it was the Sinaloa and that they have someone at DHS."

"It's pretty clear that they only want *her* alive," said Loyal.

"Agreed," said Trinity. "Has she told you anything?"

"Not really," said Loyal. "She's all smoke and mirrors."

"I have questions for her," said Trinity.

"Let's hold off until we are farther away from Mulege," said Loyal.

"I don't think that is wise," said Trinity. "I'll give it one more hour, Loyal. Then I want some answers."

He was silent for a beat, then said, "Maggie gave me some maps detailing back roads and trails. I've been studying them. I can get us to Guerrero Negro without using the highway. I haven't studied them any further than that."

"Rodger mentioned something about Ensenada," Trinity said. "I think we should try to get there."

Loyal reached out and grasped Trinity's hand. "It's really good to see you," he said. She gave his hand a slight squeeze. "You too," she said with a small smile.

As they were walking back to the buggy Trinity saw something that stopped her in her tracks.

"You have got to be kidding me," she said.

She could see Brandi, her suitcase open, was leaning down by the side view mirror applying makeup. Loyal actually chuckled.

"It is just how she is Trinity," he said. "You'll get used to it."

The good feeling she had been enjoying with Loyal just a moment previously dissipated. Trinity's mouth set in a hard line. "I highly doubt that," she said. She turned to Loyal. "I want the back seat. I don't want her sitting behind me." She paused, then added, "I don't trust her."

98

PATRICK O'KEEFE

P at had heard Trinity pick up the SAT phone, then he had heard gunshots. He had called out what he thought to be the most important information, that the Sinaloa were after them and that there was an informant at DHS. Trinity had dropped the phone, so the connection had not been lost. Pat had heard more gunshots, then the King Air's engine as the plane began to move. He listened for any sign of Trinity's survival, but heard nothing. He heard the door of the airplane being closed, then silence. Eventually he had disconnected. He instructed Schreiber to get in the driver's seat and get them back to the Sheriff's Station as fast as possible. He explained what he had heard as Schreiber drove.

Pat entered the station and took the stairs two at a time. He ran down the hall and burst into Captain William's office without bothering to knock. The captain was sitting behind his desk. Len Hammond, a homicide detective who Pat detested, was sitting in the guest chair opposite the captain.

"I need to speak to you Captain," Pat said through labored breaths. "Privately."

"If it is about Truesdale you can speak freely in front of Hammond," said the Captain. "I've just spent the last twenty minutes convincing him Truesdale should not be a suspect in the kidnapping or murders."

Pat looked at Hammond for a moment, then sat down in the chair next to him. He explained the chatter he had heard through Stingray, and the action he had heard over the SAT phone.

"I need to get in touch with Agent Glass' agency." He told the Captain. "They need to know what is going on."

Hammond leaned forward in his chair. "I don't know Captain," he said. "That all sounds pretty unbelievable."

"Believe it," said Pat leaning forward. "They need help."

99

TRINITY GLASS

Loyal rearranged things so that Trinity had room in the back seat. She watched in silence. When he had created enough space, she slid in, directly behind Brandi, who was already in the buggy. Loyal slid in the driver's seat and pulled the maps out to review them quickly before heading out into the desert again. As Trinity watched, Brandi slid her left hand onto Loyal's shoulder and leaned in close to look at the maps with him. She thought she saw Loyal flinch, but wasn't sure. What she was sure of was that she had had enough of Brandi Kendrick.

Trinity stood and slid out of the buggy.

"I have questions," she said. "And I'm asking them now."

She grasped Brandi by her right upper arm.

"Step out of the buggy Ms. Kendrick," she said. "You and I are going to have a talk."

Trinity did not look at Loyal. She kept her focus on Brandi's brown eyes. Brandi looked toward Loyal, but when he said nothing, she slid out of the buggy. Trinity maneuvered the two of them so that Brandi's back was against the rock outcropping, Trinity in front of her. Trinity was about 4" taller than Brandi and she knew how to use the height to intimidate. Her face was just inches from Brandi's, her voice hard.

"I know you know more than you are saying," Trinity said. "What are the things in the backpack? Do you know Regina Krause or Joel and Corinne Amos? Why are the Chinese after you?"

Brandi was shrinking back against the hard rock, almost collapsing in on herself. Her eyes were wide. Trinity took a deep breath and drew back.

Brandi inhaled, and let the breath out slowly. Their eyes remained locked.

"Ms. Kendrick," Trinity said, "if I'm going to get us out of Mexico alive, I need to know the whole story."

Brandi took another deep, shuddering breath in, then let it out.

"They are digital wallets," she said.

Trinity leaned back even further. "Thank you," she said. "I bet that feels better, telling the truth. Your sister sent them to you. Why?"

"I don't know," said Brandi. "She wrote a short note telling me to keep them safe and that she would contact me." She paused and finally broke the eye contact. "But she never did."

Trinity paused a moment. The desert air was still and silent. She could tell without looking that Loyal had stopped studying the maps and was focused on their conversation.

"What kind of currency do the wallets hold?" asked Trinity quietly.

"Cryptocurrency," said Brandi.

Trinity thought for a moment then asked, "What is the value of the backpack, Ms. Kendrick?"

"I don't know," said Brandi. "It is everything Jodi had, so I think it is a lot."

100

LOYAL TRUESDALE

oyal listened to Trinity's questions and Brandi's answers. He was surprised Brandi had opened up to Trinity. He supposed it was self preservation kicking in. Brandi didn't do things for anyone but herself. He turned slightly in the buggy so that he was able to see the two women. Their posture spoke volumes. Trinity stood ramrod straight above Brandi, who was sitting against the outcropping.

"We need to move," he said. "Get back in the buggy."

Trinity gave him a long look. He couldn't tell what she was thinking. Brandi stood and walked to the buggy. She slid in without a word. After a full minute, Trinity did the same. Loyal put the buggy in gear and drove slowly into the desert.

No one spoke for a very long time. The engine noise and the breeze were the only sounds. Loyal followed Maggie's map. The mountains in the West grew larger and more distinct as they approached. When he could stand it no longer, Loyal pulled over near a stand of cacti. He turned off the ignition and slid out.

"We need to eat," he said. He turned to Brandi. "How many beers do you have left?"

She slid out of the buggy and opened the cooler, which was stored in the very back behind Trinity.

"Eight," she said.

"Get three out," said Loyal.

He looked at Trinity, who was still sitting in the backseat.

"Come on Trinity," he said. "Let's call a truce."

Trinity slid out of the buggy and went to stand beside Loyal. He slung his arm over her shoulder and leaned in close to her ear.

"She gave you something," he said. "Now might be the time to act just a little more friendly."

He kissed her cheek, then moved away. He had never seen this side of Trinity, and while he understood it, he didn't think it was the right approach with Brandi. He pulled the dry box and the soft sided cooler out of the buggy. He removed bread and sandwich meats and prepared three sandwiches. He indicated a bit of shade provided by the cacti and sat. The two women joined him. Brandi passed a beer to Loyal and then to Trinity before settling crosslegged on the sand. Loyal sat to Brandi's right with his back against the rear right side tire, his legs stretched out in front of him. Trinity settled in the sand to Loyal's left. They ate and drank in silence.

Trinity spoke first.

"Ms. Kendrick," she said, "I found video surveillance footage from the boat in Oceanside Harbor."

Brandi, who had been drawing designs in the sand with a stick, sat up a little straighter and looked at Trinity.

"I didn't understand what the older man was trying to do, but I get it now. He was trying to access the currency."

Brandi nodded, "I think so."

"Are the wallets encrypted?" Trinity asked.

Brandi nodded, "Yes."

"Do you have the codes?"

Again Brandi nodded. "I haven't tried them," she said, "but I think so."

101

PATRICK O'KEEFE

Loyal Truesdale and Len Hammond had a long history. Pat was aware of only the most recent events that had occurred while Hammond and Loyal were investigating the same case. He was hoping Loyal would survive to tell him more about the past. Pat's opinion of the Hammond was low. He had seen him stoop below the law on at least one occasion, and was quite sure there were more times Hammond had stepped outside the legal limit. He didn't want to waste time explaining the situation.

"Captain," he said, "the chatter was clear. They only want Brandi Kendrick alive. Loyal and Agent Glass are dispensable." He watched as Captain Williams mulled this over.

"I'll reach out to her office," he finally said. "There isn't much more I can do."

"Can you pull him," Pat indicated Hammond with a nod of his head, "off of Loyal?" We all know he isn't a kidnapper or killer Captain."

"We've established that O'Keefe," said the Captain as he stood. "I think our time here is done."

102

BRANDI KENDRICK

Brandi slid back in the front seat and cracked another beer. Loyal started the buggy and drove in the general direction of the mountains to their West. She mentally reviewed the day, specifically her conversations with the agent. The woman was a hard ass, that was clear from her actions at the airport which had saved them all. Trinity Glass was tough, strong, and smart. Brandi had been fairly successful at manipulating Loyal so far, she would just have to find a way to do the same with Agent Glass. Pretending she knew nothing had not been an option with the agent. Brandi reviewed the information she had given the woman. Her conclusion was that it had been just the right amount.

Her next thoughts were about the hug Loyal and Glass had shared, and the kiss on the cheek she had seen him give the woman. Brandi wasn't too happy about that. Loyal was growing on her. Sharing him was not in her plan. She cracked another beer and settled in for the ride. Loyal had explained that it would be a long one, and she was prepared. She had her candy on her lap, a beer in her hand, and two more stashed in the footwell. They would likely be warm by the time she drank them, but she didn't care. There were two more in the cooler, enough for her and Loyal to have one together at the end of the drive. Agent Glass was on her own.

Brandi was on her third beer when the topography began to change. The mountains were close now, and the track they were following began to rise. The angle of ascent was minimal. The track followed a winding route. The desert cacti were left behind, replaced by low growing scrub brush. Brandi thought she could see stands of trees when she gazed upwards. The Sun had crossed the midpoint of the sky and was beginning its journey Westward. Loyal pulled to a stop and turned so that he could see both Brandi and Trinity.

"It is going to be getting dark before we cross these mountains," he said. "I'm going to get us as far as I can, but I think we should be looking for a good spot to spend the night."

He turned back to face the front and began driving again without waiting for a response from either of his passengers.

As they rose in elevation pine trees and what Brandi thought looked like some type of oak began to appear. The track wandered between the trees and around large rocks. When it appeared that they were close to the crest of the mountains and the sun was starting to sink in the West, Loyal pulled to the side of the track and parked under a stand of about a dozen oak trees. There was flat ground beneath the trees. He parked and slid out of the buggy.

"This looks like a good spot," he said. "Good cover from the trees and a flat spot to sleep."

Brandi slid out of the buggy and stretched her arms towards the sky. She walked around to the driver's side of the buggy and pulled some toilet paper out from behind Loyal's seat.

"Be right back," she said. She walked towards the far end of the stand of trees and positioned herself behind a large rock to go to the bathroom. When she stood, she leaned around the rock and watched Loyal and Trinity for a moment. The agent had slid out of the buggy. Loyal had moved around to the passenger side. He was facing Trinity and holding both her hands in his. They were talking quietly. Their body language told Brandi everything she needed to know about their relationship. She felt a sharp stab of disappointment. For these past few days, although in her heart she had known it wasn't true, she had felt like Loyal belonged to her.

103

TRINITY GLASS

Trinity had watched Brandi walk towards the rock at the edge of the stand of trees, then slid out of the buggy. Loyal had walked around the vehicle, stood in front of her, and taken her hands in his.

"You ok?" he asked.

"Yeah," she said, "a little stiff and sore."

"You hit hard when you jumped from the plane," said Loyal.

"I'm all right," said Trinity. She leaned in, kissed him, then leaned back again. "All I have is what I'm wearing," she said.

"What's mine is yours," said Loyal. "Let's get set up while we still have light."

Trinity helped Loyal push the buggy in between two oaks. When she looked up she saw that Brandi had returned from her nature stop. She was sitting on one of the larger rocks, a fresh beer in one hand and the nearly empty bag of candy in the other. Despite the darkening sky, she still wore the sunglasses. The backpack remained in place, although she was

wearing it correctly now, with the pack on her back rather than
her chest. Trinity wondered again, if anything had happened
between Brandi and Loyal. There was an energy between them
that made her uncomfortable. Trinity gave a little shiver. The
air was rapidly losing its heat as the sun went down. Loyal
came up beside her.

"Let's make dinner while we still have a little light," he said.
Trinity watched as he turned and walked towards Brandi. He
said something to her, then held out his hand to help her down
the face of the rock. It seemed to Trinity that Brandi held onto
his hand for a bit longer than necessary.

They ate sandwiches again. Loyal and Trinity drank water.
Brandi drank the last beer.

"I have the bottle of rum," she had said, "but no mixer."

The last vestiges of light faded while they ate. The moon
had not yet risen in the East, the faint glow on the Eastern
horizon was just becoming visible. Loyal produced a flashlight
which they used to position the two sleeping bags.

"It will be a tight fit," he said to Trinity, "but you can sleep
with me."

104

LOYAL TRUESDALE

Loyal lay in the sleeping bag, Trinity's back against his belly, and considered their options for the next day. He could feel the rise and fall of Trinity's even breathing. When they had first squeezed into the bag she had been facing him. He had listened as she brought him up to speed on the events of the past few days. She spoke without emotion, as if she was being debriefed. Loyal understood now how much danger they were actually in, and what Trinity had risked by jumping out of the plane and away from safety. When she was done talking, she had squirmed around so that her back was to Loyal. He had wrapped his arms around her and begun to tell her his story of the past few days, but had realized fairly quickly that she had fallen asleep.

He lay in the bag, holding Trinity, and trying to decide the best course of action. The leaves of the oak trees, which stood nearly fifty feet high, were blowing gently in the breeze. They rustled quietly, reminding him of the sound of the ocean. He could hear Brandi as well, in her sleeping bag about ten feet to his right, taking quiet sips out of the bottle of rum. She had made no secret of the fact that she was taking it to bed with her. Loyal mentally reviewed their situation. The Sinaloa cartel was in bed with the Chinese. Both were looking for them. Now that he understood the value of the backpack it was clear why. Trinity's assumption was that everyone on the list had some sort of cryptocurrency fortune, and that the Chinese wanted it for an as yet undetermined reason. Loyal and Trinity were expendable, Brandi was not. At least not yet. That was something he was going to try to impress upon her tomorrow. At some point she would become expendable as well.

Loyal knew that there was a checkpoint between Baja Sur and Baja Norte near Guerrero Negro. He and Brandi had passed through it just a few days previously. He supposed they had made it through just before the alert went out to be looking for them. According to Maggie's maps and notes, there was no way to avoid this checkpoint. This was a major concern. Trinity had said that the Sinaloa cartel was mixed up with the Chinese. Loyal supposed it was possible, likely probable, that the cartel and the army were connected as well. Going through that checkpoint could very well be a death sentence.

Loyal heard the cap being unscrewed and Brandi taking yet another sip of rum. He was well aware that the woman could hold her liquor, but was concerned about her ability to function the next day. He thought about getting up and talking to her, but dismissed the thought after a brief moment. He was finally laying next to Trinity again. He lowered his nose to her hair and breathed in. He loved her scent. Hell, if he was being honest, he loved everything about her. Despite the danger, seeing her in action at the airport had been spectacular. With not a wasted movement, she had jumped from the plane, rolled and retrieved a gun, then taken out three of the four men. The fact that she knew how to use an M16 wasn't wasted on Loyal. Trinity was the most fascinating person, man or woman, that he had ever met. He would do anything to keep her safe.

105

BRANDI KENDRICK

Brandi was deep into a rum induced sleep, twisting and turning in her sleeping bag in an attempt to free herself from the ties that bound her in her dream. She was on the boat again, yet she could tell by the motion of the waves that they were far out to sea. Her hands and wrists were secured with zip ties. A gag was in her mouth and the blindfold was tightly around her eyes. There was no space that permitted her even an obscured view. She could hear the Chinese talking. They spoke this time in a dialect that she understood. They had broken the encryption. They no longer needed her alive. She felt herself being lifted. She felt the cold ocean spray on her face. She was lifted up higher for a moment, then dropped. She was suspended in the air for a brief moment, then fell and plunged into the freezing sea. The water surrounded her. The zip ties cut into her skin as she struggled. She twisted and turned, trying in vain to free herself so that she could return to the surface for a breath. She opened her mouth to scream and felt the cold water rush in. It was too late, she realized. She was going to drown.

. . .

Brandi came awake with a gasp and a cry. She forced her head out of the tangled sleeping bag and sucked the pre dawn air in greedily. She was confused and forced herself to slow her breathing down. When she was calmer she took a moment to orient herself. The moon shone brightly in the dark sky above her. She could make out the shape of tree limbs silhouetted against the moon. They were swaying gently in the breeze. She rolled and looked to her left. She saw the occupied sleeping bag and the buggy beyond it, pushed into the space between two large trees. Gradually her mind began to let go of the dream and her current reality seeped back into the spaces left behind. She lay on her back and watched the moonlit movement of the oak trees. It sounded like the ocean. She supposed that might have been what sparked the dream. She thought about the dream for a while. Brandi believed dreams held messages. The unconscious mind, realizing something of great importance, was trying in the only way possible to send the message to the sleeping recipient. After some pondering, she decided her unconscious self was trying to tell her conscious self that she was not out of danger yet.

It was not yet dawn, but Brandi knew that she would not be falling back to sleep. She mentally returned to Sunday and replayed the events, counting the days as she worked her way through them. According to her calculations it was Friday morning. She lay in her sleeping bag and watched the day emerge from night. The sun was not yet visible in the East, but the rays were extending up enough beyond the horizon to create ambient light. Her eyes adjusted as the light gradually increased and pushed the dark of night away. The air was chilly. As Brandi squished herself down further into the sleeping bag her hand touched something cold and hard. She flinched, then reached out again. It was the bottle of rum. She grasped it, then pulled it out of the sleeping bag and held it up in the dim light. There was about one-third missing. She slipped it back in the bag.

"Come on girl," she whispered to herself, "just keep it together for a few more days."

She was tempted to take a sip this morning, before the other two woke up, but she knew that she would have to be more careful now that Agent Glass was with them.

106

PATRICK O'KEEFE

P at beat his alarm by four minutes and slipped out of bed without waking Olive. It was Friday morning. Schreiber was not available today, so Pat would be taking the van out by himself. Not the ideal situation, but doable. He made coffee, filled a single travel mug, and packed the cooler for one. The sun was just rising as he pulled into the rear parking lot at the Sheriff's Station. He went to his office, retrieved the keys for the van, and returned to the parking lot. He transferred his supplies to the van and left the Sheriff's Station. He returned to the spot on Melrose, thinking that perhaps this was the last day he could park here without attracting too much attention. From the outside the van looked like many other vans owned by wealthy families in the coastal cities. Still, parking in the same place every day was not a smart move.

Pat settled in to listen. Stingray was active, whether he was in the van or not. He had multiple numbers programed and the device searched for them constantly. He listened on one frequency for new activity, and at the same time reviewed anything recorded in his absence. He searched for the number he had heard the other conversations on, and was rewarded with a conversation from six pm the previous evening. He listened to the content. The Mexican man spoke first.

"We lost them in Mulege," he said. "The female, Agent Glass, overpowered our men. She killed three, one escaped."

"This is unacceptable," said the Chinese man.

"They cannot get to the United States without passing through checkpoints," said the Mexican. "We will find them that way."

"You cannot control all the checkpoints," said the Chinese man."What about your enemies?"

"The Jalisco control some," he said. "But not all. We will find them."

"You had better," said the Chinese man. "I am losing patience with you."

The connection was broken before the Mexican had a chance to reply.

Pat leaned back in his seat with a sigh of relief. They had survived the gunshots and as of six pm last night had not been found. There was still a chance they could make it back alive. He reviewed the rest of the recorded items, but there was nothing else from this number. Pat took a long sip of his coffee, pulled out a granola bar, and sat back to listen and wait.

107

TRINITY GLASS

Trinity woke with the sun. She lay still in the sleeping bag, enjoying the feel of Loyal's arms around her. His breathing was low and even. She could tell he was asleep without attempting to turn in the sleeping bag, which would surely wake him up. He had listened attentively to everything she had told him after they lay down the previous evening. She remembered turning so that her back was to him, intending to listen to his story of the past few days, but must have fallen asleep. She remembered nothing.

The morning air was cool on her exposed face. Her body, snuggled next to Loyal's, was warm inside the sleeping bag. It wasn't really intended for two people, but Loyal had insisted that they would fit. They had, with little room to spare. Trinity lay still as long as she could. She focused on the soothing sound of the oak leaves as they were stirred by the gentle breeze. She was concerned about what the day would bring. She heard movement to her right. She turned her head just a fraction of an inch so that she could see out of the corner of her eye. Brandi was inching out of her sleeping bag, clearly attempting stealth, and failing miserably. When she was fully out of the bag, she stood and stretched. She then kneeled back down and reached into the depths of the sleeping bag. When she stood she held a partially empty bottle of booze in her hand. She tiptoed to the buggy and stashed the bottle in the back. She pulled the slowly shrinking roll of toilet paper from the back of the buggy and headed toward the rock on the distance.

Trinity decided this was a good time to get out of the sleeping bag. She tried to manage this without waking Loyal, but he stirred when he felt her movement. She felt his grip tighten on her torso and relaxed into him for a brief moment. She turned half a turn, kissed him, then slid out of the bag.

"I guess it is time to get up," he mumbled. Trinity didn't say anything. She hoped that he would be able to drift back to sleep for a few minutes. Instead she walked to the buggy and leaned against the driver's side. When Brandi returned, Trinity held her hand out for the toilet paper. Brandi handed it over silently, then turned toward her sleeping bag. Trinity walked to a different rock. As she was heading back she saw that Brandi had rolled up her sleeping bag and was loading it into the buggy. Trinity approached.

"Let's let Loyal sleep a bit more," she said. "Why don't we make some food and then wake him up?"

Brandi nodded, then looked in the cooler and the dry box. "All we have are sandwiches or granola bars."

"Sandwiches it is," said Trinity.

. . .

She woke Loyal when the sandwiches were ready. They assumed the positions they had held the previous evening. Loyal sat with his back against the rear passenger side tire. Brandi sat to his left, Trinity to his right. Everyone was drinking water. Again, there was no small talk during the meal. Trinity noticed that they were all eating more slowly and wondered if they were all unconsciously putting off the start to the long day. She looked at the oak trees that surrounded them. They were tall. The bark on their trunks was gnarled and bumpy. The leaves were narrow ovals; dark green on the tops and a light shade of gray-ish green on the underside. The way they swayed in the wind reminded her of seaweed moving in the ocean current. Brandi was the first one to finish her sandwich. She stood and leaned over Loyal, digging in her suitcase for something. When she sat back down Trinity saw that she held a small bottle in her hand.

"What's that?" Trinity asked.

"Paracetamol," said Brandi. "It's like Tylenol."

"They call it that in a lot of other countries," said Trinity.

"You want a few?" asked Brandi.

"If you have enough, I could use a few," said Trinity. "I'm pretty sore."

Brandi tapped a few pills into her palm and stretched them out toward Trinity. Trinity closed the gap between the two women by leaning forward herself. She accepted the pills and used the last of her water to swallow them.

"You were pretty kick ass yesterday," said Brandi. "You looked like a stunt woman. Why didn't you keep the gun, though?"

"You don't want to be caught with a gun in Mexico, Ms. Kendrick," said Trinity.

"Call me Brandi," said Brandi as she leaned over and placed her right hand on Loyal's left knee. "Loyal does."

Trinity gave her a tight smile, but did not return the suggestion that they be on a first name basis. As far a she was concerned, Ms. Kendrick could refer to her as Agent Glass.

LOYAL TRUESDALE

Loyal saw Trinity's expression tighten when Brandi placed her hand on his knee. He brushed it quickly off, pulled his legs in, and stood. He reached a hand out to Trinity, who accepted, and helped her to her feet. He turned away from the women, and circled around the back of the buggy and to the driver's seat. Everything had been loaded already. He wanted to study the maps again before they set out. Maggie had made notes that one part of the track was pretty rough. While he considered himself a decent driver, he had not had a lot of off road experience in a buggy. He was hoping that his years on a motorcycle would be of help to him now.

Trinity settled herself in the back seat and Brandi slid into the front. Loyal added gas from one of the gas cans to the buggy's tank, slid in the driver's seat, and drove back onto the track. As he drove, he kept an eye on the rearview mirror, and Trinity. She had her head turned to her right, apparently watching the scenery. After about an hour, the track leveled out, then began its descent back to the desert floor. Slowly the trees thinned out, then disappeared altogether. The air was hot and dry, the sun's rays burning. The track became rockier and more difficult to traverse. Loyal stopped the forward motion, studied the maps again, and eased forward.

According to the maps, they would come out of the mountains just Southwest of San Ignacio. The remainder of the drive would be through the desert. They would actually cross Highway 1 at one point on their way to the checkpoint at the border of Baja Sur and Baja Norte. While Loyal was concerned about crossing the highway, where they would be completely exposed, his concerns about the checkpoint were much larger. Army members had died in Mulege. Loyal was considering these things when he heard a loud scrape from beneath the buggy. He stopped the forward motion. The buggy was tilted towards the right, the wheels on the left side were off the ground. He cautiously swiveled his torso to the right so that he could see his passengers.

"You both ok?" he asked.

Both women nodded.

"Get out as carefully as you can," he said. He watched as both women slid out of the buggy, then he maneuvered himself out as well. He walked to the back of the buggy and knelt down to look underneath. The buggy was perched atop a large flat rock that blended perfectly with the dirt on the road. Loyal stood and turned to Trinity and Brandi.

"It is propped on a large rock," he said. "It is going to take all three of us to get it up and over."

. . .

Loyal decided that he and Trinity were the strongest of the three. He put Trinity at the right rear tire, himself at the left rear tire, and Brandi leaning in the buggy at the steering wheel. He explained that he and Trinity would lift, and that Brandi would steer the buggy to a sandy patch a few feet away once it was free of the rock.

"If it feels like it's getting away from you, jump in and hit the brake," said Loyal.

Brandi nodded and grasped the steering wheel with her right hand. Loyal and Trinity took their places.

"On three," said Loyal. "One, two, three."

Trinity and Loyal lifted. The buggy was heavy. He felt the buggy rise up an inch or so. They pushed it forward. The underside scraped as it slid along the rock. Brandy steered. When the buggy was past the rock gravity took over and the buggy picked up a tiny bit of speed. Brandi gave a small cry, released the steering wheel, and fell to the ground.

Loyal watched as Trinity, in one swift movement, jumped into the back of the buggy, climbed over the seats, and slid into the driver's seat. She brought the buggy to a stop moments before it would have crashed into a large boulder just past the sandy area. He then turned his attention to Brandi, who was sitting on the ground clutching her right foot and moaning. He approached her and knelt down

"What happened?" he asked.

"The buggy got away from me," she said. "The rear tire ran over my foot and ankle."

Trinity approached and knelt down as well.

"Can you move it?" she asked.

Brandi attempted the move, gasped in pain, and broke down in tears. Trinity turned to Loyal. "Get me a shirt," she said. "Your least favorite."

Loyal returned with a button down that had been given to him by his second ex wife, Angela, and handed it to Trinity.

109

BRANDI KENDRICK

B randi clutched her ankle. Tears were streaming down her cheeks, blurring the images of Loyal and Trinity, who knelt beside her.

"Do you have anything we can cut the shirt with?" Trinity asked Loyal.

Loyal pulled a pocket knife from the pouch on the driver's side and handed it to her. She made a cut in the shirt, then used her hands to tear the thin material. She handed half to Loyal.

"Put any ice we have left in here and tie it up," she said.

She turned back toward Brandi.

"I need to wrap your ankle," she said. "You are going to have to let go of it."

Brandi released her ankle and watched through tear filled eyes as Trinity wrapped her ankle in the remaining half of the shirt. Loyal returned with the ice, which Trinity placed gently on the injured limb. Brandi flinched, but didn't move away from the cold.

.   .   .

Trinity rearranged the back seat and rear storage shelf. Loyal helped Brandi up onto her left foot, and supported her as she hopped to the buggy. He lifted her into his arms, much like a groom would carry his bride, and slid her into the back seat. Trinity reached over from the driver's side of the buggy and guided her injured ankle to the soft resting spot she had created.

"It needs to remain elevated," said Trinity. "The ice will likely melt before twenty minutes passes. Keep it on there as best you can."

Brandi, no longer crying, nodded.

Loyal inspected the undercarriage of the buggy and, satisfied that no structural damage had occurred, slid into the driver's seat. Trinity slid into the passenger seat. She turned so that she could see Brandi.

"You ready?" she asked.

Brandi nodded, Loyal shifted into first, and they drove the rest of the way down the mountain.

They reached the smooth sand of the desert without further incident. Loyal told them that Maggie had noted that this section was smooth and could be transversed with speed. It appeared to Brandi that Loyal was taking Maggie at her word. He accelerated in much the same way he had on their late night drive in San Felipe. The wind, a much more active participant in the back seat, blew her hair in all directions. Brandi attempted to contain the unruly mass, but eventually gave up. She closed her eyes and let the strands fly. When she felt the buggy decelerate, she opened her eyes. Loyal had pulled to the side of the track. He and Trinity were examining the map and speaking in low tones.

. . .

"What's up?" asked Brandi.

Loyal twisted in his seat so he could see her.

"We are almost to Highway 1," he said. "We are going to be exposed while we cross it. Just deciding on the best spot to cross." He paused. "How's the ankle? You need anything?"

Brandi thought about this. There was no more beer, and no stores in sight.

"Maybe a shot from the bottle of rum?" she asked.

She watched as Loyal and Trinity exchanged a look, much the way parents would if their teenager had made this request.

"It hurts, dammit," she said. "Unless one of you has a stronger pain reliever than the paracetamol, I'd like a shot."

Trinity slid out of the buggy with an audible sigh. Brandi watched as the agent rummaged around and came up with the bottle of rum.

"I don't think we have any cups," Trinity said.

Brandi held out her hand for the bottle. "That's ok Glass," she said. "I don't need one."

110

PATRICK O'KEEFE

Pinpointing the exact location of the phone he was listening for was high on Pat's list of things to do. Mobile phones are designed to connect with the tower nearest them that provides the strongest signal. Stingray mimicked a tower, and provided a boosted signal, so phones in the suspect area would connect to it. This is how Pat was able to hear the phone calls. Stingray could also triangulate to reveal a location. One way to accomplish this was to get the International Mobile Subscriber Identity, or IMSI, from the third party carrier. This required either the third party carrier's permission or a court order. Pat had neither of these. Alternatively, he could collect all the IMSI's in a certain area, then follow the suspect out of range. As the other IMSI's dropped off, the suspects would become clear.

Neither of these options would work for Pat because he had no permission or court order, and he did not know who to follow. He had sat in the van all morning, hoping to hear from the

Chinese and Mexican again. To entertain himself, he had activated the surveillance cameras on the exterior of the van. He could watch the outside world from the comfort of his small control center. A call came in from the target number just as he was watching a black Mercedes slide to a stop at the corner of Carillo Way and Melrose. He watched in amazement as the driver, an older Asian man, lifted a phone to his ear and spoke at exactly the same time that he heard the words "Tell me you have her" on Stingray. Pat jumped to the front seat and started the van. The light turned green and the black Mercedes made a left turn onto Melrose. Pat waited for a few cars to pass, then made a u-turn onto Melrose and took off after the man.

Following was not difficult. The man turned Left on Palomar Airport Road, Right on El Camino Real, then right on Faraday. For a brief moment Pat thought he might be heading to the Sheriff's Department, but the man turned in and parked at the FedEx Ship Center. Pat cruised past the parking lot, made a u-turn, and parked across the street. He slipped in the back and watched through the cameras as the man, carrying a small box, exited his car and entered the shipping center. Six minutes passed, then the man emerged, slid into the Mercedes, and exited the parking lot. Pat returned to the driver's seat and watched as the Mercedes turned left on El Camino Real. He put the van in gear and followed.

The man followed the same route back to Melrose, then turned right on Carillo Way. Pat followed at a distance. The Mercedes took a left on Paseo Aspada. Pat continued past the small residential street. He parked a few blocks away, stepped out of the van, locked it, and pocketed the keys. He was dressed in comfortable clothes for surveillance, a T-shirt, shorts, and running shoes. He put on a pair of sunglasses and started jogging towards Paseo Aspada. The houses were large. The ones on the right side of the street backed up to a greenbelt. Pat counted the houses as he passed them. The last one on the right, number ten, had a black Mercedes parked in the driveway. Pat memorized the house number as he passed it by.

111

TRINITY GLASS

Trinity slid back into the buggy after handing Brandi the bottle of rum. Loyal was still looking at the map.

"It looks like the highway is about fifteen miles away," he said. "After we cross it here," he pointed at the map, "we will have about twenty-five more miles until we hit the border checkpoint." He paused and looked up from the map. "I don't see any way we can avoid it."

"It is a risk," said Trinity. "The army is going to be looking for whoever ambushed their men. It is possible that they think it was me."

At that moment Trinity felt a tug on the back of her seat and turned to see Brandi's head filling the space between her seat and Loyal's.

"Do you speak Spanish Agent Glass?" she asked.

Brandi's face was close to Trinity's, her rum scented breath was warm on Trinity's face. She pushed herself back and said, "No."

Brandi smiled. "I do," she said. "You two better let me handle the checkpoint."

Trinity stiffened. "No way," she said. "Absolutely not."

"I want to get home alive as much as you do, Agent Glass," Brandi said, her face still mere inches from Trinity's. She smiled again. "Trust me."

No one spoke for a brief moment. Brandi gave a deep sigh, then lay back down in her makeshift bed in the back seat with a small thump. Trinity felt Loyal's hand on her knee. She looked over at him.

"I don't trust her Loyal," she said in a whisper.

"Yeah, I get that," said Loyal. "She's always telling me to trust her and I'm not sure that I really do." He smiled. "My mental nickname for her is Miss Trust." He squeezed Trinity's knee gently. "She did get us out of a potentially very bad situation in San Felipe though. I think we *are* going to have to trust her if things start going bad."

Trinity shook her head. "It goes against all my training."

"Mine too," said Loyal. "To be honest, I've never trained for a situation like this one. I've been making it up as I go along."

Trinity let out a long slow breath. "I trust you Loyal," she said at last. "If you want to play it this way, then I will."

Loyal gave her knee another quick squeeze, then removed his hand, shifted into first, and eased the buggy back onto the track.

They crossed the highway with no complications. The road was empty in both directions. Loyal simply drove the buggy across the two lane road and back out into the desert. Trinity sat in the passenger seat and attempted to calm her troubled mind. She was worried about giving Brandi any kind of control over the situation. Despite Loyal's attempts at reassurance, Trinity did not trust the woman. She was sure Brandi would throw them under the bus to save her own skin. She wished now that she had learned Spanish. When her brother had been stationed in Germany she had made a half hearted attempt to learn German, but she spoke no other languages. When her job took her to foreign lands she always had another agent that spoke the language to translate for her. Her other thought, she hated to admit, was that she was angry that Loyal had a "mental nickname" for Brandi. She knew that he was trying to be clever by calling her Miss Trust, but it rankled. She recognized the emotion for what it was; jealousy. She didn't like the feeling. She had told Loyal that she trusted him, and she meant it, but she didn't like thinking about the days that he had spent alone with Brandi.

112

LOYAL TRUESDALE

L oyal could feel the tension radiating off of Trinity. He watched her out of the corner of his eye. She was looking at the road in front of them, but he could tell her focus was inside. He supposed she was trying to convince herself to trust Brandi. He doubted she would have much success. He wondered if it had been a mistake to tell her the nickname. He had seen the brief flash in her eyes when he had said it. He cared very deeply for Trinity, and believed she felt the same. In truth, however, they really didn't know each other that well. He hoped he hadn't made a mistake.

The track they were following headed North, then looped West and rejoined Highway 1 less than a mile from the checkpoint. Loyal steered the buggy through the long lazy curve, then bumped back onto the highway. He could see the checkpoint up ahead. Orange cones led up to a structure that spanned the road and provided shade for the men manning the checkpoint. A white building sat to the right of the structure. As they got nearer Loyal could see tall antennas sprouting behind the building. Several armed men stood beneath the structure over the road. Loyal took a deep breath, let it out slowly, and drove up to the orange cones.

When they saw the buggy, the previously inactive men became very active. Four of them surrounded the buggy, M16's raised in front of them and ready to fire. All of them spoke at once, issuing orders in Spanish. Loyal could not understand what they said, but the guns spoke volumes. He raised his hands slowly, holding them above the steering wheel. He saw that Trinity, her face grim, had done the same. He glanced in the rearview mirror and saw that Brandi, too, had her hands in the air. He was surprised to see that she was smiling. It was at that moment that she began to speak. One of the men held up his hand. He appeared to be in charge, as the other three stopped speaking when they saw his hand. He was older than the others, possibly in his mid-thirties compared to their early twenties. He approached Brandi and rattled off something that sounded like questions to Loyal. When Brandi responded Loyal had to admit that her absolute confidence was encouraging. She spoke to the man as if they were equals. Loyal watched the entire exchange in the rearview mirror. He understood only a few words, San Felipe, Mulege, and General Javier Salvador Zepeda.

The man quieted at the mention of the General's name. He stood still for a long moment, clearly making a decision of sorts. Finally he turned to the other three men and said something. Two remained where they were, guns trained on Trinity and Loyal. The third came around to the back of the buggy and helped Brandi out. Loyal swiveled his head and looked at her with questions in his eyes.

"Everything is going to be fine," she said with a wink. "Trust me."

113

BRANDI KENDRICK

B randi leaned on the arm of the man that had helped her out of the buggy and hopped toward the white building. She had known that the General's name would carry some weight, but hadn't been sure how much. She was pleasantly surprised to see that it appeared to carry quite a bit. They entered the small white building. It was comprised of two rooms, the outer area and a small office in the back. Another door to her left was slightly ajar and she saw that it was a restroom. She was led into the office and helped into a chair. The man in charge, he had identified himself as Captain Peralta, sat behind the desk. He fiddled with some knobs on a black box, then lifted what appeared to be a square microphone to his mouth.

"Este es el punto de control Guerrero. Nosotros estamos llamando General Zepeda." He said. He repeated this several times, then sat back and waited. It took several minutes, but then the radio crackled to life. Brandi listened as Peralta requested to speak to General Zepeda. Another minute passed, then she heard the General's familiar voice. Peralta explained

the situation, and that Brandi had requested to speak to the
General. The General agreed and Peralta handed the microphone to Brandi.

The General remembered Brandi, as she was sure that he
would. She explained to him that the Sinaloa were after her.
She expressed her fear and asked for his protection. When he
pushed her for information and a reason why he should help
her she told him she had information about the incident in
Mulege for him, but that she didn't feel safe stating it over the
radio. She explained that she and her companions needed to
get to Ensenada. Could he meet her there, she asked, so that
they could speak face to face? The General agreed to provide an
army escort for them as they traveled to Ensenada. He agreed
to meet her there, but warned her that her information had
better be compelling, or things would take a turn for the worse
for her and her companions. Brandi assured him that she
understood.

Captain Peralta took the microphone from Brandi and spoke
with the General briefly. She could hear the entire conversation
and understood that, while they were getting an army escort to
Ensenada, they were by no stretch of the imagination out of
trouble. The younger man appeared at her side, helped her to
her feet, and provided balance as she hopped back out to the
buggy. Loyal and Trinity were in the exact position that she had
left them in, sitting in their seats with their arms raised. Brandi
was helped back into the buggy. Captain Peralta approached
the buggy and spoke with her briefly, then told the men with

the guns aimed at Loyal and Trinity to lower their weapons. He pointed to a dirt patch just past the office.

"He wants you to park there," Brandi said. "You need to give him the keys Loyal. Don't worry. You will get them back." Loyal steered the buggy to the dirt patch, cut the engine, and handed over the keys. Captain Peralta pocketed them and walked away. Two young men remained with the buggy, the other followed the Captain.

Loyal swiveled to look at Brandi. "What's going on?" he asked.

"I've got us an armed escort to Ensenada," she said. "I asked to speak with the General from San Felipe. He remembered me and agreed to help."

"In exchange for what?" asked Trinity, who had turned backwards in her seat so that she could see Brandi.

"He wants information about what happened in Mulege," she said. She looked at Loyal. "I told Coco about him. He works with the Jalisco and against the Sinaloa. He'll be interested to know who ambushed his men in Mulege."

114

TRINITY GLASS

Trinity hated to do it, but she grudgingly admitted to herself that Brandi had handled the situation very well. They were safe for the moment. She wasn't sure what would happen in Ensenada. She didn't think they had enough information to satisfy the General, but at least Brandi had bought them some time. Before she turned to face forward again she told Brandi that she had done a good job and thanked her. The smile that lit up Brandi's face at these words seemed genuine. Trinity found herself smiling back at her. She turned and faced forward again.

The two guards stood, unsmiling, one on each side of the buggy. They held their weapons loosely at their sides. After a few minutes Brandi started talking to the men in Spanish. She kept up an endless stream of conversation. At first the two guards ignored her, standing still with straight faces. After a while, Trinity noticed the corners of their mouths twitching. Eventually both were smiling and talking with Brandi.

Watching this brought back memories for Trinity. Several years ago, she had attended a day long seminar in Virginia. The topic was social engineering, or more accurately in Trinity's mind, manipulation of people to exact a desired objective. She saw now that Brandi was a natural. Although Trinity had no idea what they were saying, the two men were clearly responding to Brandi. Trinity wondered how much she had been manipulated by Brandi in the last twenty four or so hours, and how much Loyal had been in the last five days.

They remained in the buggy for what Trinity guessed to be a little over an hour. Neither she nor Loyal spoke, each lost in their own thoughts. The sound of engines brought Trinity back to reality. She turned to look behind them and saw two armored vehicles approaching the checkpoint. Captain Peralta came out of the office and spoke to both drivers. He walked over to the buggy and handed Loyal the keys. He spoke briefly to Brandi, then walked away.

"That's our escort," said Brandi. "One will be in front of us, and one behind us. The Captain said to stay between them." She paused, then added, "Technically we are still being detained. He warned us not to try anything stupid."

Loyal nodded, then started the buggy. One armored vehicle pulled up on the road just ahead of them. Loyal pulled out of the dirt patch and slid in behind him. In his rearview mirror he saw the second vehicle pull in behind them. He glanced at Trinity. She was facing forward, but must have felt his eyes on her because she turned toward him. She gave him a small smile, which he returned. The armored vehicle in front of them moved forward. Loyal let his gaze remain on Trinity for a moment, then faced forward and drove.

115

PATRICK O'KEEFE

P at jogged back to the van, slid in, and wrote the address on a slip of paper. He listened to a call that had been recorded by Stingray. It seemed that Loyal, Trinity, and Brandi had somehow secured an army escort along the highway. The Chinese man was furious. The Mexican had explained that a General Zepeda had ordered the escort, and that he was affiliated with the Jalisco. The Chinese man had known who Zepeda was, and said that the General had hurt their organization one too many times. He had ordered the General's death as well.

Pat drove back to the Sheriff's Station, climbed the stairs to his office, and sat in front of his computer. He accessed the public records available on the address on Paseo Aspada. It was owned by a corporation, Complete Geometrics. Pat had never heard of this company and began to research. It didn't take long to discover that it was a Chinese pharmaceutical firm. Pat leaned back in his seat and thought about this. It surely was not a coincidence that the Chinese Nationals appeared to be staying at a home owned by a Chinese company. On a whim he dialed Agent Glass' cell phone. It went straight to voicemail.

116

TRINITY GLASS

T he drive was long and hot. The desert landscape was barren. Trinity saw no plant life at all. She felt as though she was on the moon. The driver of the vehicle in front of them pulled over every three hours or so to let them stretch or find a spot to use the bathroom. He spoke only to give instructions, which Brandi translated. The sun had worked its way across the sky and dipped into the Pacific long before they arrived in Ensenada. The highway went right through the middle of the town. Trinity had no idea where they would be spending the night and was holding out hope it would not be the local jail.

The lead vehicle pulled off the highway and into what looked, to Trinity, like a small community of houses. She saw the sign just as they turned. *Quintas Papagayo Hotel by the Sea.* The driver in front parked near a sign that said *Office,* exited his vehicle, and pointed, indicating that Loyal should park in the space next to him. The rear vehicle parked on the other side of the buggy. The soldiers stepped out of the vehicles and stood near the buggy. The driver of the lead vehicle, who appeared to be in charge, went into the office. Trinity looked at the faces of the soldiers watching over them. It was dark, but the moon provided enough illumination for her to make out their features. They seemed so young. The soldier returned from the office and spoke briefly to his men. Brandi leaned forward and spoke quietly.

"This place is called Papagayo's," she said. "We will be staying in a house at the back of the compound."

The soldiers re-entered their vehicles. The leader led the small caravan down a dirt road and parked in front of a small house. Loyal pulled in beside him, the rear vehicle parked in a parallel fashion, blocking the first two vehicles in.

117

BRANDI KENDRICK

Loyal helped Brandi out of the buggy and allowed her to lean on him as she hopped to the entrance of the house. Once inside, he led her to a couch in the living room and helped her sit down. Trinity brought up the rear carrying Brandi's suitcase and Loyal's duffel. The black backpack was still strapped across Brandi's chest.

She relaxed into the couch and looked around the house. The living room had windows that faced the Pacific Ocean. The water was dark. From her position Brandi could see the kitchen in front of her, a table and chairs slightly to her left, and a hallway beyond them. The living room contained the couch she was sitting on, two armchairs with their backs to the ocean opposite her, and a coffee table in between. Loyal settled into one armchair, Trinity sat in the other. Brandi saw her squirm a bit and reach into one of her cargo pockets. Trinity pulled out a phone, pushed a few buttons, then scowled. The soldier in charge walked through the entire house. Brandi supposed he was making sure no one else was on the premises. The remaining soldiers stayed in the living room, standing, ever present MI6's hanging loosely by their sides.

When the lead soldier returned to the living room, Brandi started talking. In Spanish, she told him that she had been hurt, her ankle and foot run over by the buggy. She asked if they could they take her to a pharmacy for some pain meds, and possibly some crutches. After a brief discussion, he agreed to send two of his men to escort the buggy to the pharmacy. Loyal would drive, Trinity would remain at the house. Brandi explained everything to Loyal and Trinity. Neither seemed happy about the situation.

"At least see if they have a phone charger there for an iPhone," said Trinity. "I forgot about mine. It must have been searching for service during our entire drive." Loyal helped Brandi back out to the buggy and into the front passenger seat. He slid into the driver's seat and waited as the armored vehicle moved out of their way. Brandi watched silently as he backed the buggy out of the driveway and followed the soldiers back onto the highway.

118

LOYAL TRUESDALE

L oyal was not happy about leaving Trinity with the two soldiers. He supposed, after seeing her in action in Mulege, that she could handle herself if either of them decided to try something. He followed the armored vehicle back onto the highway. The drive took them South, back to the more densely populated parts of Ensenada. The air was cooler now that they were driving along the Pacific Ocean. After the heat of the desert, Loyal savored the fresh, salty air. The soldiers turned left on Alvarado and drove five blocks. They parked on the street in front of a building with a neon sign jutting out from the roof. It said *Pharmacy American*. An A frame sign on the sidewalk listed some of the items that were available inside.

- **Painkillers**
- **Muscle Relaxers**
- **Diet Pills**
- **Sleeping Pills**

- **Antibiotics**
- **Viagra 100mg**
- **Cialis 20mg**
- **Levitra 20 mg**

Loyal couldn't help but smile. He had heard about the ability to acquire prescription medication without a doctor's prescription in Mexico. This proved that it was true. He slid out of the buggy and crossed behind the rear of the vehicle to the passenger side. He helped Brandi out. One soldier remained with the cars, the other went into the small building with them.

The pharmacy was small and very like pharmacies Loyal had been to in America. There were rows of shelves piled with merchandise. A long counter took up much of the back wall. An analog clock hanging on the back wall informed him that it was just past 8:00 pm. He helped Brandi to the counter, then left to look for a charger for Trinity. The soldier remained at the entrance to the shop. Surprisingly, Loyal found some chargers hanging on peg board on a wall. He found one that would work for Trinity's phone, then walked back to the counter. Brandi was deep in conversation with the pharmacist. Loyal approached, placed the charger on the counter, then stepped back to give her some privacy. There was no sense in eavesdropping, he couldn't understand anything they were saying anyway. After a minute or so, the pharmacist went into the back of the store. When he returned he had a pair of used crutches in his hands. Brandi nodded and clapped her hands. She turned to Loyal.

"Can I have some money please?" she asked.

Loyal reached into his pocket, withdrew some cash, and stepped back to the counter. In addition to the charger and the crutches, there was one small pill bottle and another bottle, containing a dark liquid, on the counter. Loyal hoped she had gotten something that would put her to sleep for a while.

119

TRINITY GLASS

T rinity sat on the couch while Loyal and Brandi went to the pharmacy. She did not try to engage the soldiers in any type of conversation and they did her the same courtesy. She spent the time trying to come up with a plan. They had no valuable information for the General. She supposed he was going to be quite angry about that and wasn't sure that Brandi's skills at manipulation were going to be refined enough to get them released and back to the United States. Her one hope was that Loyal would return with a charger. Once her phone was useable again she would find a way to place a call to Caldwell. Beyond that, she had no plan.

She supposed about 30 minutes had passed when she heard the buggy pulling into the driveway. Her armchair faced the entryway. Loyal was the first person through the door. She was pleased to see that he was carrying a charger in his hand. Next came Brandi, on a pair of crutches and moving without help. Last came the two soldiers. Loyal had just handed her the charger when a cell phone rang. Trinity turned her head to see the soldier in charge pulling a phone out of his pocket and raising it to his ear. He spoke briefly, disconnected, and turned to Brandi who was sitting on the couch again. He spoke to her, then she turned to Loyal and Trinity.

"General Zepeda will be here in 90 minutes," she said. "He wants to talk to us right away."

"Ask him if I can charge my phone," said Trinity.

Brandi spoke to him, then nodded.

"He says to plug it in in the kitchen where he can see it."

Trinity rose from the couch, crossed to the kitchen, and plugged in her phone. A small battery icon appeared on the screen. Trinity knew from experience that it would take fifteen to twenty minutes before the phone was useable. She set it on the counter and returned to her chair. Across from her Brandi was holding two bottles in her hands. One was a pill bottle, the other held a liquid. Brandi was studying the labels. She looked up and said, "These are going to make me tired. I'll wait until after we meet with the General to take anything."

With nothing to do but wait, the soldiers sat at the table and talked quietly amongst themselves. When Trinity thought that enough time had passed she stood and went back to her phone. The charge indicated 36 percent. She pressed the power button and watched as the phone came back to life. She noted a missed call from Detective O'Keefe and was just about to bypass that notification in favor of calling Caldwell when her phone rang. It was O'Keefe, calling again. She looked at the soldier in charge and held up her phone with a question in her eyes. He hesitated, then nodded his assent. Trinity tapped accept.

"Glass," she said.

"Thank God you are alright," said Pat. "Where are you?"

"Ensenada."

"I've heard some conversations," said Pat. "The Chinese are doubling down. The only person they want alive is Brandi Kendrick. Everyone else is expendable. They are furious with the General who gave you the escort. Zepeda? They have ordered a hit on him as well."

"Understood," said Trinity. "I'm going to call my boss and see if he can pull any international strings to get us out of here."

She paused, then added, "This phone is our only source of communication."

"Copy," said Pat, and they disconnected.

120

BRANDI KENDRICK

Brandi listened to Trinity's side of the conversation, which didn't tell her much. She watched the face of the lead soldier. He was scowling.

"I don't think you should make any calls," Brandi said.

Trinity turned to look at her.

"It's not a good idea right now," Brandi said, then glanced at the soldiers. Trinity appeared to get the message because she simply set the phone back on the counter and walked back to sit in the armchair. They sat in silence, each lost in their own thoughts. Eventually the silence was interrupted by the ringing of the soldier's phone. He answered, then stood and walked to the front door. Moments later headlights flashed briefly into the entryway. The soldier stood straighter, then saluted as General Zepeda walked in.

Brandi fluffed her hair and sat up straighter. She watched as the General's dark eyes scanned the room. His gaze paused on Loyal, then Trinity, then Brandi, where it remained for a moment before settling on Trinity. He strode across the room and stood in front of her. He spoke to her in rapid Spanish. Brandi spoke up, telling the General that Trinity did not speak Spanish. The General glanced at Brandi, then turned back to Trinity.

"I want to know everything that happened at the airport in Mulege," He said in fairly good English.

"Your men were ambushed by the Sinaloa," Trinity said. "I managed to take out three of the four. One got away."

"What did the Sinaloa want?"

"Her." Trinity pointed at Brandi. "But they want you now too."

"What?" said the General.

"I just spoke to a contact in law enforcement in the US," Trinity said. "They are listening to conversations between someone with the Sinaloa and some Chinese Nationals. They know you helped us get this far and they did not appreciate it. The Chinese have ordered the Sinaloa to kill you."

General Zepeda was quiet for a moment.

"The pilot who left you on Mulege landed in Ensenada and was detained," he said. "I will send word to have him released to you tomorrow. He is in the Penitenciaria."

Before Trinity had a chance to respond to that news, General Zepeda turned away from her. He walked to Brandi and stood looking down at her. He reached his hand out and caressed her cheek. It took all her willpower not to flinch at his touch.

"I have no time to spend with you," he said. "You can be sure that if you come back to Mexico again, I will find you."

He spoke gently, but Brandi heard the threat behind the words. As long as General Zepeda was around, Mexico would be off limits for her. The General's fingers lingered on her cheek another moment, then he straightened and turned to his men. He spoke to them in Spanish, telling them that they were leaving the city immediately. There was a brief flurry of activity as they gathered their things and exited the house. Brandi flinched at the sound as their vehicles roared to life, then squinted as their headlights flooded the room. As quickly as the lights appeared, they vanished. Silence filled the room.

121

TRINITY GLASS

A s soon as the vehicles were gone, Trinity jumped up and crossed the room to her phone. She tapped Caldwell's contact information and raised the phone to her ear. He answered on the first ring.

"Glass," he said, "where are you?"

"Ensenada," she said. "I think Rodger is in jail here."

"He is," said Caldwell. "I'm working on getting him out."

"It is my understanding that he will be released tomorrow morning," said Trinity. "We need that King Air Doug."

"I'll make sure you are cleared to fly," Caldwell said. "What the hell is going on down there Glass?"

Trinity took about ten minutes to fill Caldwell in. She gave him O'Keefe's number and suggested that he call the detective.

"Stay in that house the rest of the night," Caldwell said. "Pick up Rodger in the morning, then get the hell out of Mexico. I'll make sure security is on hand at Brown Field when you land. I'm leaving for San Diego first thing in the morning.

Keep an eye on that Kendrick woman, Glass. I want to talk to her."

Trinity agreed, disconnected, then turned to face Loyal and Brandi.

"He says to sit tight tonight," she said. "We can get Rodger out of jail in the morning. My boss is going to make sure the plane is released to us and that we are cleared to fly." Her eyes met Loyal's and she smiled. "We are going home."

"Let's celebrate," said Brandi. "I've got enough rum left for each of us to do a healthy shot." Brandi looked at Loyal.

"Get it out of the buggy?" she asked. "I'll find some glasses in the kitchen."

Trinity watched as Brandi crutched awkwardly across the room and into the kitchen. She opened a cabinet, pulled out three glasses, and set them on the counter. Loyal returned with the rum and a handful of granola bars. He set the rum on the kitchen counter and carried two granola bars across the room to Trinity. She turned as he approached so that she was facing the window. He put his arm around her and she leaned into him. It was late enough that the moon was high in the sky. Its light reflected off the dark Pacific, the motion of the waves barely visible in the glow. The view was mesmerizing. They ate their granola bars and Trinity felt the energy drain from her body, replaced by a blanket of fatigue.

"Ready," said Brandi.

She and Loyal turned to see three glasses, half full of amber liquid, sitting on the counter. Brandi slid two in their general direction, then picked up the third. Loyal looked at Trinity.

"Why not?" he said.

Trinity nodded and they crossed the room together. They each lifted a glass.

"A toast," said Brandi, holding her glass in the air. "To my heroes."

Trinity and Loyal raised their glasses. All three met with a gentle clink. Trinity swallowed the rum in two large gulps. The sting of the alcohol brought tears to her eyes.

"To us," she said.

122

LOYAL TRUESDALE

Loyal's dream was causing him pain. A monster, or more accurately a massive ogre, was squeezing his head. The creature stood in front of Loyal, facing him, and had its huge hands wrapped around Loyal's head. The pain was excruciating. Loyal merged from sleep to awareness in a strange way. He realized he was awake, but wasn't cognizant of the moment that the transition had occurred. The dream was over, but the ogre still squeezed. He had a headache of massive proportions. Loyal opened his eyes and took stock of his situation. He was sitting on the couch in the house at Papagayos. The curtains were open and he could see the sparkling Pacific out the window. He became aware of a pressure on his shoulder and turned to see that Trinity sat next to him. She was still asleep. Her head rested gently on his shoulder.

Loyal eased her head up, swiveled so that his knees were on the ground, then eased her head down to the cushion where he had been sitting. He picked up her legs and placed them on the couch as well, so that she was laying on the cushions. He stood and the ogre squeezed again. Loyal faltered as a wave of dizziness and pain coursed through his brain. He leaned forward, placing his hands on his thighs, and struggled to find equilibrium. When he felt he could handle it, he straightened slowly, one vertebrae at a time. Eventually he stood completely upright. He shuffled to the bathroom, relieved himself, then turned to face the mirror. His hair was mussed and his face was pale. He had slept with his mouth open, his tongue felt sticky and dry. He must have drooled as he slept. A single dry line tracked down his chin. It reminded him of the track they had followed through the desert, one solitary line against the expanse of his skin. He turned on the faucet, cupped some water in his hands, and splashed it on his face. He wanted to wash his mouth out, but was fearful of putting Ensenada's water in his mouth and getting Montezuma's revenge. He ran his wet hands through his hair, then used the hand towel to wipe his face.

Loyal knew that Trinity was on the couch, but he hadn't seen Brandi. There were two bedrooms at the end of the hall. He assumed she was sleeping in one of those. He exited the bathroom and walked down the hall. Both bedroom doors were closed. He tried the door to his left first, easing it open and peeking inside. The curtains were open, allowing light into the room. A king sized bed dominated. It was pristine, not a wrinkle or dent, and clearly had not been slept in. Loyal closed the door and turned to the one across the hall. He turned the knob quietly and leaned his head in. The curtains in this room were closed and it was very dark. Loyal found the light switch and turned it on. This room, too, was empty and appeared to have not been used.

. . .

Loyal closed the door and walked back down the hallway. As he entered the kitchen, intending to look in the fridge for a bottle of water, he saw Brandi's crutches leaning against the counter. Both medication bottles and a small stack of twenty dollar bills were placed on the counter just beyond the crutches. Loyal stopped his forward motion. The ogre was still crushing his head and he was finding it hard to think. Something was wrong with what he was seeing. It took a moment for him to realize that it was the money. He had held on to all the cash the entire trip, doling it out to Brandi when she needed something. He reached his hand into his right pant's pocket. It was empty.

"No," Loyal said.

He walked to the front door and opened it. The driveway was empty. His buggy, and Brandi, were gone.

123

TRINITY GLASS

Gentle pressure on her shoulder brought Trinity out of a dreamless sleep. She opened her eyes, winced at the pain in her head, and quickly shut them again. She counted to ten, then opened them again. She found herself looking directly into Loyal's brown eyes.

"Hey," he said.

"My head," said Trinity. "The pain. What happened?"

"Brandi and the buggy are gone," said Loyal.

Trinity maneuvered herself into a sitting position, wincing as another flash of pain flowed through her head. Loyal, who had been kneeling, stood, then sat down beside her.

"I'm pretty sure she drugged us," he said. "I'm sorry Trinity, I knew she was a liar, but I never figured her for something like this."

Trinity leaned against him for a moment, then stood.

"She fooled me too, Loyal."

. . .

Trinity walked to the bathroom, relieved herself, and washed her face. When she walked back down the hall she found Loyal in the kitchen, leaning against the counter. He was holding the liquid medication bottle in his hand, studying the label.

"What is that?" Trinity asked as she moved to stand next him.

"Liquid Oxycodone," said Loyal. "The pills are Vicodin. There is one pill missing, she probably actually took that." He held up the liquid bottle. "There is a bunch missing from this," he said. "I think she put it in the shots."

Trinity took the bottle from Loyal's hand, read the label, and studied the remaining contents. With a sigh she set it back on the counter. She turned to Loyal. "I guess we better make a new plan," she said.

Just as Loyal was opening his mouth to say something, her phone, which was sitting on the kitchen counter, rang. Trinity picked it up and checked the caller ID. "Rodger," she said to Loyal as she tapped accept.

"Rodger," she said.

"I'm out of jail," he said. "Caldwell said you were in Ensenada."

"We are," said Trinity.

"Well, when they took me in they took all my belongings," said Rodger. "I got everything back but my money."

"We'll come get you," said Trinity.

She put the phone on speaker, then accessed Google maps.

"It looks like we are about twenty five minutes away. We'll get there as fast as we can."

"I'm on a stone wall by the parking lot," he said. He disconnected before Trinity had a chance to reply.

. . .

"He's pissed," said Trinity. "We need to go get him."

Loyal nodded. "We can go to the office and have them call us a taxi."

He picked up the bottles of medication.

"What do you want to do with these?"

"Trash them," said Trinity.

She watched as Loyal dumped the bottles in the trash. He gathered his duffel and together they walked to the door. The air outside was fresh and tinged with salt. Trinity breathed in deeply, savoring the scent. They walked to the office, asked the young man behind the desk to call them a taxi, then went outside and sat on a bench to wait. Several minutes passed, then a bright yellow van slid into the parking area and squealed to a stop. A young man, Trinity wondered if he was even sixteen, slid out of the driver's seat and came around to open the sliding door for them. Loyal threw his duffel in and slid across the bench seat.

Trinity slid in beside him, then turned to the driver and said,"Penitenciaria Ensenada." The young man nodded and slammed the door shut.

The drive to the jail, or more accurately the prison, took them through the middle of town. Traffic was heavy. The driver moved in and out of lanes, honking and swerving around other vehicles and pedestrians. Trinity held onto the door handle tightly. She supposed the kid wanted to avoid an accident even more than she did. After all, this was his livelihood. Rather than commenting on his driving, she kept her mouth closed and simply held on. She glanced at Loyal. He was very pale and beads of sweat were glistening on his forehead. She wondered if he was going to be sick. She reached out and took his hand. He turned to look at her for a moment, squeezed her hand, then faced forward again.

124

LOYAL TRUESDALE

The Penitenciaria Ensenada was located on the Eastern edge of the town. High stone walls surrounded the perimeter. Guard towers, strategically placed, rose above the wall. The driver entered the parking lot and Loyal saw Rodger right away. He had never met the pilot, but there was only one man sitting on the stone wall. Loyal leaned forward, tapped the driver on his shoulder, and pointed at Rodger when the young man swiveled his head in response to the tap. He nodded, and steered the van to the wall. Trinity opened the sliding door and slid out. She waved at Rodger, who stood and walked to the van. He slid in the front passenger seat and said, "Ensenada Airport," to the driver. He turned and looked into the back seat. "You must be Truesdale," he said to Loyal. Without waiting for a response he turned to Trinity who was back in the backseat

"Where's Kendrick?" he said.

"Gone," said Trinity.

He looked back at Loyal. "Rodger Stuart," he said. Then he faced front again.

. . .

The airport was on the Western edge of the city. Loyal gritted his teeth and endured another hair raising trip across town. In addition to providing general aviation services, the airport was an official port of entry into Mexico and also functioned as a military airbase. Rodger directed the driver to the military facilities offices. When he had parked, the driver slid out and ran around the van to open the doors. Loyal followed Trinity out of the van. He paid the driver, then turned to Rodger.

"What now?" he asked.

"You have any money left?" Rodger asked. "I'm probably going to have to pay some "fees"." He used his fingers to put quotations around the word fees. Loyal held out the rest of his cash.

"This is everything I have," he said.

Rodger counted the four remaining twenties, then shrugged. "I guess this will have to do. You guys wait here." With that he turned and entered the office building. Loyal supposed that half an hour had passed when Rodger exited the building and rejoined them.

"Someone must have greased the wheels," he said. "That was a lot easier than I expected." He turned to Loyal. "They still took all of your money."

Less than an hour later Rodger was in the pilot's seat of the King Air, Trinity and Loyal were in the cabin, and the plane was accelerating down the runway. The takeoff was to the West, straight out over the ocean. Loyal looked out his window as Rodger banked and turned North. Loyal was on the right side of the plane so when he looked down he saw the Pacific and the city of Ensenada beyond. The sun was bright in the sky and reflected off the water, shimmering and dancing on the waves. Loyal turned and saw that Trinity was looking out her window as well. Her view was pure blue sky. He reached his hand over and placed it on hers. She turned to him.

"We are going home," he said.

She nodded.

"I'm going to find her, Loyal," she said.

He nodded. "If anyone can, it's you," he said.

Trinity faced forward, leaned her head back, and closed her eyes. Loyal did the same. He did not let go of her hand.

125

TRINITY GLASS

The jolt of the King Air's wheels hitting the runway woke Trinity. She opened her eyes and looked at Loyal. He looked as if he was just waking up as well. She looked down at her hand and saw that he was still holding it. She gave his hand a little squeeze, then released it. They sat in a comfortable silence as Rodger taxied off the runway and parked in front of customs. He shut the engine off and entered the cabin.

"You are not on the manifest," he said to Loyal. "That might give us some trouble. Follow my lead, okay?"

Loyal nodded. Rodger opened the door and actuated the stairs. As she was waiting for them to descend completely Trinity saw Caldwell approaching the plane. Two men and a woman walked behind him. Trinity felt a wave of relief crash over her. She hadn't known whether he would be able to make it to San Diego in time to meet them. Her faith in him was absolute. He was here, and they would be fine.

. . .

The two men walking behind Caldwell were Customs officials. They had questions and spent some time with Rodger and Caldwell getting those questions answered. Trinity and Loyal waited in the King Air. The woman waited at the base of the stairs. She did not speak to them. Eventually Caldwell and Rodger returned.

"You three," Caldwell pointed at Trinity, Loyal, and Rodger, "are going to ride with me. This is Julia Reynolds." He indicated the woman. "She is going to fly the King Air back to Western Flight."

"Where are we going?" asked Trinity.

"DHS," said Caldwell, "you need to be debriefed."

The drive from Brown Field to DHS took just under a half hour. Caldwell drove the black Suburban, Rodger sat in the front seat, Loyal and Trinity in the rear. Caldwell called ahead and there was a young woman waiting in front of the building. Caldwell pulled over and slid out of the driver's side. He left the door open and the young woman slid in to take his place. Rodger, Trinity, and Loyal slid out of their seats, closed the doors, and watched as she drove the car away.

"Parking is tough around here," said Caldwell. "She'll find a spot." He pointed at the front door of the building.

"Let's go," he said.

They were escorted to the third floor of the building. Caldwell took Rodger into an office and closed the door. Trinity and Loyal were placed in separate offices and told to wait. Trinity was well aware that this long day was far from over.

After what felt like an eternity, but was likely less than an hour, the door to the room Trinity was in opened and Caldwell walked in. He sat in a chair opposite her and leaned forward, his forearms on his thighs.

"Tell me everything Glass," he said. "Start from the very beginning."

Trinity did just that. She started with her initial visit to DHS, the boat in the Oceanside Harbor, her discovery of the list, and the trips to Tahoe and Hales Grove. She explained Loyal's connection, described the trip across Mexico in the buggy, and detailed the circumstances of Brandi Kendrick's escape. She told him about Detective O'Keefe and the conversations he had captured using Stingray. She explained the connection between the Chinese Nationals and the Sinaloa Cartel. And, lastly, she told him about the cryptocurrency wallets in Brandi Kendrick's backpack.

PATRICK O'KEEFE

P at often ate lunch in his office. Olive always packed him something. The house they were renting was small and they were hoping to buy a home of their own within the next year. Buying lunch every day was not in their budget. Pat didn't mind. Olive's lunches were far better than any fast food he could find near the Sheriff's Station. He had worked through his regular lunch hour. It was just past 4:00 when he popped the last bite of a BLT on sourdough into his mouth. Just as he began to chew Captain Williams stepped into his office. Pat continued to chew, and then swallowed as quickly as he could.

"Agent Glass and Truesdale are safely back in the U.S.," the Captain said. "I don't have any details. I received a call from Agent Glass' boss, Director Caldwell. He wants to see us today at DHS in San Diego."

Pat nodded. He logged off his computer, stood, and plucked some keys off of a hook. He looked at the Captain and said, "I think we should take the van."

LOYAL TRUESDALE

Loyal's debrief with Caldwell lasted just under an hour. He found the man to be intelligent, competent, and confident. He told Caldwell everything. While he was waiting alone in the office, Loyal had considered what he should tell and what he should keep under wraps. The more he thought about it, the more he realized he should just tell everything. Holding things back was a habit from his days on the force. It was no longer necessary. When he had told the entirety of his knowledge, Caldwell stood, shook his hand, and offered to have someone drive him home.

"Has Agent Glass left yet?" Loyal asked.

"I don't think so," said Caldwell.

"I'll ride with her," said Loyal.

He met up with Trinity in the lobby of DHS. The same young woman who had parked Caldwell's Suburban drove them back to Carlsbad. Trinity asked that they be dropped at Western

Flight. It was nearly 6:00. The sun was still up, but had started its nightly descent towards the ocean. Loyal and Trinity walked to her car and slid in. Before she started the vehicle, she turned to him and said, "Caldwell wants me back here at 6:30 tomorrow morning. We are going to Hales Grove for my debriefing and to get my gun back, then straight to Quantico."

"On Saturday?" Loyal asked.

"Weekends are just the same as weekdays to him," she said. "We've got a lot in play now. We need to keep our forward momentum."

Loyal nodded his understanding. He placed his hand on her thigh.

"Let's get your stuff and stay at my place tonight," he said.

She smiled and nodded, then started the car and exited the parking lot.

The moment they walked into the condo Trinity declared that she was starving and needed food at that exact moment. Loyal agreed. It had been nearly twenty four hours since either of them had eaten. He sat at the table while Trinity heated a can of soup and grilled two cheese sandwiches. She joined him at the table when their impromptu meal was ready. They ate quickly and in silence. When she was finished, Trinity leaned back in her chair with a satisfied sigh.

"Better," she said.

Loyal nodded his agreement.

"I'll wash the dishes," he said. "You get your stuff together and let's get out of here."

By the time he had washed and dried the dishes and replaced them in the cabinet, Trinity was ready to go. He helped her carry her things to the car, then slid into the passenger seat. She slid into the driver's seat and headed towards the freeway.

128

PATRICK O'KEEFE

P at found a secure parking garage just over a block away from DHS. He and Captain Williams walked briskly back to the the building and entered. They identified themselves, produced ID, and waited in reception for an escort. After just a minute or two a man in his mid thirties, with close cropped black hair and wearing a dark blue suit approached them. He identified himself as Agent Zimmer and asked them to follow him. He led them to a bank of elevators, pushed the up arrow, and stepped back to let them enter before following them in. They rode to the third floor in silence. Agent Zimmer escorted them down the carpeted hallway, gave two sharp knocks on a door on the left, then opened it and stepped aside so that they could enter. Leaning in the doorway, he said, "Captain Williams and Detective O'Keefe."

Pat heard the door close behind him, but kept his eyes on the man in front of him. Director Caldwell had stood and stepped out from behind the desk that dominated the room. He approached with his right hand extended. He shook Captain Williams hand first, then Pat's.

"Gentlemen," he said. "Thank you for coming down here on such short notice." He turned and gestured towards the guest chairs in front of the desk. "Please have a seat."

Caldwell returned to his chair behind the desk and sat. Pat and the captain did the same. Caldwell folded his large hands on the desk and leaned forward a bit.

"Agent Glass suggested that I speak with you," he said. "It appears we have intersecting cases."

Captain Williams gestured at Pat.

"I think you will want to hear what Detective O'Keefe has to say."

Caldwell turned his gaze towards Pat.

"Let's hear it Detective," he said.

Pat started from the beginning. He told Caldwell about Truesdale, Kendrick, and the initial meeting with Agent Glass. He explained about the van and its incredible technology, then summarized the conversations intercepted by Stingray, and the connections between the Chinese Nationals and the Sinaloa. He included his hunch that the Chinese Nationals and the Sinaloa were pumping fentanyl into the US, but was clear that he had no admissible proof yet. He concluded with the newest information, the house on Paseo Aspada in Carlsbad.

Caldwell listened with intention; focused on Pat's every word. When Pat finally fell silent, Caldwell leaned back in his chair, folded his hands in his lap, and closed his eyes. He remained in this position for about a minute. When he opened his eyes he looked at Pat.

"Where is the van?" he asked.

"It's here," said Pat. "We drove here in it."

Caldwell picked up the phone on his desk, and asked that Agent Park, Agent Malone, and Agent Nash be sent to his office immediately. The men arrived and Caldwell summarized Pat's information, then began giving orders.

"Get a warrant for the house on Paseo Aspada," he told Park, who immediately glanced down at his watch. "Interrupt a judge's dinner to get it signed," said Caldwell. "Whatever it takes. I want that house and I want it today." He turned his attention to Nash. "You go with O'Keefe in the van." He turned to Pat. "Locate the Mexican's phone," He said. "If he's in the United States, find him and arrest him."

"Stingray is inadmi..." Pat began to speak, but Caldwell cut him off.

"I know the law, Detective," he said. "Locate him, liaise with the local police wherever you find him, and arrest him. I'll make sure you have admissible charges."

Caldwell paused for a breath then turned his attention to Captain Williams.

"Don't worry Captain," he said. "I don't want visibility here. Your department will share all the credit."

129

LOYAL TRUESDALE

When Trinity turned into the small alley behind his apartment, Loyal was shocked by what he saw. His buggy was parked in front of his garage. Trinity saw it at the same time as he did. She braked sharply and turned to him.

"How does she know where you live?" she asked.

Loyal shrugged. "The registration I suppose."

Trinity looked at the stairs to his apartment then asked, "Do you think she's up there?"

"It is possible," said Loyal. "She has my keys. It doesn't look like any lights are on. If she is up there, she's sitting in the dark."

Loyal looked at Trinity. Her hands were tight on the steering wheel, her expression full of anger.

"Maybe I should check on my own?" he suggested.

"Oh hell no," said Trinity. "If she's up there, I'm finding a reason to arrest her."

. . .

Trinity eased her car in next to the buggy. They both slid out and mounted the stairs. Loyal tried the door handle. It was locked. He asked Trinity to wait there and went to the manager's office. Tom Wilson answered the knock quickly.

"Mr. Truesdale," he said, peering at Loyal through his thick glasses. "The Detective said he had permission to go into your apartment for the evidence."

"He did," said Loyal. "I've just misplaced my keys and I was wondering if you could open my apartment for me."

Mr. Wilson disappeared into his his own apartment for a moment, returning with a set of keys. He followed Loyal to his door, his eyes widening at the sight of Trinity.

"Well, hello there," he said extending his hand. "I'm Tom Wilson."

Trinity introduced herself and shook his hand. Mr. Wilson unlocked Loyal's door and swung it open. He looked at Loyal.

"Well, there they are," he said pointing a bony finger.

Loyal looked where Wilson was pointing. Sure enough, his keys were right there, sitting smack dab in the middle of his kitchen table.

Loyal thanked Mr. Wilson, then he and Trinity entered the apartment. It was a one bedroom, small, and easy to search. Brandi was not there. Loyal and Trinity stood in the living room, looking at the keys on the table. Eventually, Loyal picked them up and hug them on a hook in the kitchen. He walked back to Trinity and pulled her in for a hug. He held her tightly for a moment, then leaned down and gave her a kiss.

"Let's shower, find a little more food, then go to bed," he said.

"How about shower, bed, then food?" she said with a smile.

Loyal smiled. Trinity's order of operations sounded much better than his.

130

PATRICK O'KEEFE

I t was just past midnight when Pat pulled into the driveway of his small rental. He turned off the headlights and cut the ignition, then sat in the dark listening to the engine clicking quietly. Caldwell was a man of action. True to his word, he had not wanted any public acknowledgment for himself or the Office of Strategic Investigations. He had worked behind the scenes, securing three warrants. The first had been for the house on Paseo Aspada. Agent Park had worked in conjunction with the Carlsbad Sheriff's Department and had successfully detained the four remaining Chinese Nationals. Last Pat had heard, none of them had said a word.

The second warrant had been for the IMSI number for the Mexican's phone. Once Pat had the identifying number, finding the Mexican's location had been fairly easy. He had been in a small house on the corner of H Street and 2nd Avenue in Chula Vista. Ironically, the Chula Vista Police Department was located on 4th Street, only two blocks away. The third warrant

Caldwell obtained was for a raid on the house on the corner of H and 2nd. Pat and Agent Nash had participated in the raid, along with the Chula Vista PD. Pat had practiced for this type of event, but never participated in one. Even now, hours later, his adrenaline was spiked and flowing through his veins.

The raid had been very successful. Not only had they captured the Mexican, Jose Gonzales, but they had confiscated over $15,000 in cash, multiple guns, and large amounts of meth-amphetamine, heroin, and fentanyl. Pat was hoping that the drugs could be connected to the overdoses North San Diego County had been experiencing. Either way, Gonzales, who turned out to be on San Diego's wanted list, would be going to prison for a very long time.

Pat rubbed his hands over his face, slid out of his car, and entered his house. He made the rounds, checking that all doors and windows were locked. He stopped by each of his children's beds, straightening their covers and kissing their warm cheeks. He worried for their, and their unborn sibling's, futures. Their was so much bad in the world. He hoped that he and Olive would be able to steer them toward the good. Pat took a quick shower, dried, and slid into bed. He wrapped his arms around his sleeping wife, cradling her swollen belly. He breathed in her scent, grateful for their love and their life. Just as he was drifting off to sleep, his hands on her belly, the baby gave a little kick. Pat couldn't help but smile.

131

TRINITY GLASS

T rinity's alarm sounded at 5:45. She had set it as late as possible in order to maximize her time with Loyal, even if they were sleeping. She silenced the alarm and leaned back into him. Her back was to his belly, his arm was wrapped loosely around her. A part of her wanted to call Caldwell and tell him she couldn't leave until Monday. She knew that would never work with her boss. And, truly, his work ethic was one of the things she so admired about the man.

She felt Loyal's arm tighten around her. He kissed the back of her neck, then turned and slid out of the bed.

"You don't want to be late," he said. "I'll make the coffee, you get ready."

Trinity sighed, turned on her back for a long stretch, then sat up and slid out of bed as well. She watched Loyal as he slid on shorts and a T-shirt and headed for the kitchen. Trinity walked to the closet and retrieved a dark gray pantsuit she had hung there the previous evening. Everything else was packed in her suitcase and ready to go.

Once she was dressed and her hair pinned up in a neat bun, she followed the scent of coffee into the kitchen. Loyal stood facing her, his back against the kitchen counter, a mug of coffee in his hand. Another mug was on the counter beside him. He lifted it and held it out to her. She crossed the room and took it from him, then leaned against the counter next to him, their shoulders touching.

"At least we got one night," said Loyal.

Trinity nodded. Loyal set his mug down and put his arm around her.

"You saved my ass, Trinity," he said. She leaned in to him.

"We make a good team," she said. She turned and looked up at him.

"I'll text you when I'm back to Quantico."

"Call me," said Loyal. "I like to hear your voice."

"It will be late," Trinity said.

Loyal pulled her closer and kissed the top of her head.

"I don't care," he said.

132

LOYAL TRUESDALE

L oyal walked Trinity down the stairs and watched her get into her car and drive away. He hated these good-byes. He walked back up the stairs and into the empty apartment. He had moved here after the divorce from Angela not really intending to stay very long. The years had passed quickly. Loyal sat down on the couch and looked around. He wanted something more, something permanent. He realized that sitting around moping wasn't going to do him any good. A glance at the clock told him he still had time to make breakfast at Lake Wohlford with Bruce and Winnie and the Meyers Manx gang. He quickly changed into a button down and nicer shorts. As he walked down the stairs to his buggy he wondered if Brandi had left any gas in it. She didn't strike him as someone who would leave a full tank. Sure enough, the tank was nearly empty. He lifted the gas cans in the back seat and found that one still had a gallon or so. He poured that into the tank, drove to the gas station and filled up, then headed East to Lake Wohlford.

. . .

Despite having spent nearly a week in the buggy, Loyal found himself enjoying the drive. It was early on a Saturday morning. The sun was out, the sky was blue, the wind was still fairly cool, and traffic was light. Loyal had kept his promise to Maggie. Her GPS had spent most of its time in Mexico in his shirt pocket. When they first arrived at Papagayos in Ensenada, he had transferred it to his duffel. It was tucked safely into his shirt pocket now. On a whim he pulled over in Northern Escondido and called Maggie. She answered on the second ring.

"Loyal, are you ok?" she asked.

"Yes," he said. "Safely back in the US. I'm actually heading to breakfast at Lake Wohlford. Are you going? I have your GPS and maps."

"I was just sliding into the buggy," said Maggie. "Let me run back inside and get your gun. I'll see you there."

Loyal pulled back onto the road and continued his drive. He pulled into Lake Wohlford's parking lot and parked. Minutes later Maggie pulled in and parked her bright yellow buggy next to his. She slid out, leaned down behind the driver's seat, then straightened and handed Loyal his belly band and gun. He strapped them on immediately. He reached into his pocket, withdrew her GPS, and handed it to her.

"Your waypoints literally saved our lives," he said. She took the small machine with a smile. Loyal leaned into his buggy, removed the maps from the side pocket, and handed them to her as well. She accepted them with a smile, turned, and stowed everything in her buggy. She straightened and looked back at Loyal.

"Brandi?" she asked.

"Rescued, then disappeared," said Loyal.

"Will you tell me the story one of these days?" asked Maggie.

"I'll tell you what happened if you tell me what happened last year in Las Vegas," said Loyal.

"I'll have to think about that," said Maggie.

"Think about it, Maggie," said Loyal with a smile. "My story is a good one."

Maggie and Loyal entered the restaurant, located the buggy club in the right hand corner, and found seats at the far end of the table. They waved hello to Bruce and Winnie and the rest of the group. Loyal noticed Verne was there, just a few seats away from him. Verne saw Loyal, stood, and approached him. He leaned down and said, "Can we talk for a minute after breakfast?" Loyal nodded. The waitress came and took everyone's orders. The food was delivered quickly. Conversation centered on the Big Bear Bash. It was hard for Loyal to believe that only one week had passed since the event.

"The next one in California is Mammoth Lakes in September," Bruce called down the table to Loyal. "You should go."

"Sounds fun," Said Loyal. "I think I will."

The group broke up quickly after breakfast. Loyal and Maggie walked to their buggies, hugged, and agreed to meet for lunch the following Tuesday. She slid in her buggy and Loyal turned to look for Verne. He was just exiting the restaurant, walking with Bruce and Winnie and laughing about something one of them had said. They said their goodbyes, then Verne crossed the parking lot to Loyal.

"Did she contact you?" Loyal asked.

Verne nodded. "I picked her up at Pizza Port," he said. "Apparently it is near your apartment."

"Where is she now?" asked Loyal.

"No idea," said Verne. "I dropped her in San Diego at the airport. She's long gone by now."

They stood in silence for a moment.

"Did she tell you what happened?" Loyal finally said.

"Her version of it," said Verne. "I've known Brandi long enough to know I rarely get the full story."

"Yeah, I figured that out," said Loyal, "but not soon enough."

Verne reached into the pocket of the windbreaker he was wearing and pulled out a small padded manilla envelope. He handed it to Loyal.

"She asked me to give this to you," he said.

Loyal took it from him. Verne held out his right hand and they shook, then he turned and walked to his buggy. Loyal stood and watched him go.

When Verne had exited the parking lot Loyal slid into his own buggy and looked at the envelope. His name, penned in loose flowing cursive, was written across the front in blue ink. He could feel that the envelope held a small object. He peeled back the adhesive and upended the contents into his hand. For a moment he didn't breathe. He was holding a Ledger Nano S cryptocurrency wallet, a short cord to connect to a computer, and two folded pieces of paper. He opened the first piece of paper and found a note, unsigned, but presumably from Brandi. It had four words written on it:

.   .   .

Payment for services rendered

There was a small heart drawn just below the words. Loyal opened the second piece of paper. It held a single line of numbers, letters, and symbols. Loyal knew it was an encryption key. He slowly slipped everything back into the envelope and pressed the adhesive to re-seal it as best he could. He slid the envelope into the pouch on the inside of the buggy door. After thinking for a moment, Loyal pulled out his phone and searched his contacts for the personal cell number of his lawyer and friend, Maynard Lily.

BRANDI KENDRICK

I first met Mei Hua when I was living with my father in China. He hired her to teach me the language, but they also used me as a mule of sorts, delivering purloined secrets from Boeing to her and money to him. When I left China she hugged me goodbye and whispered, "We will meet again." At that time I very much doubted we would. Imagine my surprise when she called me nearly a month ago. She spoke to me in Chinese and seemed pleased when I responded in her language. She told me she was giving me one chance to save not only my life, but the life of my sister as well. She wanted to know where Jodi was. She wanted her bitcoin. At the time I thought I was doing the right thing by telling Mei Hua how to find Jodi. Turns out I was very wrong.

The backpack arrived the next day. When I saw what was inside, I hid two digital wallets, then picked up the phone to call Mei Hua and tell her that I had the cryptocurrency and she didn't need to bother with Jodi. Just as I was about to tap her number, there was a knock on my door. When I opened it I found two homicide detectives and a chaplain on my doorstep. In this way I learned that Jodi and Travis were dead. The Detectives had questions and I answered them as honestly as I could. When they left I retrieved the two wallets I had hidden and added them back to the backpack. I packed a small suitcase and wrote down a few important contacts. I placed my phone on the nightstand intending to leave it behind, when it rang. It was Verne, my only true friend besides Jodi. I had to answer. He mentioned the trip to Big Bear. At that time I did not commit to the trip. When our call ended, I left the phone on the nightstand and drove away. I bought a burner phone and checked into a hotel.

My name is Brandi Kendrick, but I have another identity that I have carefully maintained for many years. My father had paid someone for a false birth certificate upon our return from China. I suppose he was worried about me since he had exposed me to Mei Hua and their illegal dealings. He never said, and I never asked. He got me a passport in that name, and when I was sixteen I got a drivers license. When Jodi started bringing in lots of money, I opened bank and credit card accounts. I renewed the documents when required, and used the credit cards and bank accounts periodically. When I checked into the hotel after Jodi's death, I used that name. Mary Alice Dalton.

When I called Verne to give him my new number he repeated the invitation to accompany him to Big Bear. Getting out of town actually sounded like a good idea, so I agreed. Again, a poor choice on my part. I suppose they were monitoring my original phone. Mei Hua told me, when I was captive on the boat, that the Chinese government was making a run at world currency. They needed the billions of dollars of bitcoin that existed around the world. Thank God for Loyal Truesdale, my unwitting hero. Without him I'd be at the bottom of the ocean instead of floating on top of it. Going to Mexico with him was one of the best choices I ever made. I didn't mind drugging the agent, Trinity, but felt bad about drugging him. I truly trusted Loyal, and I don't trust easily. I left Ensenada, drove through the wine country, and crossed at Tecate. More accurately, Mary Alice Dalton crossed at Tecate. The rest was easy. I dropped the buggy, called Verne, and walked to Pizza Port to wait for him. He brought me an envelope for Loyal's "payment" and drove me to the airport. And just like that, Mary Alice Dalton flew away.

I made several stops around the world before settling here, on this tiny island. It is private and warm. I bought a house on the beach and spend most of my time the way I am right now, floating on a raft, one hand tethered to the dock the other holding a strong cocktail. I miss Jodi desperately, but once she was gone there was no way I was giving up the backpack. It is worth a fortune. I can easily live the rest of my life here. I only wish I could see the look on Loyal's face when he figures out how much that digital wallet is really worth.

AUTHOR'S NOTE

My husband has given me many thoughtful gifts over the years. The idea for this story is one of his most generous. Brett came up with the germ of an idea while I was writing my first novel, A.I. Smith. Not wanting to muddy the creative waters, he wrote the idea down and hid it away. When A.I. Smith was complete, I already had the idea for Loyalty, so Brett patiently waited for the right time to share his idea. That time arrived with the completion of Loyalty.

Brett gave me his idea with no strings attached. Never once during all the hours he listened to me read Mistrust aloud, did he ever try to influence what was being written. In his typically generous way, he gave his idea to me completely and fully, allowing me to run with it in whatever direction I chose. For that, I thank him.

ACKNOWLEDGMENTS

My first thanks are to the readers of my books. Many have shared with me that the characters I have created have become very real to them. What joy that brings me!

Sincerest thanks to Detective Terry Coker, LASD (ret.) who patiently answered any questions I sent his way.

Thank you to my cold readers: Sarah Binau, Terry Coker, Madison and Edith Cooper, Hayley Helms, and Mark Palmerton. This book is better because of you.

A big thank you to Marta Palmerton for her faith in me, and for editing the proof.

Gratitude to Kym McNabb for creating another amazing cover.

Several people allowed me to use their names or likenesses in the book. Thank you to Bruce and Winnie Meyers, Mike and

Lori Ann Dario, Jim and Nancy Chamberlain, Andy, Cassidy, and Rodger Stuart.

I would also like to thank Bruce and Winnie Meyers for introducing Brett and I to the buggy lifestyle. What fun we have in ours!

Made in the USA
Las Vegas, NV
17 August 2021

28319418R00223